the pattern

FIC
PEA

201558

the
pattern

the american quilt series

LIBRARY OF THE
FIRST BAPTIST CHURCH
PRESCOTT, ARIZONA

ZONDERVAN®

ZONDERVAN.com/
AUTHORTRACKER
follow your favorite authors

We want to hear from you. Please send your comments about this book to us in care of zreview@zondervan.com. Thank you.

The Pattern
Copyright © 1996 by Jane Peart

Value Edition, 978-0-310-29214-2

Requests for information should be addressed to:
Zondervan, *Grand Rapids, Michigan* 49530

ISBN 978-0-310-24900-9

Internet addresses (websites, blogs, etc.) and telephone numbers printed in this book are offered as a resource to you. These are not intended in any way to be or imply an endorsement on the part of Zondervan, nor do we vouch for the content of these sites and numbers for the life of this book.

All rights reserved. No part of this publication may be reproduced, stored in a retrieval system, or transmitted in any form or by any means—electronic, mechanical, photocopy, recording, or any other—except for brief quotations in printed reviews, without the prior permission of the publisher.

Edited by Robin Schmitt
Interior design by Sherri L. Hoffman

Printed in the United States of America

08 09 10 11 12 13 14 • 23 22 21 20 19 18 17 16 15 14 13 12 11 10 9 8 7 6 5 4 3 2 1

Part One

Chapter One

᠃᠊᠊᠊᠊

Johanna Shelby, eighteen and recently having returned home from boarding school, stood looking out through the rain-smeared bedroom window. It had started raining early in the morning and had continued steadily all day. Now it was coming down in sheets.

Sighing impatiently, she turned back into the room. She gave a rueful glance at her new scarlet taffeta party dress hanging on the ledge of her armoire. She was looking forward eagerly to wearing it tonight at the first party of the holiday season, held at the home of her best friend, Liddy Chalmers. But if this kept up, it might be impossible to get there, country roads being what they were.

On her way across the room, she practiced a few dance steps, ending up by holding on to one of the bedposts, where she twirled around a couple of times before plopping down and bouncing onto the feather mattress. There she sighed again.

Although she had only been home a few days, she already felt restless, at loose ends. Why? At school, she couldn't wait to get home for Christmas. And now it certainly was not that she missed school! For a free-spirited girl like Johanna, the rules, regulations, routine, the tedious hours in needlework class, and the memorizing endless verses to recite in the weekly elocution programs were boring and meaningless. In fact, Johanna was determined not to go back. That is, if she could convince her parents that she was quite "finished" enough. After two and a half years at Miss Pomoroy's Female Academy in Winston, she had had enough!

No, it certainly wasn't the lack of boarding school schedule that made her feel so fidgety. It was that she couldn't seem to settle down now that she was home. She felt so betwixt and between. She had changed more than she realized while being away. She'd gone off to school when she was sixteen and didn't seem to fit back into the family nest so neatly.

Johanna didn't really know what made her feel so uncomfortable back in the Shelby family circle. Maybe it was her prickly relationship with her sister Cicely, the next oldest. After her first greeting, Cissy had slipped back into her old adversary role with Johanna. Of course, Elly, the youngest, was adorable and as loving and lovable as ever. It was something else Johanna couldn't define. Even though she tried, she had the uneasy feeling she didn't really belong here anymore.

That is why after only a few days, Johanna found herself strangely at odds with everyone. It wasn't that she didn't love them all. It was just that she had the strangest feeling, as if she were on the brink of something, something unknown, something that was both exciting and a little daunting.

Johanna walked over to the window again. Putting her palms up against the steaming panes, she pressed her face against the glass. Just then the sky seemed to split open with a jagged streak of lightning that zigzagged down through dark, purple-edged clouds, sending the bare trees outside into stark silhouettes in a blinding flash. This was followed by a loud crackle of thunder that caused Johanna to jump back from the window in alarm.

In a panic reaction, Johanna turned and ran out of the room and down the stairs into the parlor, where the rest of the family was gathered, in time to hear her mother declare, "My good gracious, that was quite a jolt. It's a regular downpour. The roads will be rivers of mud by evening. I've a mind not to set out in this weather—"

"Not *go?*" a chorus of protest came from both the other girls. Cissy ran to stand beside her mother, peering out the window. Elly jumped up from the hassock, dropping her cat, which she'd been holding in her lap, to exclaim, "Not go to the *party?*"

"Oh Mama, surely you don't mean *that!*" cried Johanna, looking at her father for support and mainly concerned about having another evening confined at home and about losing the opportunity to wear her new dress.

"Well, I don't know. . . ." Mrs. Shelby's voice trailed into uncertainty. "Just getting from the carriage to the house, we'll get drenched for sure."

"Oh, it will be all right, Mama. We can bundle up and wear boots and carry our slippers 'til we get inside," Cissy assured her. At fifteen, she was the practical one.

"I suppose." Mrs. Shelby's voice still sounded tentative.

"Please, Mama, don't say we can't go!" wailed Elly, who at nearly eleven had been promised this treat, her first time to attend a really "grown-up" party.

"Oh, come now, Rebecca," boomed Tennant Shelby, the girls' father, who had caught Johanna's pleading look. He laid aside the book he had been reading to say chidingly to his wife, "Can't let a little rain deprive these pretty young ladies of the first party of the holiday season."

His wife gave him a cautionary look. Tennant was so indulgent of their three daughters, especially Johanna, that it was *she* who sometimes had to exert discipline or take the stern parental role. However, she was already inclined to put

9

aside her own misgivings about the weather. The Chalmerses'
party *was* the first of the holiday season. After all, she wasn't
yet too old to remember what fun a dancing party could be.
More to the point, with three daughters to eventually marry
off, it was important that they get out socially. Particularly for
Johanna, their oldest, home after her years out of circulation
here in Hillsboro. Now eighteen, ready to be launched into
society and ready for a serious courtship and marriage proposal. Not that it would be much of a problem. Johanna was
pretty, vivacious, and bright. Any number of eligible young
men would no doubt find her attractive. It was only a matter
of choosing the right one.

Rebecca felt all three pairs of anxious eyes upon her.
Waiting an appropriate length of time, she said slowly, "Well,
I suppose it will be all right. If we leave early enough and you
make sure Thomas drives carefully." This admonition was
directed at her husband. Her decision was greeted by excla-
mations of relief and delight by her daughters.

By dark, the icy rain had turned to sleet, and once more
Mrs. Shelby voiced her doubts about the wisdom of ventur-
ing out over rutted roads in the stormy night. Again she was
the lone dissenter, and again she was coaxed, cajoled, persuaded. Finally, at half-past seven, swathed in hooded cloaks,
shod in sturdy boots, their portmanteaus containing dainty
slippers into which they could change upon their arrival, they
were at last ready to leave. In high spirits, the three Shelby
girls climbed into the family carriage. Inside the narrow interior, settling their crinolines, they seated themselves opposite
their parents. As the carriage jolted along the country roads
now running with streams of mud, the girls chattered merrily,
giggling at whatever nonsensical things one or the other of
them said. Elly, squeezed between her older sisters, was wildly

excited to have been allowed to come along. She was ecstatic at the prospect of the evening ahead.

∗❧∗

Upon reaching the Chalmerses' house, Thomas, the Shelbys' coachman, pulled up as close to the covered side porch as possible. With Rebecca issuing warnings to be careful, the three girls, giggling with nervous excitement, descended from the carriage. Jumping over puddles, they ran through the pelting rain up the front steps of the house, through the door opened by the jovial Mr. Chalmers, and into the front hall.

The warm, candlelit house was already filled with the sound of fiddle music, lighthearted laughter, and happy voices. Someone took Johanna's cape, and as she stood there for a minute looking about, Liddy Chalmers, her closest friend from childhood, came rushing up to her. "Oh, Johanna! I'm so glad to see you! I was afraid you might not come! Isn't this weather dreadful?" She gave Johanna's arm an excited squeeze. "Come on. You can primp in my bedroom before we go in to dance." She lowered her voice significantly. "Burton Lassiter's been pacing up and down like a madman, waiting for you to arrive! I hid your dance card so he wouldn't fill up every slot."

Liddy propelled Johanna back through the narrow hall to her downstairs bedroom, chatting all the while. "I absolutely *love* your dress, Johanna! It's a perfect color for you."

Sitting on the mounting steps to the high, four-poster bed, Johanna bent to pull off her boots and get her dancing shoes out of her bag. Liddy continued to talk as Johanna took out the red satin slippers with the tiny silk roses on the toes and slipped them on her feet.

11

"It's going to be such a fun party. I wish you could spend the night so we could stay up till all hours and talk." Suddenly Liddy clapped her hands. "Maybe the weather will worsen and you'll have to! Anyway, come along. Papa's about to call the first reel."

At the entrance to the parlor, now cleared of furniture for dancing, the eager Burton Lassiter was quick to find Johanna and claim her as his partner for the Virginia Reel, which was usually the dance to open a party.

When they finally came to a breathless halt after the lively dance, Johanna's gaze swept the room. It was then she became aware of the young man leaning against the pilaster in the archway.

He was very tall and his dark shaggy hair needed a good trim. He was not handsome, and his features were too irregular, with a strong nose and a determined mouth. However, the combination was oddly attractive. His gray eyes, regarding her so steadily, were intelligent yet held a hint of humor.

As the stranger glanced at her, Johanna experienced the strangest sensation, as if somehow they knew each other, as if they'd met somewhere. Of course, that was impossible! Yet the strong feeling lingered.

She and Burton took their places with other couples lining up for the quadrille. The music struck up and she was swept into the promenade. Again Johanna caught sight of the stranger, and to her immediate confusion, found he was looking at her as well.

Who was he? she wondered curiously. In spite of her odd sense of recognition, she couldn't place him. In as small a town as Hillsboro, a stranger stood out. Surely Liddy would know. For some reason, Johanna felt an urgency to find out. Fanning herself briskly, she told Burton she was perishing from thirst and sent him off to fetch her a glass of punch.

Then she quickly darted to Liddy's side. Taking her by the wrist, she led her aside and whispered, "Come with me. I have to talk to you!"

Puzzled but compliant, Liddy followed Johanna's lead down the hall to her bedroom. Some of the other girls were already there, restoring hairdos and primping in front of the mirror as they came in.

"What is it?" Liddy asked.

"Who is that tall fellow standing beside Dr. Murrison? Is he new in town? A relative? A nephew? Who?"

"That's Dr. Murrison's new assistant."

"What's his name?"

"His name is Ross Davison. He's been with Dr. Murrison for a few months now. He came after you left for school in September."

"Where's he from?"

"If you heard him talk, you wouldn't have to ask where he's from," a voice behind them said with a snicker. Unaware that they'd been overheard, both girls turned around. Emily Archer, a girl Johanna had never liked very well, was standing in front of the full-length mirror. Her face in the glass had a know-it-all smirk. But at the moment, she had the information Johanna wanted, so Johanna swallowed her dislike to ask, "What do you mean? Is he a foreigner?"

Emily giggled shrilly. "No, silly, he's from the *mountains*!"

"Mountains?"

"From Millscreek Gap, for pity's sake!" Emily fluffed her corkscrew curls and patted her skirt, turning this way and that as she surveyed herself in the mirror. "I suppose he *must* be educated—I mean, to be a doctor and all," she remarked indifferently. "But he still has that hill twang." Emily mimicked, "*You kin jest tell*."

13

Johanna frowned. She suddenly remembered why she had never liked Emily very much. Emily had a sharp tongue. She was always quick with a snide remark, a mean comment, or a sly innuendo. For some reason, it made Johanna cross to hear Emily make fun of that young man with his serious expression and deep-set, thoughtful eyes. But Johanna let it pass, not wanting to appear too interested in the newcomer. Emily had a razor-like tongue, liked nothing better than to tease. Johanna was not about to become her target by giving her anything to turn into a joke.

"Come on," she said to Liddy. "Burton's waiting for me with punch." She slipped her hand into Liddy's arm and they made their escape.

"What a cat that Emily is!" commented Liddy as they hurried out into the hall. "Actually, Dr. Davison is very well mannered and pleasant. Dr. Murrison sent him over when my little brother Billy had croup, and he couldn't have been nicer."

Back in the parlor, Burton was nowhere in sight, and Johanna allowed her gaze to seek that of the young doctor. As her eyes met his, he turned and spoke to Dr. Murrison. Then, to her surprise, they both crossed the room. "Well, Johanna, my dear, it's nice to see you home from Winston and looking so well," Dr. Murrison said. "I don't believe you've met my new assistant, Ross Davison."

Johanna's heart gave a little leap. "No, Dr. Murrison, I've not had the pleasure. Good evening, Dr. Davison," she managed to say, fluttering her fan to cool her suddenly flushed face.

"Good evening, Miss Shelby. I trust you are having a pleasant time?"

His voice was deep. There *was* a trace of the mountain twang to it, as Emily had said. However, Johanna did not find it at all unpleasant.

"Yes, indeed. And you?" As she looked up at him, Johanna felt a tingling in her wrists and fingertips.

It was uncanny, Johanna thought, this feeling of recognition. As though somehow they had been parted a long time and were, at this very moment, seeing each other again. The sensation was bewildering.

"If you have not already promised it, may I have the next dance?" His question brought her back to the present moment.

Even though she *had* promised the next three, Johanna simply put her hand in Ross's, felt his fingers close over it. He bowed from his great height, and she moved with him out onto the polished dance floor as the first notes of the next set began. Out of the corner of her eye, she saw Burton, looking bewildered and a little indignant, glancing around in search of his missing partner. But she didn't care. She knew she was exactly where she wanted to be, dancing with this tall newcomer.

Ross was not the best of dancers. He was a little unsure and stiff, his height making him rather awkward. It did not matter to Johanna. She felt as if she were floating, her head spinning as fast as her feet. They circled, his hand firmly on her waist, her face upturned to his, and she could not remember ever feeling so happy. The piece ended and as they waited for the next one, they smiled at each other—as if they had danced together many times before.

The music started again, and again they seemed to move in perfect step. At length the melody ended. Yet, they remained facing each other. Mr. Chalmers's booming voice jovially announced, "Line up, ladies and gentlemen, for musical chairs."

Reluctantly Ross stepped back, bowed slightly, and relinquished Johanna. A row of chairs, numbering one less than the assembled guests, was placed down the middle of the long room.

The musicians started playing a lively march, and the company began moving in a circle around the room, giggling, shuffling a little, attempting to anticipate when the music would stop and they would have to rush for a seat. As one by one a chair was eliminated and one or more persons had to drop out, the circle grew smaller and the fun and hilarity of the suspense grew louder. Every once in a while Johanna would catch Ross's glance. He was so tall and lanky that watching him scramble for a chair was comical. What pleased her the most was that he seemed to be thoroughly enjoying himself and had lost that slight awkwardness. Although his shyness touched her, she was elated that he could enjoy such fun.

Soon there were only a handful of marchers left, Ross and Johanna among them. The musicians, enjoying the sight as much as the onlookers clustered around the periphery of the room, changed the tempo from fast to slow to trick the hopeful remaining players. Johanna was almost weak with laughter, and once when the music stopped abruptly, she and Ross landed unceremoniously on the same chair. In a gentlemanly manner, he shifted and stood up, leaving her seated while a more boisterous young man slid into the only other chair left empty. Ross joined the spectators as Johanna stayed in the game. With two chairs and three people left, the room became noisier than ever, people cheering on their favorites. When the music halted, Johanna made a dash for a seat, and as she did she lost her balance and went crashing, sending the chair sliding, herself collapsing in a heap with upturned crinolines and taffeta ruffles. One small dancing slipper, with its tiny heel, went skittering across the polished floor and out of sight.

Burton ran to help the laughing Johanna to her feet. Leaning on his arm, she hopped to the side of the room, where someone pushed a chair for her to collapse into. Johanna's laughter suddenly came to a swift halt when, from across the room, she saw her mother's disapproving expression. Johanna felt a sinking sensation, which was quickly replaced by one of rebellion. What had she done that was so horrible? Just played a silly game to the fullest. What on earth was wrong with *that*? She turned away from the admonishing face just as Ross came up to her, bearing her small satin shoe in his open palm.

He knelt to slip it back on her foot. As his hand held the arch, Johanna felt a tingle running up from her foot all through her. Involuntarily she shivered. He glanced up at her, and for a single moment their gazes met and held, as if seeking an answer to an unspoken question. Then people gathered around, and their voices crowded out the sound of Johanna's heart beating so loudly she was sure everyone could hear it.

❧

Hours later Johanna was sitting in front of her dressing table, dreamily brushing her hair, when her mother entered her bedroom.

Johanna had been reliving the evening. At least the part after she had been introduced to Ross Davison. Following that, the rest of the party had simply faded into a backdrop. She hardly remembered the carriage ride home, the excited voices of her sisters discussing the evening. She had seemed to float up the stairs and into her own bedroom on some kind of cloud. Now her mother was talking to her in a tone of voice that was edged with severity, chiding her about something. Johanna blinked, looked at her mother, and tried to concentrate on what she was saying.

"I simply cannot believe it, Johanna! I thought your years at Miss Pomoroy's had taught you some reticence, some proper behavior. I am shocked to see that—given the opportunity—you are as much a hoyden as ever!"

Johanna, outwardly submissive, listened to her mother's lecture while continuing to brush her hair. *Eighty-two, eighty-three, eighty-four*, she counted silently, wondering if her mother's tirade would end at the prerequisite one hundred strokes.

"I expect you to set a good example for your younger sisters, Johanna. This was Elly's first grown-up party, and she worships you, you know, imitates everything you do: your mannerisms, your likes, dislikes—unfortunately, your bad traits as well as any good ones you might exhibit. I am thoroughly ashamed of your lack of decorum tonight, Johanna. And with that—that rough-hewn young man, whose parlor manners also need a great deal of improvement." All at once Rebecca realized Johanna was not really listening. Hadn't she heard a word? Maybe the child was tired. Perhaps this could wait until tomorrow.

"You *do* understand, don't you, Johanna? Anything you do reflects on the family. People are ever ready to gossip or spread untrue rumors. I would not want anyone to get the idea—" Again Johanna's expression looked faraway. Her sweetly curved mouth was—smiling. Rebecca's voice sharpened. "Johanna!"

"Yes, Mama. I do. I didn't mean to—I was just having fun."

"I'm sure that was all there was to it, dear. But we can't give the wrong impression—you see?"

"Yes, Mama," Johanna replied demurely.

Rebecca leaned down and kissed the smooth brow, cupping her daughter's cheek for a moment with her hand. Her eyes swept over her daughter. Johanna was fulfilling her childhood promise of beauty. Her complexion was lovely, her eyes, with their sweeping lashes, truly beautiful, Rebecca thought fondly. *But we must be careful that her gaiety and vivaciousness aren't misunderstood.*

As soon as the door closed behind her mother, Johanna put down her hairbrush and studied her reflection in the mirror. Was it possible? Did she really look different? Something had happened tonight, and she seemed changed somehow.

In a way, that shouldn't have surprised her. She *felt* different. Ever since she'd come home less than a week ago, she had felt oddly displaced. The familiar seemed unfamiliar. Even getting used to being with her parents and two younger sisters again had presented problems. However, Johanna knew it was something more than that. Deep inside, there was a heart hunger she couldn't explain or even understand. A need for something to give her life meaning and purpose.

Johanna blew out her lamp, climbed into bed, and pulled the quilt up to her chin. She shut her eyes, squeezing them tight, and the image of Ross Davison came into her mind. He was different from most of the young men she knew, the ones she'd smiled at and teased at picnics, flirted with and danced with at parties.

He might be a bit awkward and unsure of himself socially, perhaps not good at small talk or such. He was already into a man's life, a doctor, healing the sick and injured, saving lives. It made the lives of most of the other young men she knew seem shallow by comparison.

Up until recently Johanna's life had been that of a schoolgirl—simple, uncomplicated, filled with friends, fun, light flirtations. Now Ross Davison had stepped into her life. His eyes seemed to look into her very soul. It had been almost as if he recognized that longing within her she had not ever spoken of to anyone.

Suddenly Johanna saw a possibility of something deeper and more important. She wasn't exactly sure just what happened tonight. She only knew that something had and nothing would ever be the same again. It both excited and frightened her.

Chapter Two

*A*t breakfast the following day, Rebecca announced, "Johanna, I want you to take the fruitcakes around to the aunties. You may take the small buggy. If you don't dawdle or stay too long at each house, you should be back by noon. No later, because I shall need it myself this afternoon when I go to help decorate the church for Advent services."

Delivering fruitcakes to her cousins was Rebecca's holiday custom. Since she used a secret Shelby family recipe handed down to her by her mother-in-law, she knew that this was one thing none of them could duplicate. Fond as they all were of each other, nonetheless an unspoken but very real rivalry existed among the cousins.

"Yes, Mama, I'll be happy to." Johanna cheerfully accepted the errand, glad of the opportunity to get out of the house and thus escape some of the household chores Rebecca daily allotted to each daughter.

Immediately Cissy protested. "Why does Johanna get to do all the fun things?"

The difference in their ages always rankled Cissy. It was something she had not had to deal with while Johanna was away. After her first welcome to Johanna at her homecoming, Cissy had reverted to petty jealousy. Rebecca sent her a disapproving glance. "Because Johanna can drive the trap, for one reason. For another, the aunties haven't seen her since she came home." Then she added, "And stop frowning. Your expression is as unbecoming as your attitude." To Johanna she said, "I'll put the fruitcakes in a basket and then have Thomas bring the trap around."

Her mother's reprimand subdued whatever else Cissy might have argued. At least temporarily. However, when Rebecca left the table, Cissy stuck out her tongue at Johanna, who ignored her and went to get her hooded cape. She was pulling on her leather driving gloves as Rebecca emerged from the kitchen area carrying a willow basket packed with the gaily beribboned rounded molds of fruitcakes. Johanna drew a long breath, relishing the combined smells of brandied fruit, cinnamon, nutmeg. "Umm, smells delicious, Mama."

"Take care, and try to be back on time," her mother's voice followed her as Johanna took the basket and started out.

"Yes, Mama," Johanna promised as she opened the front door. She gave a cheery wave to her sisters, a pouting Cissy and a resigned Elly, both assigned to polishing silver.

Outside, Thomas, the Shelbys' "man of all work," waited beside the small, one-seated buggy at the front of the house, holding the mare's head. Thomas was husband to their cook, Jensie, brother to Bessie, the maid. All three had worked for her family as long as Johanna could remember.

"Morning, Thomas," Johanna greeted him, then paused to rub Juno's nose and pet her neck before climbing into the driver's seat.

"You be careful now, Miss Johanna. She's feelin' mahty frisky this mawnin'," Thomas cautioned, handing her the reins.

"Thank you. I will," she said. She gave the reins a flick and started down the winding drive out onto the county road.

The morning was bright, sunny, the air crisp and clear, and Johanna felt lighthearted and free. She was glad to be home, back in Hillsboro, after the long months away. At boarding school, her independent, happy-go-lucky spirit felt hopelessly surpressed by the strict rules. She had the secret intention that during this Christmas vacation, she would persuade her indulgent father to let her stay home rather than go back to the academy. She felt she'd had enough education and enough of the restrictive life at school. Cissy could go in her place!

As they moved along at a brisk pace in the winter sunshine, Johanna enjoyed traveling over the familiar roads, breathing deep of the pine-scented air. She was actually looking forward to having a visit with each auntie as she delivered her mother's special holiday gift.

Johanna's "aunties" were not *really* her aunts. They were her mother's first cousins. And they all had the same first name: Johanna. Their grandmother, Johanna Logan, had five daughters and one son. Each daughter named their first daughter Johanna in honor of her. The only one not named Johanna was Rebecca, the daughter of the son. *His* wife, the only daughter-in-law in the family, had refused to have *her* daughter christened Johanna. All the first cousins named Johanna were called by other names to distinguish them from each other. Thus there was Aunt Hannah, Auntie Bee, Aunt Jo McMillan, Aunt Honey, Aunt Johanna Cady.

Thinking of the aunties, Johanna often wondered if her mother ever resented the fact that *her* mother had broken with tradition and not named her Johanna. She never said and somehow Johanna had resisted asking. Her mother rarely talked about her childhood or her life before marrying. It was as if everything began for her when she became Mrs. Tennant Shelby. It seemed she had become part of his life and left her own completely, proud of her husband's prominence, their place in Hillsboro society.

Families were funny things, Johanna mused as she turned off the main road and took the rutted lane that led to the Breckenridges' home, the one closest to the Shelbys', her first stop. She and her sisters were the only girls in the family. The other relatives on both sides who had children had boys. Johanna had never given it much thought, but recently she had noticed that her mother quite bristled when the other aunties talked—or the better word was *bragged*—about their male offspring. Would her mother have rather had sons? Johanna wondered. However, she'd heard several of the aunties sigh and verbally declare they pined for a daughter, making such remarks as, "such comfort, so companionable, considerate in old age." So maybe it all evened out in the end, Johanna decided as she pulled up in front of her Auntie Bee's. She knew this would be a happy reunion. Auntie Bee, childless herself, doted on the Shelby girls, and secretly Johanna was her favorite "niece."

Winding the reins around the hitching post, Johanna ran up the porch steps. She raised the brass knocker and banged it a few times before Auntie Bee, who was somewhat hard of hearing, opened the door. "Why, Johanna, how lovely to see you! Come in, dear!" she said, beckoning her inside. "My, you get prettier every time I see you."

Johanna gave her a hug, relishing the familiar fragrance of violet eau de cologne she always associated with this aunt. "I've brought you Mama's Christmas fruitcake!"

Looking as surprised as if receiving it weren't an annual event, Auntie Bee declared, "How dear of her! And I know it's delicious. Let's slice a piece and have some tea. You can stay for a visit, can't you?"

"I probably shouldn't. Mama wants the trap back by noon."

"Not just for a wee bit?"

"Well, I guess—why not!"

"Why not, indeed! Come along inside. No mistake about its being December, is there? Lots of frost this morning when your Uncle Radford set out for his office." Auntie Bee took Johanna's cape and hung it up, saying, "Now you go right on in the parlor, where I've a nice fire going. That'll take the chill off you after being out in the cold air. I'll get our tea and slice the cake."

"Can I help you, Auntie?"

"No, dearie, you just go on in and make yourself comfortable. I won't be but a minute." Auntie Bee bustled out to the kitchen.

Auntie Bee's quilting frame was set up in the cozy parlor, and Johanna went over to examine the one she was working on. When her aunt came back in carrying the tray with tea things, Johanna told her, "This is very pretty, Auntie, and I like the colors—what's the pattern called?"

"It's called the Tree of Life. In the Bible, a tree is the symbol of all the good things of life: plenty, goodness, and wisdom. All God's gifts to humankind we're to enjoy on this earth—our families, our home, what he provides—the abundant life the Scripture speaks about."

Johanna regarded her aunt's serene expression, the sincerity with which she spoke. Surely she never had a doubt or an uncertainty, unlike Johanna, who always questioned everything. "You really believe that, don't you, Auntie?"

"Of course, dearie. What's not to believe?" Bee put one hand on the open Bible on its stand beside her quilting frame. "As it is written in Proverbs 3, 'Happy is the man that findeth wisdom. She is a *tree of life* to them that lay hold upon her.'"

24

After consuming a large piece of fruitcake and a cup of tea, Johanna turned down her aunt's urging for a second helping of each and departed for her next stop.

As she drove away, waving her hand to her plump aunt standing on the porch waving back, Johanna wondered: had her aunt never had a rebellious thought, a longing for something different than a placid existence? Was she always so at peace, as perfectly content as she appeared? Johanna sighed. She herself had so many unfulfilled dreams, so many romantic fantasies and desires. Perhaps her aunt's kind of serenity came eventually with age? She didn't really know. In her own heart a restlessness stirred, a deep yearning for an experience that did not even have a name. Was she to constantly search for something she might never find?

❧

As she approached Aunt Hannah Mills's house, Johanna hoped she would not have to listen to a prolonged recital of her aunt's ailments. Aunt Hannah tended to complain at length of various aches. The consensus of family opinion was that most of them were imaginary. Today Johanna was in luck. At her knock, the door was opened impatiently, and Johanna got the immediate impression she had come at an inopportune time. The household was in the midst of holiday cleaning. Behind Aunt Hannah, through the door to the parlor, Johanna saw Suzy, the maid, kneeling at the hearth, polishing the brass fender, the fire tools, and the andirons. The frown on her aunt's face faded at once when she saw Johanna.

"Why, Johanna, child! What a surprise!" she spoke, trying not to sound irritated by the unexpected visit. This aunt was known in the family as a fuss-budget about her home— for her, cleanliness was truly next to godliness—and twice a year the entire house was scrubbed, cleaned, polished to a

LIBRARY OF THE
FIRST BAPTIST CHURCH
PRESCOTT, ARIZONA

fare-thee-well. Christmas was one of those times. Yet since hospitality was a cardinal rule practiced by all the family, she welcomed Johanna inside.

"One of your mother's lovely fruitcakes!" she exclaimed with feigned surprise as Johanna handed it to her. "My, my, I don't see how your mother manages to do all she does. A houseful of girls to look after, a large household to run, all the entertaining she does, besides her charitable activities. Of course, *she* has been blessed with good health!" Aunt Hannah sighed lugubriously. "Not like some of us." She drew her small bottle of smelling salts from her apron pocket and inhaled. "I have felt quite unwell since . . . well, I believe I overdid it when—"

"I'm sorry to hear that, Aunt Hannah," Johanna said brightly, determined not to be an unwilling audience to a long list of Aunt Hannah's hypochondriac complaints. "I do hope you will take care so that you won't miss the holiday festivities. New Year's dinner is at our house this year."

Aunt Hannah looked aghast. "Miss our family dinner? Of course not! I wouldn't miss *that* even if—"

Before she could add the phrase "if I were on my deathbed," which Johanna anticipated might be next, Johanna said quickly, "I must be on my way, Aunt Hannah. I have the other fruitcakes to deliver, and Mother explicitly told me to be back home by noon. She is expected to be at the church to help decorate."

"Go along then, child. How I wish I had the strength to volunteer for such active things, too, but I just haven't felt up to it—"

Johanna moved to the door. One hand on the knob, she said, "Do give Uncle Roy my love. We shall see you on Christmas Day at Aunt Honey's." The door was open now.

"Yes. That is, if—"

Before her aunt could finish her sentence, Johanna stepped outside onto the porch, into the crisp, cold morning.

Aunt Hannah gasped, saying, "Oh, I must shut the door quickly, Johanna, or I'll catch my death—"

"Sorry, Auntie," apologized Johanna, then she ran down the porch steps and climbed back into the buggy. Glad to escape, she picked up the reins with a long sigh of relief. Next stop was Aunt Cady's. Johanna Cady was what Johanna called her "fashionable aunt." She was exceptionally attractive and youthful looking, with fine hazel eyes, silvery blond hair. She had a distinct style, impeccable taste, and a rather superior air. As Johanna arrived, she saw her aunt's carriage in front of the house, and when her aunt answered the knock at her door, she was dressed and ready to leave. Her peacock blue faille ensemble was elegant, and her bonnet sported curled plumes and velvet ribbon.

"Oh, dear me, Johanna, I'm just about to depart," Aunt Cady said. "With the holidays upon us, I moved up my visiting day so as to get all my calls in before I get caught up in the season. Munroe and Harvel will be home from college day after tomorrow, you know—and then there'll be no end to it!" She threw up her hands in mock dismay, but Johanna knew her aunt was looking forward with great pleasure to the arrival of her two handsome sons.

"It's all right, Aunt Cady. I just came to leave Mama's gift."

"Oh, how nice." Her aunt accepted it distractedly, placing it on the polished Pembroke table in the hall behind her. "When the boys come, we shall have to have some kind of party, invite all their friends—I don't know just when, but we shall of course let you know. They shall be so pleased to see you, Johanna." Her aunt's gaze traveled approvingly over her. "The boys will be amazed to see how pretty and grown up you are since last year!"

Johanna wasn't so sure. Her older boy cousins had always rather ignored her, being busy with their own social activities. Years ago it might have mattered to her to be noticed by her two attractive cousins, but somehow now at the mention of them, she mentally shrugged.

"Do tell them hello for me, and of course, tell Uncle Madison," she said as she went back out to the buggy.

"We'll see you at church on Christmas Day and at dinner afterward. And be sure to thank Rebecca for me, won't you, dear?" Aunt Cady called after her.

Johanna had one more stop to make before heading home. She had purposely saved this one till last, because Aunt Johanna Hayes was her favorite. She was called Aunt Honey, because that was the name her husband Matt called her in his loud, jovial voice. He was a large man, measuring at least two feet taller than his petite wife. That name suited this aunt perfectly, Johanna thought as she approached the fieldstone and frame house surrounded by tall pines at the end of a lane. Honey had remained a great deal like the lighthearted girl she had been, frivolous, charming, fun-loving, the pampered pet of her husband and three strapping sons.

Up to her elbows in flour, Aunt Honey was making the decorated Christmas cookies of all sorts of shapes and sizes for which she was famous in the family.

"Darling girl, how happy I am to see you! But you've just missed Jo," Honey told Johanna. Her plump face showed dismay. "She'll be sorry to miss you. But she would go out riding! I told her I thought it was too cold, but you know how she is!"

Aunt Jo was spending Christmas with the Hayeses. Johanna knew Aunt Jo was an excellent horsewoman and no matter what the weather, she would go riding. "Yes, I know. I'll leave her fruitcake from Mama anyway and see her another time."

"Ah yes, there'll be plenty of family get-togethers during the holidays," Aunt Honey agreed. "Want to sample one of my cookies?"

"I can't stay, Aunt Honey, but I'll take one along to munch on."

"Of course. Come along into the kitchen with me. I have a batch almost ready to take out of the oven."

Suddenly a startled look crossed Aunt Honey's face, and she sniffed the air suspiciously. "Oh, my! I'd better get them out quick, or they'll be burned."

Johanna followed her into the deliciously fragrant kitchen. Aunt Honey scurried over to the stove and slipped out the tray of bell- and tree-shaped Christmas cookies. "Uh-oh, they're a bit brown at the edges!"

"They'll be fine, Aunt Honey," Johanna consoled. "Once you've covered them with colored sugar."

"What a clever girl, you are, Johanna," her aunt declared happily. "That's just the thing."

"I really must go, Auntie."

"Do tell your mama thank you for our cake. Matt always looks forward to Rebecca's fruitcake," Aunt Honey said as she walked to the door with Johanna. "Your mother is so organized, no one can keep up with her! And here I am, not finished with my baking, not by half. I'm hopeless, it seems, no matter how early I start."

"You're just right, Aunt Honey." Johanna gave her a hug and went out the door. "And we'll see you on Christmas!"

Her errands done, Johanna decided to ride through town on her way home. With only a half-formed thought in her mind, she slowed her horse to a walk as she went by Dr. Murrison's house. Ever since the Chalmers' party, Johanna had spent a great deal of time thinking about the tall, young doctor with his slow smile and disturbingly penetrating eyes.

However, as she passed the brown-shingled house, there was no one in sight. She felt disappointed, but then, what she had hoped for? A chance to talk to him again? There was just something about Ross Davison. . . .

In no hurry to get home, where household chores awaited her, Johanna decided to do a little shopping. She had a good half hour before her mother expected her back. Why not stop at the little notions shop that carried ribbons and lace and look around for a bit? She had started making handkerchief cases in needlework class months ago as Christmas gifts for both her sisters. As usual with such things, she had lost interest in the project, and she had brought them home with her, unfinished. With Christmas only a few days away, maybe she could find some lace or trim to add a finishing touch.

She found a space in front of the shop and, hitching Juno to the post, went inside. It didn't take long to find what she wanted. Her purchases made, she was just leaving the store when she saw him crossing the street, coming straight toward her!

At the exact same time, Ross Davison saw *her*. Her scarlet cape, caught by a sudden wind, swirled up behind her like a bright fan, framing her dark, flying hair. He thought Johanna the loveliest thing he had ever seen.

"Miss Shelby," he greeted her. "What luck!"

"Luck?"

"Yes, quite a coincidence."

Or a hopeful wish come true, Johanna thought, amazed. Trying to conceal her pleasure, she teased, "Don't tell me you just happened to be thinking of me!"

"As a matter of fact, I *was*."

Johanna was taken aback. Most young men of her acquaintance were not so frank expressing their feelings. In her social circle, an unwritten law was never to say what you meant—a game played equally by ladies and gentlemen. Johanna had always thought it ridiculous nonsense. Ross's frankness was as refreshing as it was startling.

"Yes," he said, "I *was* thinking about what a good time we had at the Chalmerses' party—"

"Musical chairs, you mean? Yes, it was fun." She laughed and Ross thought Johanna was prettier even than he had remembered, her face all glowing and rosy, her smiling mouth showing small white teeth.

"I hope we may enjoy other such times, or"—he frowned suddenly—"will you be returning to school after the holidays?"

Although she had not launched her planned campaign to persuade her parents to let her stay home instead of going back to the academy, she hesitated. "I may not be going back. I hope to be through with all that—"

"With boarding school? Or learning in general?" he grinned.

"Oh, there are lots of things I want to learn—*outside* the schoolroom." Her eyes sparkled with mischief.

"I see." Ross regarded her so seriously, she began to feel uncomfortable. Recalling her mother's recent lecture on deportment, she hoped that her remark did not sound too flippant, too flirtatious. An awkward silence stretched between them. To break it, Johanna asked, "And why are you not going about doing good, curing illnesses, and that sort of thing, Dr. Davison?"

"At the moment, it seems most of Hillsboro's citizens are in good health or too busy with Christmas preparations to be sick."

For a minute, they simply stood smiling at each other. Since she could think of no plausible reason to delay longer, Johanna shifted and moved as if to go. "Well, I must be on my way, Dr. Davison."

"May I help you with your packages, Miss Shelby?"

There were so few, it seemed an almost ridiculous suggestion. But grasping at anything to prolong this chance meeting, Johanna just as ridiculously replied, "Why, thank you, Dr. Davison."

"Where's your buggy?"

It was right in front of them, a matter of a few steps. "Over there."

"I'll see you to it," Ross said quite solemnly. His hand slipped under her elbow, and they walked over to where Juno patiently waited. Ross helped her climb in, then said with obvious reluctance, "Well, I have patients to see—"

"Yes, and I'd better get home."

Before relinquishing her small parcels, he asked, "When may I hope to see you again?"

"Perhaps at church on Sunday," Johanna blurted out impulsively, then blushingly amended, "—that is, *if* you attend?"

"Not always, but"—he looked amused—"*this* Sunday I will."

She picked up the reins. Their gaze still held. Johanna was amazed that so much had been said, and yet so much remained unspoken but somehow understood. At last she said, "Good-bye, then. Until Sunday."

"Yes, 'til Sunday. Good-bye."

Feeling unreasonably happy, Johanna started for home.

~~∾ೞ∾~~

The following Sunday, Johanna was already up when her mother came into her bedroom to awaken her with a cup of hot chocolate. In fact, Johanna was standing in front of the mirror trying on her new bonnet while still in her nightie. Surprised, Mrs. Shelby raised her eyebrows but said nothing.

Johanna was usually the hardest of the three girls to get up and moving in the morning. What had prompted this early rising? Surely it wasn't sudden religious fervor? Rebecca regarded her oldest daughter curiously.

Rebecca was inordinately proud of her three pretty daughters, and this morning as they made their way to church, she noted that Johanna looked especially attractive. Her new bonnet of russet velvet, with a cluster of silk bittersweet berries nestled on green velvet leaves on the band, and wide brown satin ribbons tied under her chin, was most becoming. She was also being extremely amiable and sweet-tempered, moving over at Cissy's demand for more room in the carriage, looking demure with folded hands over her prayer book. Something was stirring, Rebecca felt sure, but she could not pinpoint what it might be.

As for Johanna, when they reached the churchyard, her heart was pumping as fast as if she were on her way to a ball. When they all got out of the carriage, she saw Dr. Murrison and his tall assistant mounting the church steps. She dared not look to the right or left to try to locate where they were seated as she followed her parents down the aisle to their family pew, indicated by the small brass identifying marker engraved SHELBY.

Before she sat down, she glanced around as casually as possible and saw that the two were seated toward the back of the church. Then she remembered it was well known that Dr. Murrison always sat in the rear near the door in case a medical emergency called him away from divine service. She ducked her head, studying the hymn book. After reading the same line over at least three times, none of it making sense, she realized she was much too aware of the young man three pews behind her. It became suddenly hard to breathe, much less sing.

Somehow Johanna got through *this* Sunday's seemingly endless service. When her mother stopped to chat with friends on the way out of church, she had to curb her irritation. *Oh, please don't let him leave,* she prayed. Stepping outside onto the church steps, to her delight she saw her father engaged in conversation with Dr. Murrison, and Ross stood quietly beside him. She heard her father saying, "But of course, you both must join us. Am I right, my dear?" He turned to Rebecca as she and Johanna approached them. "Wouldn't we be pleased to have Dr. Murrison and his assistant join us for dinner on New Year's?"

Dr. Murrison, a ruddy-cheeked, gray-whiskered man with a gruff manner that his small, twinkly blue eyes belied, demanded, "But wouldn't we be intruding? A family occasion, surely?"

"Not at all, my good fellow," Mr. Shelby denied heartily. "Holidays are no time to be alone. Now, we'll say no more about it. But expect you both."

Rebecca murmured something appropriate. Johanna shyly smiled at Ross. His eyes seemed to light up, replacing his serious expression with one of pleasure. A few more pleasantries were exchanged, then good-byes were said.

Once in the family carriage, her father announced, as if in explanation of his impromptu invitation, "Couldn't let Alec spend the most festive day of the holidays alone, could we? He used to spend the holidays with his sister over in Clayton County. But she passed away last summer—and that young fellow, Davison, he'd never get to his home in the mountains in this weather. Snow's made the road up to Millscreek impassable."

Johanna did not listen to the rest of her parents' discussion. She was too happy planning what she would wear when Ross Davison came to the house for dinner. Ten days seemed a long time to wait.

Chapter Three

"I don't want to go!" pouted Elly at the breakfast table. "I don't want to have my music lesson. Why do I have to do it during the holidays? I didn't think I'd have to go to lessons at all, with Johanna just come home."

"That will do, Elly," Mrs. Shelby said sternly. "You will take your music lessons as usual. Miss Minton is paid for each pupil's lesson. If you don't go, she doesn't get paid. She is the sole support of her invalid mother, and it is only right and proper that you go. Besides, I heard you practicing yesterday, and you certainly *need* the instruction. You fumbled quite badly on your piece. Now, that's all I have to say. Go and get ready."

Elly's lower lip trembled and tears filled her eyes.

"I'll take Elly over to Miss Minton's, Mama," offered Johanna. "And maybe we can go have a little treat afterward. You'd like that, wouldn't you, Elly?"

Her little sister's face brightened. "Oh, yes!" She jumped up from her chair.

"That's very generous of you, Johanna." Mrs. Shelby looked approvingly at her but added, "Still, I believe, Elly must learn responsibility without the promise of reward. *This* time, however, it will be all right."

Within twenty minutes Johanna and Elly were on their way. Elly took Johanna's hand, swinging it happily.

"I've missed you, Johanna. It's really lonely at home without you."

"I missed you, too, punkin." Johanna smiled down at the rosy, upturned face.

"I hate taking piano lessons. But Mama insists. She says every young lady should play a musical instrument and must have accomplishments." Elly had some trouble with the word. "When I ask *why*, Cissy says, 'So that suitable gentlemen will want to marry you.' As if I cared about *that*," she sniffed disdainfully. "But Cissy *does*. She plays the flute and *she* likes it. She can't wait 'til she's old enough to have beaux." Elly looked sideways at Johanna. "Do you have beaux, Johanna? I mean, someone special you want to marry?"

"Not really, Elly," Johanna laughingly replied, but a small, secret smile played around her mouth as she thought of Ross Davison. Although she couldn't as yet consider him a beau—or even a would-be suitor, there was something tucked deep inside her heart that whispered "possibility."

Caught up in thoughts of the mysterious, unknown future, Johanna was surprised when they reached Miss Minton's house in what seemed to her like no time at all. Elly yanked the leather thong, setting the pewter doorbell clanging and bringing a flustered-looking Miss Minton.

When she saw Johanna, she gave a her head a little jerk. Johanna had not been one of her best students nor a favorite. Too restless, too uninterested, and one who had not progressed much, in spite of all Miss Minton's efforts. In her opinion, *she* had not been at fault—it was simply that Johanna had not applied herself.

"Well, Johanna, I see you're back from school. Were *they* able to give you some appreciation of the value of a musical education?"

Trying to keep a straight face, Johanna replied, "I *was* in choir, Miss Minton, but that's about all."

"Humph. Let's hope they were more successful than I at teaching you to sing on key," was Miss Minton's rejoinder. "Come along, Elinor. I hope you're prepared today. Go in the front room. I have another student in the parlor." From inside the house, the scratchy sound of a squeaky violin could be heard. Johanna suppressed a wince. She certainly didn't intend to remain here listening to Elly's stumbling fingers on the piano, accompanied by the agonizingly dreadful rendition of the violin student. Helping Elly off with her coat and bonnet, she whispered, "I'll go do some errands and be back for you in an hour. Then we'll go have our treat."

Elly threw Johanna a hopeless look. No prisoner on the way to the gallows could have looked more desperate. Before Elly reluctantly followed Miss Minton's rigid back down the narrow hall, Johanna gave her a little wave and a sympathetic smile.

Outside in the crisp winter morning, Johanna walked briskly toward the center of town. She had no particular place in mind to wile away the hour Elly was enduring her music lesson. Johanna window-shopped at the milliner's and manteau maker's, then went to the stationer's. Browsing the displays of handsome desk sets, she wished she could buy one for her father as a Christmas gift. Of course, they were all much too expensive, some elaborate silver ones consisting of inkwells, sealing stamps, quill holders. She sighed. She would probably have to finish embroidering the spectacle case she had started and never completed, for his birthday, and give it to him for his Christmas present.

Outside again, she walked slowly down the street, in the direction of Dr. Murrison's residence. A wooden sign with his name and the words "Physician and Surgeon" underneath swung on the gate. In smaller letters, another name—Dr. Ross Davison—had been painted by a different hand. She put out a tentative hand and traced the name over a couple of times with her gloved finger.

"Miss Shelby!" a deep male voice called and she whirled around. Ross Davison was running out from the side entrance of the house, without his coat, his hair tousled by the wind. Johanna felt her face flood with color.

When he reached her, Johanna saw obvious happiness in his face. He leaned forward on the gateposts. His eyes shone, his smile wide.

"Miss Shelby, what brings you out this chilly morning?"

"Yes, it is chilly." She raised her eyebrows, noting he was in his shirtsleeves, as if he had come flying out when he saw her, in too much of a hurry to put on his jacket.

To her amazement he stated, "I saw you from the window and was afraid you might pass by without my having a chance to speak to you."

What honesty! What lack of pretense or guile! Johanna thought of all the silly chitchat most young gentlemen dealt out in conversing with young ladies. Ross Davison was certainly different.

"As to what I'm doing out," she replied, "I'm on my way to fetch my youngest sister from her music lesson." Johanna laughed. "Actually, I should say *rescue* her. She was very reluctant to go, and only the promise of a treat afterward would persuade her."

Ross was spellbound. Just looking at her, her lovely eyes sparkling with merriment and her cheeks as glowing as twin roses, listening to her voice, her laughter, made his heart happy. As a doctor, he was aware of his own physical reaction at the sight of her. His heart rate had quickened alarmingly, and probably his blood pressure rose as well. Diagnosis: decidedly unmedical. He knew he was in fine health, so there must be another explanation.

A little uneasy under his steady gaze, Johanna said, "I must be on my way. It should be nearly time for the prisoner's release."

"Can you wait until I get my coat?" he asked. "I'd like to accompany you, if I may? Maybe buy both of you a treat?"

"Why, thank you, Dr. Davison. That would be very nice." Johanna was too delighted to dissemble.

"Good. Then, I'll be right back," Ross promised and, turning, ran back to the house. A minute later he emerged, still thrusting his arms into his coat sleeves. He twisted a long knitted scarf around his neck and fell into step alongside her, breathless.

"My goodness, Dr. Davison, you could win a marathon!"

"I'm what town folks call a 'ridge runner,'" he laughed heartily, turning the word used often as a derogatory name for mountain folk into a matter of pride.

On the short walk over to Miss Minton's, they talked and laughed easily, as if they had known each other a long time. Being with Ross was so natural, Johanna felt relaxed and happy. Elly, her snub nose pressed against the window next to the front door, was already anxiously awaiting Johanna's arrival. Her coat was buttoned crookedly, her bonnet jammed on her head, its strings tied carelessly into a crooked bow.

Miss Minton stood behind her, arms folded. Seeing that Johanna had not returned alone but accompanied by a young man, her eyes sharpened disapprovingly behind her spectacles.

Johanna made quick work of the introductions, then took Elly's hand, and the three of them hurried down the path and out the gate. "Dr. Davison has kindly offered to stand for our treat, Elly," Johanna explained.

"What would you say to a candied apple on a stick, Miss Elly?" Ross asked. "When I was in the bakeshop earlier, they were making them. And the smell of brown sugar, cinnamon, and apples was almost too much."

"Sounds wonderful, doesn't it?" Johanna squeezed Elly's hand.

Elly's eyes lit up and she smiled shyly, nodding her head.

The trio were blissfully ignorant that behind a stiff, lace curtain, the watchful gaze of Miss Minton was following them.

Miss Minton's mouth pressed in a straight line. What a bold baggage Johanna was! And that young assistant of Dr. Murrison. Shouldn't he be tending sick folks instead of gallivanting around with that Shelby girl? Miss Minton intended to pass on her opinion to the next mother who showed up today with one of her pupils.

Outside, the subjects of Miss Minton's negative consideration were having a merry time. They stopped to get their candy apples, then walked down to the duck pond while they ate, the sweet, sticky coating blending deliciously with the tart taste of the juicy apples. The three of them carried on a jolly conversation. Both Johanna and Ross included Elly, giving her attention as an equal.

Finally Ross said he had to go back to his office. "But I've had a wonderful morning, thanks to you two. You don't know how much it means to a doctor to be with healthy, happy folks for a change."

Elly looked wistfully at the tall departing figure and sighed. "Isn't he nice? I'd like him for a beau, wouldn't you, Johanna?"

Out of the mouths of babes! But Johanna didn't dare admit her wholehearted agreement with Elly's opinion. The little girl might just pop out with something at the wrong moment. For now, Johanna wanted to keep her still uncertain feelings about Ross Davison to herself. So not answering, she just gave her a quick hug and said, "Come on, Elly, I'm cold. I'll race you home." Then picking up her skirt, she started to run, forgetting altogether that she was now a young lady and this was unseemly behavior for someone who was eighteen.

～♥♥～

For the next few days, Johanna's thoughts swirled, circled, and whirled around Ross Davison. It was a delicious secret that she hugged close, too precious to share with anyone. Was it real, had it truly happened? Her inner happiness softened and sweetened her, touching everything she said and did with a remarkable gentleness.

Rebecca thoughtfully noted this "weather change" in her oldest daughter. Perhaps some of Miss Pomoroy's influence had taken its hoped-for effect on Johanna. Usually when Johanna was home, she created all sorts of small tempests. Frequent spats between her and Cissy, careless neglect of household duties, a general disregard for anything but her own pleasurable activities. Maybe all the trouble and expense she and Tennant had lavished on Johanna was at last reaping some benefits. Johanna certainly seemed to be maturing. Of course, she had always been generous, cheerful, maybe too fun-loving but certainly a joy to be around. Now if she could just become more interested in the womanly skills that would be necessary assets when she married. Of course, there was still time for that. Johanna had another year to complete at the academy. . . .

Unaware of her mother's concern, Johanna was fully enjoying her vacation, free from ringing bells, boring lessons, required stitchery classes. Every day, she received fistfuls of invitations to holiday parties. Each one a potential chance of seeing Ross Davison, now a part of the social circle of Hillsboro's young people. Whatever people like the snobbish

41

Archers might say, an eligible bachelor was always welcome, and as the respected Dr. Murrison's assistant, Ross had an assured acceptance.

As she wrote her replies to these invitations, Johanna could never have guessed that her next meeting with Ross would be pure "happenstance" or that it would have such unexpected repercussions.

Two days before Christmas it snowed. Snow in Hillsboro was unusual. Snow of this depth and of such lasting quality was really rare. The temperature dropped and the foot or more of snow that blanketed the town formed an icy crust, perfect for sledding. Elly was beside herself with glee, and Johanna was still young enough to love the snow and see its possibilities for enjoyment.

Excitedly they got out the seldom-used wooden sled and waxed the runners. Bundled up with scarves and mittens, Johanna and Elly went to join some other adventurous ones who had made a sliding track on the hillside.

The air was as keen and stimulating as chilled wine, stinging the eyes and turning noses and cheeks red as ripe cherries. Up and down the winding hill the girls went, swooping down the slopes and shouting at the top of their voices as they sped to the bottom.

It was when they reached the bottom for about the fourth time and were starting the slow climb back up to have another spinning ride that Johanna spotted Ross coming along the street. Holding on to the brim of his tall hat with one hand and his doctor's bag with the other, his head bent against the wind, he plowed along the path through high drifts on either side.

Unable to resist the impulse, Johanna bent over, quickly scooped a handful of snow, formed it into a ball, and sent it winging through the air. It hit its target exactly, knocking

Ross's hat clear off. Startled, he halted and spun around, looking for the culprit. Then he saw Johanna and Elly holding on to each other as they convulsed with laughter. His first puzzled expression instantly broke into a wide grin. "You rascals!" he shouted. Dropping his bag, he swiftly rounded a ball of snow with both hands and threw it. It landed on Johanna's shoulder as she turned to avoid being his target. There followed a fierce snowball fight, two against one. Elly and Johanna alternately fashioned snowballs and pelted Ross while he struggled valiantly to return as good as he was getting. Finally it ended in a laughing truce, with Ross pulling out a large white handkerchief and waving it. He retrieved his hat, dusted the snow off its brim, and picked up his medical bag. Smiling broadly, he approached the two girls, who were still laughing merrily.

"Enough! I surrender. I have sick people who are down with the croup, chills, and fever!" Ross pleaded submissively. "How can you two justify delaying me on my rounds of mercy, waylaying me and attacking me so viciously?"

For an answer, Johanna reached down and molded another snowball and tossed it with all her might, only to be hit by one herself as she turned her back and started running out of range. Her laughter was ringing out in the air when unexpectedly she heard her name spoken admonishingly. She whirled around to see Emily and Mrs. Archer approaching along the side of the street. Emily's mother had a shocked look on her face. Johanna blushed scarlet, feeling like a child caught with a hand in the forbidden cookie jar. Not only was she positive Mrs. Archer would relay *this* escapade she had observed to everyone, including Johanna's mother and aunties, but Johanna knew Emily was delighted to have a spicy tidbit to pass along to her chosen friends. Johanna Shelby and the young doctor carrying on in broad daylight on the street!

Emily's eyes were wide with curiosity as she and her mother came to a stop within a few feet of both Johanna and Ross.

Johanna attempted a semblance of poise and started to make introductions but did not have a chance. With lifted eyebrows Mrs. Archer said coolly, "Oh, we've met Dr. Davison, Johanna. I wasn't aware *you* two were acquainted."

Emily interjected too sweetly, "Don't you remember, Mama? Johanna and Dr. Murrison were the last left playing musical chairs at the Chalmerses' party." She glanced over at Johanna with the look of a tabby cat licking a bowl of cream.

Johanna flushed, gritting her teeth. That Emily! What a spiteful person she was. However, Ross, unaware or undisturbed by the fact that Emily was trying to embarrass them, bowed slightly, acknowledging Mrs. Archer. Then he laughingly declared, "That was the most fun I've had since I was a tadpole."

Mrs. Archer gave him a cold look that might have chilled a lesser individual. "*Really?* How odd, Dr. Davison." Then, turning to her daughter, she said, "Come along, Emily. We must get on with our errands." She added pointedly, "Johanna, do give your dear mother my kind regards." With that parting jab they walked off. Johanna bit her lip in frustration, knowing for certain she would hear about this later.

Ross seemed hardly to notice their departure. His mind was too taken up with Johanna. Did she have any idea how pretty she was? Her dark curls escaping from the red knitted cap tumbled onto her shoulders. The rosy laughing mouth. The blue, blue eyes shining with fun.

After exchanging a few more silly jests, Ross set his hat straight and gave them a small salute. "Good day, Miss Shelby, Miss Elly. Regrettably, I have work to do while *others* may play!" He made an exaggerated bow. "And may I take this opportunity to wish you both a very happy Christmas."

"I like him," Elly declared as she and Johanna started back up the hill.

"I do, too," said Johanna, knowing it was much more than that.

"He doesn't seem at all like a stuffy old doctor, does he?"

"No," replied Johanna. They went back to sledding, the playful incident with Ross part of a happy day. A day when Johanna had seen yet another side of Ross Davison. A side that appealed to her own fun-loving self.

~~❧~~

This year Christmas dinner was at Aunt Bee and Uncle Radford's home. Since it was also their twentieth wedding anniversary, the whole family was in an especially festive mood for the double celebration. As they gathered around the table for dinner, Aunt Hannah's husband, Uncle Roy, who was an elder in church, was asked to say the blessing. All heads bowed as it was ponderously intoned, and afterward the light buzz of conversation resumed as plates and platters were passed.

Then something happened that startled Johanna. During one of those lulls that sometimes occur even in the most congenial company when everyone is simply enjoying the good food, Aunt Hannah remarked, "By the way, Johanna, Emily Archer's mother said the strangest thing to me when I saw her the other day." Aunt Hannah pierced her with a sharp look. "She mentioned that she had seen you and Dr. Murrison's assistant in quite a rowdy display, throwing snowballs at each other in broad daylight on the street! I told her she must be mistaken, that I thought it unlikely that a girl with your background and breeding and so recently come from Miss Pomoroy's establishment would be making a spectacle of herself in public!"

The silence that followed was so absolute that one could have heard the proverbial pin drop. Johanna felt her cheeks

45

flame as everyone either looked at her or avoided doing so. Worst of all, she felt her mother's gaze rest upon her. What could she say in her own defense? Besides, it was true. It had happened, there was no use denying it. Johanna opened her mouth to explain, but as it turned out, it was Elly who did.

"Oh yes, Aunt Hannah. It is true! Johanna and I both did. It was ever so fun! Dr. Davison is so kind and jolly. Johanna and I had such a good time."

Aunt Hannah looked a trifle sheepish at the little girl's enthusiastic explanation, but she still had the last word. Giving a little clucking sound of disapproval, she said, "One would hardly expect a *physician* to engage in such sport."

"And why not?" boomed Uncle Matt. "He's a young fella, even though a man of medicine! I admit to feeling like frolicin' myself sometimes in the snow!" he chuckled heartily.

There was a murmur of amusement at this around the table, then a general, noncontroversial conversation continued.

Johanna cast her uncle a grateful look, then glanced at Aunt Hannah. Known in the family for a talent of turning a joyous occasion into something else, she had certainly been true to form today. Thankfully, Uncle Matt, was jolly enough to make up for it.

Johanna avoided her mother's questioning eye, knowing she would have some explaining to do later. Inwardly she fumed. The Archers had wasted no time carrying their tidbit of gossip to willing ears. However, evidently Aunt Hannah's *informant*, Mrs. Archer, had failed to tell her that her younger sister was there, too.

Although the meal proceeded without further ado, Aunt Hannah's acid remark about Ross had spoiled the family holiday dinner for Johanna. Auntie Bee's lemon meringue pie could have been cardboard for all Johanna could tell.

At least her little sister had saved the day. And Uncle Matt's comment had dashed some cold water on Aunt Hannah's criticism. But only temporarily. Back at home, as Johanna had known she would, Rebecca came into Johanna's bedroom. "Why didn't you mention seeing Dr. Davison and having a snowball fight the day you took your sister sledding?"

"I didn't think it was important." Johanna shrugged. "It was just a silly game—"

"It seemed important enough to Mrs. Archer for her to speak of it to Hannah. You know how it upsets me to have my daughters the subject of criticism or comment."

"Oh Mama, you know Emily's mother is a terrible gossip. She was just trying to find something to talk about. Why is she so interested in what other people do? I say she's much too inquisitive. She should mind her own affairs."

"Don't be disrespectful of your elders, Johanna," her mother corrected sharply, then added with a raised eyebrow, "Besides, the only people who mind others being inquisitive are those who have something to hide." She paused. "Do you have anything you'd like to tell me, Johanna?"

"No, Mama, I don't." Johanna pressed her lips together stubbornly.

Rebecca sighed and went to the door. Her hand touched the knob and was about to turn it, when she glanced again at Johanna.

"Remember, Johanna, anything you girls do or say reflects on us—your parents, your home, your upbringing."

Without looking at her, Johanna replied, "Yes, Mama, I know."

Chapter Four

❧⸲❧

Coming as it did at the end of the festive holiday season, New Year's Day had always been rather a letdown for Johanna. After the round of parties and festivities, it used to mean her reluctant return to the strict regime of Miss Pomoroy's. This year was different. After much pleading, she had received parental permission to remain at home.

Johanna, jubilant with that victory, had other reasons to be happy. This year it was the Shelbys' turn to host the traditional family gathering, and the fact that Dr. Murrison and his assistant had been invited to share it with them made it special.

Since this was Rebecca's first time in six years to have everyone at Holly Grove for the holiday dinner, everything had to be perfect. Right after Christmas, preparations began to ready the Shelby house for the occasion. Ordinarily Johanna dreaded the uproar of housecleaning. However, this year she pitched in with energy and enthusiasm that surprised Rebecca. The fact that Ross would be a guest was, of course, the spur.

Rebecca directed the work, allotting certain tasks and jobs to everyone. Their cook, Jensie, asked her sister, Aster, to come over and help Bessie with the heavier work of cleaning. Every nook and cranny had to be thoroughly dusted, every piece of furniture polished, the pine floors waxed. The

Shelby girls were all put to work as well. All the silver had to be shined, brass candlesticks polished, the Christmas greenery refreshed, and the red bayberry candles replaced on the mantel sconces and windowsill lamps.

Cissy frequently complained of fatigue, of being overworked, and begged to rest. Elly sighed and dawdled over every task assigned. However, Johanna's mood was merry as she hummed at any job she was asked to do. Her cheerful attitude made her sisters alternately resentful or suspicious and mystified her mother. Even so, Rebecca appreciated her willingness to help with everything. For the time being, Rebecca's mind was concentrated on the result of her efforts: perfection. The annual New Year's Day dinner was an unadmitted competition among the ladies, each one trying to outdo the others when it was her turn. Secretly Johanna thought the beginning of a new decade was terribly exciting. *1840!* What would the next year hold? The next *ten*? She had been a mere child at the beginning of the last—now she was a young woman with everything to look forward to. The possibilities seemed endless. Johanna's imagination went soaring. Heavens, she would be twenty-eight at the end of another decade. All sorts of things would have happened to her by then.

At last all was in readiness. The house sparkled and shone. The smell of lemon wax, almond paste, the fragrance of balsalm potpourri from bowls set about the rooms, the spicy aroma of cinnamon, ginger, and nutmeg from baking pies, mingled with the scent of cedar boughs and evergreen pine wreaths still hanging at the windows.

New Year's Day dawned with overcast skies. Gray clouds hovered with the promise of more snow. Before leaving for the special New Year's Day services at noon, Rebecca made a last-minute survey of her domain, satisfying herself that all was in perfect order. She anticipated that her cousins would give the

Shelby household a polite yet precise appraisal. At length, everything met her approval, and the family went off to church.

Johanna hoped she would see Ross there. Although the shape of her bonnet kept her eyes reverently toward the pulpit, precluding any possible sidelong glances, under her jade velvet pelisse trimmed with beaver, her heart raced. He might be there observing *her*! But there was no sign of him, either in the back pews as they left or in the churchyard. An emergency of some sort? A sick child? A dying patient? A doctor's life was full of such unexpected happenings. What might have prevented his attendance at church could also cause him not to come to dinner. Such a possibility dismayed her.

Johanna had no time to dwell on such a catastrophe, because no sooner had the Shelbys reached home than the aunties and their husbands began to arrive.

Each lady brought her very best culinary effort to add to the veritable feast Rebecca and Jensie had prepared. Each cousin prided herself on being a fine cook, so each dish presented was to be profusely praised. By the time everyone gathered in the parlor for a holiday libation, all were in a good mood, ready to see the old year out and welcome in the new.

Although she circulated among her relatives, chatting with each in turn as her mother would have her do, Johanna kept stealing surreptitious glances at the grandfather clock in the hall. Each time she passed a window, she glanced out hopefully, longing to see Ross coming through the gate. Even while trying to respond to some of the parlor conversation, she strained her ears for the sound of the knocker on the front door.

She knew dinner was planned for five o'clock. *Please don't be late*, she prayed. Delaying dinner would upset her mother, and she wanted Ross's first visit to come off well. Even a medical emergency would not be an excuse if her mother's sweet potato soufflé collapsed.

In an uncharacteristic state of mind, Ross Davison walked through the gathering winter dusk on his way out to Holly Grove. This would be the first time he would see Johanna in her own home, one he knew was far different from his own. During his time in Hillsboro, he had been in enough homes of people like the Shelbys to realize just how different their backgrounds were.

Ever since he'd met Johanna, his feelings both daunted and excited him. Every time he saw her, his pulse rate was erratic, his heartbeat accelerated. He had to ask himself a dozen times a day what kind of madness this was. His hopes were probably impossible. All week he had debated whether or not to find some way to get out of the invitation Dr. Murrison had accepted for them both. He had argued both sides, vacillating. It would be wiser not to go, something told him. However, the thought of missing a chance to see her, be with her again, proved too much. Now here he was, on his way.

Holly trees lined the curving driveway up to the impressive house of pink brick with white columns and black shutters. Standing at the gate, Ross looked up at the Shelby home. In the twilight, all the windows, adorned with scarlet-bowed wreaths, were lit with candles.

He swallowed hard, then opened the gate and went forward, up the porch steps. At the paneled door, there was another moment of hesitation. Then resolutely he raised his hand to the gleaming brass knocker in the shape of a pineapple, the traditional symbol of southern hospitality.

When Johanna opened the door for him herself, Ross was caught off guard. In a red and green plaid dress that rustled crisply, she looked so enchanting that it quite took his breath away. "Oh Ross, I'm so glad!" she said impulsively, then attempted to regain a proper manner. "Good evening. Do come in." She stepped back so he could enter.

Feeling tongue-tied. Ross struggled for words. He fumbled to take off his hat, held it awkwardly until he realized she was holding out her hand to take it so she could place it on the rack by the door. "Where's Dr. Murrison?" she asked.

"He'll be along soon," Ross assured her. "Just as we were leaving, an old patient stopped by to bring him a Christmas present, and nothing would do but that he come in for some cheer. You know how it is at holiday time."

A burst of laughter and the sound of voices floated out from the parlor. Ross glanced in that direction, an unmistakable look of alarm on his face. Johanna caught it and realized how shy he was. Immediately she sought to put him at ease. "Don't look so startled. It's only family. Of course, there *are* quite a lot of them," she laughed gaily. "But they're all quite harmless." She lowered her voice conspiratorially. "Just try not to sit down by Aunt Hannah, or she'll regale you with all her symptoms. I'll seat you by Auntie Bee. She's a dear and will want to know all about you." Smiling encouragingly, she took his arm and led him into the parlor.

To Ross the elegantly furnished room seemed filled with dozens of pairs of eyes, all turned to him. Johanna began to introduce him. The names went in one ear and out the other, the faces all became blurred. Ross was grateful to sit down at last. A jovial, gray-whiskered gentleman handed him a cup of eggnog. Later he unobtrusively placed it on the small pie crust table at his elbow. He was sure it contained spirits, and he was not a drinking man.

Seated across the room, between Uncles Matt and Radford, Johanna looked at Ross fondly. Even his awkwardness touched her. However, Johanna tried to see him through the appraising eyes of her mother, her aunties. Johanna knew they would probably not consider him handsome in the slightest. However, to her there was such strength in his rugged features, sensitivity in his expression, depth of intelligence in his eyes, that she thought him one of the finest-looking men she had ever seen.

Within twenty minutes the front door knocker sounded and Dr. Murrison arrived. He and Tennant Shelby were old friends and he knew the others, so he was completely at ease. At once he was drawn into the general conversation of the group. The Shelbys, Millses, Hayeses, Cadys, McMillans, and Breckenridges never lacked for topics to discuss, debate, or argue about. The fact that the young doctor was sitting quietly, observing Johanna, went quite unnoticed—*except* by her mother.

Rebecca had excused herself to give her beautifully set table a last critical look before inviting the company to come into the dining room. Pleased that her best china, with its sculptured edge of flowers, gleamed in the glow of candles in two six-branched silver holders, she gave a final touch to the centerpiece, an artistic arrangement of fruit and pinecones. Then Rebecca returned to the parlor. She stood at the threshold, waiting for the appropriate moment to invite everyone to come in and be seated. It was then, with a sudden sharpening of her senses, that she saw Ross unabashedly staring at Johanna.

It struck her with that alertness one recognizes as impending threat or danger. Immediately she glanced at her daughter. Her face illuminated by firelight, Johanna was indeed lovely. Her dark hair, parted in the middle, with bunches of curls on either side of her face, was tied with crimson ribbons. A fluting of ruffles framed her face and slender neck. However, it was her expression that caused Rebecca's intake of breath. Johanna was gazing across the room at the young doctor, with the same raptness in her eyes as *his*!

Johanna's eyes held nothing back. Their glance was softly melting. Rebecca knew her daughter so well. *Why, the girl's in love!* Rebecca felt heat rising into her face. *How in the world did that happen?* There was only time for those fleeting thoughts. No time for her awareness to do more than register. Just then, Tennant caught her attention lifting eyebrows in a silent question. At her nod, he got to his feet, announcing, "Well, ladies and gentlemen, I believe my dear wife has come to fetch us in to dinner."

Seated across the table from him, Johanna watched Ross from under the fringe of her lashes. She felt a tenderness she had never known for anyone, along with the realization that he was feeling uncomfortable. He moved the lined-up silver-ware at his place nervously as he tried to pay close attention to what Uncle Madison Cady was expounding. Ross seemed so stiff, so different from the joking, laughing young man she had danced with, pummeled with snowballs, and talked with so freely at other times. Of course, it was meeting all her relatives. That must be hard on a stranger. Her sympathy came to the surface as she watched how he remained mostly silent after answering a few questions politely put to him. But to Johanna, everything about him seemed somehow so endearing and sweet. For example, how he had bent his head considerately to speak to Auntie Bee so that her deafness would not demand his repeating.

Rebecca's practiced glance passed over the table, her hostess's eye making sure everyone was enjoying the meal. Her gaze rested upon Johanna and, alerted, moved quickly across to young Dr. Davison, then back to her daughter. Neither of them were eating! Johanna had hardly touched her food! Where was her normal hearty appetite, an appetite that Rebecca had often claimed was *too* hearty, unladylike? She was only nibbling, pushing her carrots around her plate with her fork.

Something was going on between those two. Rebecca remembered she had felt that same little dart of alarm watching them together at the Chalmerses' party earlier in the month. But she thought her word of caution to Johanna about her frivolous behavior had settled it. Even as that thought passed through her mind, she saw an exchange of glances between Johanna and the young doctor. Rebecca knew that look, recognized it for what it was. Surely not *love* but certainly romantic *infatuation*. A twinge of possible problems pinched Rebecca. No question about it, she must speak to Johanna *again*.

Dinner finally came to an end, with everyone declaring they had eaten too much and enjoyed it immensely. They all returned to the parlor and settled back into chairs, on sofas, and a kind of desultory conversation ensued. For a few minutes Rebecca lost track of the topic everyone seemed to be discussing. She was distracted by the sight of Johanna and the young doctor sitting together at the other end of the room, conversing. Johanna's attitude was that of someone intently listening to Dr. Davison's every word. The scene had the look of intimacy Rebecca felt inappropriate. If she could have overheard their conversation, she would have been even more upset.

Ross was saying, "There are some things I've been wanting to talk to you about—some things I'd like you to know about me. Maybe I'm speaking out of place—I don't know. I don't have all the social graces I know you're accustomed to—I know your family, your background, is a great deal different from mine." He hesitated. "But Miss Shelby, I come from good folks, honest, hardworking, God-fearing folks with a lot of pride. I am the oldest in my family. My father died— was killed logging, actually. I didn't get much schooling after that. That is, until a friend of Dr. Murrison's, a teacher, saw something in me—a hunger to learn, maybe—and talked my mother into letting me come with him into town, live with his family, go to school. I always wanted to be a doctor—I don't know why—always wanted to help things that were hurt, animals, children, anyone who was sick." Ross halted. "I wanted most of all to learn doctoring so I could go back to the mountains and minister to my people. I've seen children die that didn't need to, men die from blood poisoning, women—well, all kinds of sicknesses and disease nobody knew how to treat or cure. And since I got my chance, I want to give something back. Can you understand that?"

"Oh, yes!" Johanna said breathlessly, completely entranced by his earnestness. No young man had ever spoken to her like this, about serious things, important things, things that counted. She was amazed and touched and thrilled that Ross Davison wanted to share these things—evidently so dear to his heart—with her.

"You may wonder why I'm telling you all this. I don't usually talk so much, not about myself anyway. But I needed to tell you. I felt you'd understand, Miss Shelby—"

"Oh, please, call me Johanna!"

Ross looked doubtful. "I've never known anyone like you before. I haven't had much time for socializing. When I was at college, I had to work, and then there were my studies. I'm not much at dancin'"—his eyes twinkled—"as you found out!"

"You did quite well," Johanna smiled, "experienced or not!"

Ross paused for a moment. "I was looking forward very much to coming to your home tonight. Your mother was very kind to include me. She didn't have to just because Dr. Murrison is an old family friend."

"But you couldn't be alone on New Year's Day!" exclaimed Johanna. "It's such a special occasion."

"Yes, I suppose it is. We never made much of holidays at home—" He then stopped. "Anyway, it was very gracious—"

"It was lovely to have you."

Rebecca decided it was time to interrupt. The two were completely absorbed in each other. Someone was bound to notice, then there'd be questions. She would ask Johanna to go to the kitchen, bring back fresh coffee to replenish everyone's cup. Before she could put idea to action, Dr. Murrison rose, declaring he must take his leave. Immediately his assistant also got to his feet. Reluctantly, Rebecca was sure, from the way his gaze lingered on Johanna.

After bidding everyone good-bye and thanking Rebecca for her hospitality, the two physicians went toward the hall. Mr. Shelby accompanied them, and before Rebecca could invent some excuse to stop her, Johanna quickly followed.

While Dr. Murrison and her father finished up their conversation, Ross asked her shyly, "I wondered if you'll be going to the taffy pull at the Chalmerses' next Wednesday?"

"Yes! Will you?"

"Miss Liddy was kind enough to invite me."

"Then we shall see each other there," Johanna said brightly.

"Yes," Ross replied solemnly. "I shall look forward to it."

When the door closed behind them and her father returned to the parlor, Johanna spun around a couple of times in an impromptu dance. She felt her spirits soaring outrageously. Spinning to a stop, she suddenly *knew*. Why, *this* was falling in love!

The night of the Chalmerses' party, Johanna had felt something happen between them. She hadn't quite known what. Startled, her lips formed the words: I love him! To her own astonishment, she knew it was true.

Chapter Five

—•—

The evening of the taffy pull, Johanna was invited to stay overnight with her friend Liddy.

Winter taffy pull parties were one of the most popular kinds of social get-togethers for young people. Although it was not openly admitted, the romantic potential of such an evening was widely accepted. At least, the young people themselves regarded it as romantic. If their parents did not, it was only because their memories were short. Often such a casual, spontaneous evening of two-by-two candy making developed into a more serious courtship. Under the laughter and gaiety and visible adult supervision, it afforded a means for couples to pair off without raised eyebrows. Within the guise of making candy, there was the chance for a quick hug and kiss in an alcove or corner. In fact, it was one of those well-circulated sayings, part joke and part truth, that a winter night of pulling taffy often resulted in a June wedding.

For that reason alone, knowing Ross had been included in the guest list, Johanna was particularly looking forward to the evening. Without being closely observed by chaperones, there was a real possibility of having another private conversation with Ross.

She was thrilled he'd confided in her about his family, his life, his hopes, his ideas of being a doctor. None of the other young men she knew had ever talked to her that way; as if she were an equal, as if she had intelligence to understand serious things.

As Johanna was about to leave on the afternoon of the party, Rebecca had a moment's uneasiness. Johanna had been to dozens of taffy pulls, and Liddy had been her friend since childhood. Why was she acting so excited, so eager to be on her way?

Although, ever since gaining permission not to return to Miss Pomoroy's, Johanna had been a shining example of obedience, cheerfulness, and helpfulness. She did her chores without complaining, was tolerant of Cissy and kind to Elly. Then, why did Rebecca feel troubled? It was the dreamy look she sometimes saw in Johanna's eyes, how she went about smiling as if she were listening to music. Instead of the volumes of history her father had assigned for her to study in order to continue her education in lieu of going back to school, Rebecca had found an open book of poetry on Johanna's bedside table! Poetry, indeed! Still, she did not see any tangible evidence that there was anything to chastise Johanna about.

Of course, Rebecca had no idea of how many "happenstance" meetings there had been with the young doctor on the days Johanna had eagerly volunteered to do errands for her mother.

So Johanna kissed her mother's cheek and went gaily off in the buggy that had been sent for her, neither of them dreaming that this evening would be a turning point in both their lives.

A big iron pot filled with sorghum was already boiling and bubbling on the stove in the Chalmerses' kitchen when

Johanna arrived. She knew almost everyone there, and there was much chatter, everyone exchanging news and telling each other about their Christmases. They gathered around the stove, waiting for when the sugary mixture reached the proper consistency, while Liddy's father, red-faced, perspiring, shirtsleeves rolled up to his elbows, kept stirring. Suddenly he bellowed, "Get your plates buttered, folks!"

Mrs. Chalmers and the other mothers in attendance stood by the kitchen table, handing out solid white ironstone plates on which butter had been slathered. One by one, people filed up to the stove, and Mr. Chalmers ladled out dipperfuls of the syrupy liquid onto the greased plates, where it had to cool. When it was cool enough to be lifted off with the hands, the fun of pulling began.

With much laughter and conversation, everyone rubbed their hands with lard. Then the boys selected a partner and the pulling started. At first the molasses was stiff and hard to handle, but once it got started, it was easier to work, and it would be stretched into a kind of rope. The boy would grab the rope in the middle and pass the end on to his girl partner. Of course, sooner or later a few of the girls managed to get all mixed up in the rope of taffy. When this happened, the boy had to get his arms around the girl, standing behind her to free her hands from a wad of taffy. The point of the pulling was *supposed* to be to make the taffy more brittle and tasty. The longer it was pulled, the whiter it got. This was done with a great deal of giggling, squealing, and laughter, the hilarious "shenanigans" all taking place under tolerant chaperonal surveillance.

When Mrs. Chalmers felt the "tomfoolery" had gone as far as it should, she called for the taffy to be coiled onto the buttered plates. There was provided a second round of fun as people twirled and swirled the candy, making designs of hearts and links, and fashioning a fancy final assortment of the hardening taffy. When the taffy was ready for breaking up, couples took their pieces and, pairing off, went to find a place to chat, eat, and enjoy.

As it turned out, Johanna didn't have the worry of wondering how Ross would get into all the playing around. For the first part of the evening, she kept watching for him. Her distraction annoyed her partner, Burton Lassiter. "Pay attention, Johanna! Pull! Stretch it before it hardens," he told her in vain.

Johanna was finally rewarded when Ross arrived. She saw him before he saw her. He stood in the doorway with Liddy, appearing to listen to whatever she was saying while his gaze searched the room. When he saw Johanna, he distractedly excused himself from their hostess and came straight across the room to her. Suddenly everyone else in the crowded room simply disappeared for her. He was standing right in front of her, his thick hair and his shoulders glistened with raindrops. Had he come out in this storm without a coat, forgotten his hat? Johanna wondered.

"Good evening, Johanna. I'm sorry to be late and I cannot stay, but I must speak to you." Ross held out his hand and she put hers into it. He looked around and, seeing an unoccupied corner in the crowded room, led her over to it.

They sat down. Still holding her hand, he said, "I have to leave soon. The Barlow children are pretty sick. I saw them earlier today, but I'm uneasy about them. I want to check on them again."

"I understand," Johanna said, nodding her head.

Neither of them cared if curious eyes were upon them as Ross covered both her hands with his and leaned toward her, saying earnestly, "But even if it were only for a few minutes, I didn't want to miss the chance of seeing you. You see, Johanna, there is something I must say to you. Something important. In fact, I can't think of anything else." He paused. "I know this isn't the proper time or place—could you possibly meet me tomorrow? Say about two in the afternoon? I should be finished with office hours by then—"

"Yes. Where? You didn't say."

Ross's heavy brows drew together. "Someplace where we can talk without—what about the bandstand in the park near the skating pond past the stone bridge? You know where I mean?" His hands tightened on hers. "And if anything should delay me, will you wait?"

"Of course I'll wait," she said. "No matter how long." She was already planning what excuse she'd use to get out of the house that time of day. She felt wildly happy. Secret meetings, the stuff of romance novels. Johanna reveled in the excitement of it.

For a full minute they simply gazed into each other's eyes. What she saw in his told her what she had longed to know. Johanna was suddenly breathless.

Reluctantly Ross said, "I have to go. It may seem impolite to Liddy, but I don't want to disturb the Barlows by coming by too late."

"I'll walk out with you," Johanna offered, rising. She waited while he made his apologies to Liddy, then, ignoring Liddy's puzzled glance and Mrs. Chalmers's soaring eyebrows, she followed Ross out the front door.

They came out onto the porch. It had stopped raining but the night was cold and damp. Johanna shivered. Immediately Ross was concerned. "You shouldn't be out here. You'll get chilled."

"I wanted to come."

They moved closer to each other. She half turned toward him, and the moment was vibrant with all that was between them yet undeclared. Then, in a low voice, Ross spoke.

"I love you, Johanna."

That was what she had hoped, wished for in her heart, but now that it had been said, it startled her. She drew in her breath, then with something like relief whispered, "I love you, too, Ross."

"Oh, Johanna." He held out his arms and she went into them. He drew her close, held her tight. Her cheek rubbed against the scratchy texture of his rough wool coat. Her ear was pressed hard against his chest so that she could hear his pounding heart. "Oh Johanna, I love you so much—" Then, almost in a groan, he said, "But it's impossible."

She pulled back, looked up at him. "*Impossible?* What do you mean, impossible?"

"How can I make you happy?"

"You already have."

"I mean—what have I to offer someone like you?"

"Yourself. That's all I'll ever want," she replied softly.

Ross put his hands on either side of her face, raising it so he could look deeply into her eyes. Then he gently lifted her chin, leaned down, and kissed her mouth. His lips were warm in the cold air and the kiss was sweet. There was a kind of desperation in his voice when he asked, "What are we going to do, Johanna?"

<hr />

When Ross left, Johanna went back into the party. For the rest of the evening, Johanna moved as if in a daze. She spoke to others, laughed, pulled taffy, and chatted merrily with everyone. She felt as if she were in a puppet show, mouthing lines spoken by someone else, with somebody pulling the strings. She didn't remember what she said once the words were out of her mouth. Liddy kept glancing at her curiously, Burton sulked, and Mrs. Chalmers gave her several disapproving looks. It didn't matter. Johanna knew now that what was between her and Ross was no mere flirtation. It wasn't only her own dreams and fantasies about him. Ross Davison was in love with her.

Ross had asked, "What are we going to do, Johanna?"

Do? What did he mean, *do?*

❧

In the Chalmerses' guest room, Johanna propped the lavender-scented pillows behind her and sat up in bed. She was not the least sleepy, even though, with an exaggerated yawn, she had discouraged Liddy from coming in to gossip and chitchat as they usually did after a party. Liddy had gone away miffed, and although Johanna was sorry about that, she needed to be alone. Something important had happened between her and Ross tonight, and she wanted to think about it, sort out her feelings.

Everything she felt was so new. Yet there was a sweet familiarity about Ross. The odd feeling that they had known each other for a long time lingered. It was as if she had been waiting for him all her life.

She heard the steady patter of rain on the windowpanes. Where was Ross? Was he home yet? Or driving back to town along some country road? Or was he still with those sick children? Her heart felt tender as she thought of what a good doctor he must be. Was he thinking of her, as she was of him?

How conscientious Ross was. Her heart softened further as she contemplated his innate nobility. Yes, nobility. That best described him.

It made her feel humble that such a man *loved her*! She still couldn't quite believe it. She must change, become *worthy* of his love. She needed to mold herself into something better, stronger. Johanna closed her eyes in remembered delight of his kiss. She hugged her knees and smiled. Being in love was so wonderful!

Again Ross's question came into her mind.

"What are we going to do, Johanna?"

Do? Although she wanted to keep this happy secret to herself for a little while, of course in time they would tell everyone, share their happiness. That's all they would *do*. She couldn't imagine what else Ross meant.

Johanna slid down into the pillows, shutting her eyes at last and, with a happy sigh, went to sleep.

Chapter Six

~❦~

*H*urrying through the blustery January afternoon, Johanna hugged her happiness close. Oh, how wonderful it was to at last be free to say "I love you" and mean it! Ross was everything she had ever dreamed of in a lover—more, even! How had she been so lucky? She had never been so happy in her life. She had gone to meet him today from Liddy's house, where she had stayed overnight after the taffy pull party. She had invented an errand so that she could go alone. Liddy had seemed suspicious. Johanna could not share her secret—at least, not yet. Promising she would return so that she would be there when Mr. Chalmers arrived from town to drive her back to Holly Grove, she had rushed out without further explanation.

Ross was waiting for her at the appointed place. Johanna rushed toward him, but instead of looking happy, Ross looked worried. He hadn't slept, he told her. He had been wrong to speak of love to her as he had last night, he began. But she would not let him finish.

"No, no, it wasn't! I love you, too, Ross. And I know it's right."

"But what can we do, Johanna?" The words seemed wrung from the depths of his heart.

His question puzzled her. What would they do? What did any two people in love do? They got married.

He acted as if there were insurmountable problems. She wouldn't listen to any he tried to tell her about. He had house calls to make, and nothing was really settled as he hurried away.

She was so happy, she felt her heart might burst. She couldn't wait to tell her parents. Of course, they did not know Ross very well, but they knew Dr. Murrison. He was an old family friend. They certainly knew and respected Dr. Murrison and must realize he would not have chosen Ross from among all the medical students he could have brought in as his assistant, if he had not been convinced of his character and ability.

And of course, her parents would probably be surprised, call theirs a whirlwind romance, but what was wrong with that? After their first surprise, they would be happy for her. She was sure.

Johanna could not have been more wrong.

The minute the words were out of her mouth, Johanna knew she had made a mistake. She saw the stricken expression on her mother's face. Immediately Johanna was contrite. She was furious with herself for having upset her mother so much. But even though she realized she had not picked the right moment, she hadn't expected this intense opposition.

"It's out of the question. You're much too young and I won't hear of it."

Her mother's reaction chilled Johanna with its cold vehemence. Perhaps it was mostly because she would be the first one to leave the nest. At first Johanna did not realize that the real problem regarded her choice.

Though her father was surprised, his objections were milder. "Well, Johanna, I thought it was young Burton Lassiter you were interested in. He certainly has hung about here looking at you with calves' eyes long enough. What's wrong with Burton? Good family, nice fellow."

"Oh, Burton!" Johanna scoffed. "I don't love Burton. I never could. You can't make me love someone I don't. You certainly can't make me marry someone I don't love."

"Who was talking marrying?" Tennant protested. "Anyway, I agree with your mother. You're far too young to be thinking about marrying anyone."

"Mama was seventeen when she married *you*, Papa. And I'm eighteen and will soon be nineteen."

"That's quite enough, Johanna," her mother interrupted sharply. "We'll speak no more about it. And we will certainly make our wishes plainly known to Dr. Murrison that we do not appreciate Dr. Davison's attentions to our daughter without our permission."

Johanna turned pale. "Oh Mama, you wouldn't! That would humiliate Ross, and he is so sensitive."

Rebecca looked at her coldly. "He should have had the good manners to address your father before he spoke to you of love, Johanna—assuredly before he spoke of marriage. It is just more evidence that he has neither the breeding nor background that we would accept in a prospective husband for our daughter—any of our daughters. And as I have told you many times, as the oldest it is up to you to set the example for your younger sisters. Now, that is all. I suggest you go to your room and give some thought to your rash, reckless behavior and the upset you have caused your parents."

Mute with misery, speechless with frustration and resentment, Johanna turned and went out of the room, ran upstairs and into her bedroom, letting the door slam behind her. She flung herself down and, in a torrent of tears, wept into her pillow for some time.

She knew she had done everything wrong, had approached her parents in the worst way. She'd ruined everything! She had foolishly hoped they would be happy for her. She had not thought of all the objections her mother had listed. It seemed so petty, so cruel, to judge Ross on such shallow measurements. What could she now do to put things right? To make Ross acceptable to her parents?

She woke the next morning with a blotched complexion, eyelids puffy from her frequent bursts of tears during the sleepless night. When her mother sent Cissy to call her down for breakfast, she pleaded a headache and said that she was going to stay in bed. When her mother peeked in the door later in the day, Johanna pretended to be asleep. She had lain there through the hours trying to come up with a new way to present Ross to her parents, to ask them to try to get to know him, to discover his fine qualities. If they did, she knew they could not help but be impressed with the same things she saw and loved in him.

The winter afternoon darkened, and Johanna knew her father would soon be home. When she heard the front door open and her father call out "Rebecca!" as he always did when he entered the house, she tiptoed out of her bedroom, leaned over the banister, and heard the murmur of her parents' voices. She felt sure they were discussing her. She crept downstairs, in her nightie and barefooted, and huddled on the steps, straining to hear what her father and mother were talking about.

She heard her mother say, "She's buried herself in her room all the day, won't eat a bite, determined to be stubborn. She has upset the whole household over this foolish thing. She won't listen to me. She won't listen to anybody!"

"It's her fondness for melodrama, that's all. It will all be over in a few weeks, I'm sure."

At her father's rejoinder, Johanna stiffened indignantly. If there was anything that infuriated her, it was indulgent amusement, that her earnest pleading could be dismissed as a whim not worth considering.

Her father was always inclined to be amused at whatever Johanna did. All her life, when she had popped up with something she had just discovered or thought, he had looked at her indulgently. She could remember numerous times when he had done exactly the same as he had last night when she broke her news about Ross. He had smiled at her, stood up, and patted her on the head as if she were a recalcitrant child who needed to be pacified and reassured that somehow, in time, she would get over her silly notion.

Well, *this* time he was wrong. He'd see. They'd both see. She was serious. She loved Ross Davison, and in spite of anything they said, she was going to keep on loving him and someday they would marry.

Then she heard her mother say firmly, "You must speak to Alec Murrison, Tennant. That's all there is to it. I am sure he would not countenance his assistant pursuing a courtship that was unwelcome. Even if it is only a matter of our friendship, I am sure he will see that our wishes are respected."

Johanna's hands balled into fists and she pressed them against her mouth. Oh, no! That would hurt Ross so dreadfully. He revered and admired Dr. Murrison so much. To have him rebuke him for—what? For loving her! It was too awful. Johanna crept back upstairs and into her room, choking back new sobs.

❧

Across town in the house of the town's physician, another conversation was taking place. Remembering that this was the man who had taken him in, treated him like a son, rendered the hospitality of his home, given him the benefit of his own knowledge and skill, been his mentor and his instructor, Ross hesitated. Perhaps it was too much to ask for Dr. Murrison to champion his cause. Perhaps Dr. Murrison would be risking his friendship with the Shelbys if he gave his blessing to Ross's asking for Johanna's hand in marriage. But how else could this ever come about? At least he could ask Dr. Murrison if he should try.

"I want to marry Johanna Shelby. Do you think there is any hope? I don't want to take advantage of you, sir, but I do need your opinion."

Dr. Murrison pursed his mouth as if giving the statement considerable thought. He knocked his pipe ashes on the stone edge of the fireplace, took his time refilling it and lighting it again before answering Ross's question.

"Have you addressed the young lady herself as yet?"

"Not formally asked her to marry me. However, truthfully, I have told her I love her." He paused in anguished embarrassment. "I couldn't help myself. But I didn't speak of marriage. I wanted to talk to you first, and if you think it would be all right, I would then, of course, approach her father and ask his permission."

"Well, that certainly is the usual way of things," Dr. Murrison agreed, but there was a degree of hesitancy in his words that sent a cold chill through Ross. Something more was coming, and instinctively he braced himself for it.

Then Ross suddenly decided that whatever it was—and he suspected what it *might* be—he didn't want to hear it. Abruptly he got to his feet and said, "I shouldn't have taken advantage of our relationship. I was wrong to place you in an awkward position. Forgive me." Without waiting for Dr. Murrison's reply, Ross left the room.

He went quickly upstairs to his room. He sank into the one chair in the sparsely furnished space and stared at the flickering light shining through the door of his small stove. Why had he been so stupid? Why hadn't he seen what should have been obvious to him from the first? The Shelbys, one of the most prominent families in Hillsboro, accepting a poor, backwoods doctor with no future for the husband of their daughter? He gave a short, harsh laugh. For that's what it was—laughable! Ridiculous. Impossible. How could he have been foolish enough to entertain such a thought—to dream?

At church the following Sunday, Johanna was sitting in the family pew, beside her mother. Rebecca's head was bowed in private prayer before the service. Johanna bowed her head also. She wasn't praying, exactly—she was pleading in anguish and fear. Fear that what she wanted most in the world would not be allowed her. *Please, please, God.*

While her mother stopped after the service to compliment the minister on his sermon, Johanna stepped outside, looking for Ross or Dr. Murrison in any of the groups of men gathered in the churchyard, talking. But the tall figure she hoped to see was nowhere in sight.

It was bitterly cold and frosty, and when Johanna's mother joined her on the church steps, she took her arm, urging sharply, "Come along, Johanna. Get into the carriage. It's too cold to stand around in this wind."

Chapter Seven

❧❦❧

Rebecca, her back very straight, sat at her quilting frame in the parlor. Seven stitches to the inch, in her hand the needle, poised daintily, moved expertly in and out. She had placed a lot of hope in Johanna. Much careful thought and consideration had been given to her rearing. Expense too, sending her to a fine female academy for the kind of education necessary for a girl who would assume the role of a wife in a prestigious marriage. Johanna had shown little interest in housewifely skills. She had acquired exquisite manners and social graces, could set a beautiful table, and was a graceful dancer and a gracious conversationalist. Of course, if she married someone from a wealthy family, such as Burton Lassiter, she would have plenty of servants. However, a woman still needed to master all sorts of tasks to enable her to teach her servants, show them how the work was to be done.

Rebecca gave a small shudder. Although her face was expressionless, she was concerned about her oldest daughter. Through the years, Rebecca had learned to conceal her emotions—disappointment, hurt, anxiety. Pride might be her besetting sin, but it was also her shield.

One deep wound she had suffered and tried to conceal was that she was the *only* one of all Grandmother Logan's granddaughters not to bear her name—Johanna. As if that weren't humiliation enough, then there was her own failure to produce a son for her husband. After two miscarriages and one stillborn, with much difficulty she had delivered Johanna. Three years later Cissy, and five years after that, Elly. But no male to carry on the family name.

Thinking of her own mother, Rebecca had to suppress her resentment. Why had she refused to follow the tradition of the family she married into? Rebecca had hardly known the rebellious young woman who had been her mother. She had died when Rebecca was only four. But of course, the story of her own christening had been told to Rebecca by anxious "do-gooders" and busybodies. It was a family scandal that could not be hushed up, because it had been witnessed by so many. A whole churchful, as a matter of fact. Possibly the whole congregation. The time had come for the minister to ask the question, "And by what name shall this child be known?" and instead of replying as expected, "Her name shall be Johanna," her mother, dark eyes flashing, had responded in a clear voice, audible to the very rafters of the small stone church, "Rebecca." There had been, Rebecca was told, a collective gasp of shock.

The story had been repeated many times to Rebecca over the years, and she grew to dislike hearing it. She'd had to live with the legacy she had been left. It had, in a way, made her the outcast. She had tried to make up for it by excelling in many ways, always competing for attention among her cousins, for her grandmother's affection. But in the end, no one really seemed to care. Bee and Honey and Jo McMillan and Johanna Cady and even Hannah never mentioned it.

Was blood thicker than water? Had somehow Johanna, her carefully taught daughter, inherited the wildness of her maternal grandmother? The rebellious spirit? Flaunting what was expected, falling foolishly in love with an unsuitable man? Ross Davison might be a fine young man—certainly Alec Murrison thought the world of him. Still, he was not the right husband for *her* daughter. Johanna Shelby had been reared to marry a man of wealth, society, good family, refined background.

Well, it would not be. She would not allow it. Not let all her dreams, hopes, plans, go amiss because of a foolish girl's fancy.

Rebecca bent her head again over her work. This quilt, on which she was spending hours of meticulous care, tiny stitches outlining the lovely pattern, was for Johanna. Her wedding quilt. Rebecca had carefully traced the pattern from the ancient design, adding some of her own creative interpretations. It was called the Whig Rose by most, although the more romantic name was Rose of Sharon, which was taken from the beautiful Scripture in Song of Songs, the love song of Solomon to his bride, a part of the Bible that was now taught to describe Christ's love for the church.

As the Rose of Sharon, the pattern was a dazzling declaration of human love, the joy and passion between man and woman, honoring the sacredness of marriage. Secretly that is how Rebecca thought of it as she appliquéd the delicate scrolls, the buds, stems, and leaves, white thread on white. To her it represented all those hidden expectations she had brought to her own wedding, the special dreams of happiness she had hoped would be fulfilled. Now, years later, she was a mature woman who had survived the cares and concerns, the sorrows and losses, the disenchantments of life. As she sewed, Rebecca reflected on her own memories. If all those hopes and dreams had never been fully realized, still she had experienced a satisfying life, once she had faced realities, put away fanciful dreams. As she stitched into this quilt for her daughter renewed promises that yet might be for her happiness, Rebecca's mouth tightened. Rebecca rapped her thimbled finger on the edge of her quilting frame resolutely. *I won't let her make some stupid mistake, throw her life away.*

❦

The following afternoon was the cousins' weekly quilting session. Alternating homes, the ladies of the family gathered to work on each other's quilts. Each cousin had her own special quilt in progress on which the others sewed. Of course, this was more than simply a sewing session. It was a time to exchange events and town gossip, discuss relatives and friends and upcoming plans, or contribute a bit of interesting news. Dessert and coffee and tea were served, perhaps a new recipe to be tasted, commented upon, and enjoyed. It was always a congenial time, and Rebecca always looked forward to it with pleasure. However, in her present state of mind, she was tempted to promote her slightly scratchy throat into a full-fledged cold to avoid going.

These get-togethers had started before they all had married, at the time all were working on quilts for their hope chests. Now it had become a weekly ritual in their lives. Nothing but a serious illness or a life-and-death crisis was an acceptable excuse for not attending. To not go was bound to cause concern of one kind or another.

Only the most unobservant person could have missed the effect of Hannah's remark at Christmas about Johanna's snow frolic with Dr. Davison. Since not one of her cousins could be qualified as that, Rebecca was also sure her canny relatives had noticed Johanna's obvious gaiety brought on by the arrival of the young doctor on New Year's Day. Surely one of them had guessed her high spirits were prompted by something other than a family gathering.

Nothing in the family was ever a private matter. Although kept within the family enclave, everything that happened or was about to happen or needed to be decided was always discussed at length among the cousins. Rebecca was sure someone, some way or other, would mention Johanna's escapade, her interest in Dr. Murrison's assistant.

Although Rebecca felt ill-prepared to answer any probing questions, at length she decided she had to go. There was no possible way out. However, she was determined to maintain a discreet silence on the subject, no matter what the provocation. She anticipated that if there were any, it would most probably come from Hannah. With no children of her own to make excuses for or explanations about, Hannah had an insatiable curiosity about others' offspring.

Resignedly Rebecca hooked the braided fastenings of her mauve pelisse, settled her bonnet on her head, tying its brown satin ribbons firmly under her chin, and set out. Today's meeting was at Johanna Cady's house, only a short distance from the Shelbys'. The brisk walk would clear her head for whatever lay ahead.

As she stepped inside her cousin's door, she was greeted by the usual buzz of conversation from the already assembled ladies, which only halted briefly as she was welcomed. The hostess for the day, Johanna Cady—called Josie by her cousins—rose to take Rebecca's cape, compliment her bonnet, and relieve her of her muff.

"You're late, Rebecca. I thought something might have happened."

"I'm sorry. A little delay, that's all."

"Well, you're here now, and that's all that matters." Josie lowered her voice. "You missed all the discussion about the new pattern we're starting. Of course, Hannah had to have her say, which took a while. So we got started later than usual."

Rebecca took her place at the quilting frame, between Honey and Hannah, and threaded her needle. The pattern stretched out was called Caesar's Crown. It was an array of geometric shapes forming an intricate design, on which Hannah was unfavorably commenting, "Why ever did you pick such a complicated one, Josie?"

"Because it's beautiful. Why else?" Josie retorted, adding tartly, "When it's done properly."

Honey, always the conciliator, spoke up. "I've seen one or two of these finished, and they're outstanding."

"Did Munroe or Harvel use drafting tools to cut your material from?" Hannah persisted.

"No. As a matter of fact, I did it all myself. I used bowls and teacups and folded paper," Josie said with a little toss of her head. "It just takes a little imagination."

"Well, I prefer the Double Wedding Ring pattern to this—it's every bit as handsome and much simpler," sniffed Hannah, anxious to have the last word. Then, in order to keep Josie from another sharp rejoinder, Hannah turned her attention to Rebecca, asking, "Has Johanna finished her twelve quilt tops yet, Rebecca?"

Traditionally, a young woman completed twelve quilt tops for her hope chest. A quilt was supposedly finished by the time she was ready to be engaged. Before Rebecca could think of a noncommittal answer, Bee appeared with the tray of cakes and the tea service. "Let's take a break, ladies," she suggested, and the ladies left their sewing for a welcome time of refreshment. Hannah's question was left dangling.

Rebecca had always been provoked by Johanna's lack of interest in quilting and needlework of any kind. Cissy was much more amenable in every way toward the womanly arts so necessary in a genteel woman's preparation for marriage. If only Johanna were more diligent and less imaginative and adventurous. If she *were*, there would certainly not be this need to worry over her.

Josie used Hannah's comment to introduce a subject she wanted to bring up. "Speaking of the Double Wedding Ring pattern, I think we should start working on one soon," she smiled smugly and sat back, waiting for her cousins' eager curiosity.

"What do you mean, Josie?" asked Bee.

"Well, it isn't official," she began tantalizingly, "but I think Harvel is about to propose to Marilee Barrington. He's just spoken to her father over in Cartersville, and—"

She was immediately the target of enthusiastic inquiries, demands for a description of the young lady, the possible date of the nuptials, and other pertinent questions. Of course, it was Hannah who had to put a chill into the happy conversation. She pierced Rebecca with a long look and pursed mouth, remarking morosely, "What a shame we couldn't be planning a lovely quilt for Johanna!"

Every eye, albeit tactful ones, turned expectantly toward Rebecca. She could easily have said something scathing to silence her cousin, but that would only have revealed her own inner upset. Instead, keeping her voice even, a tolerant smile in place, she replied, "No news from that corner, I'm afraid." Inside she was indignant at her cousin's bluntness. Somehow Hannah always managed to strike a sour note.

For the rest of the afternoon, Rebecca sewed quietly, not adding much to the hum of conversation that flowed around her. Her mind was busily plotting a sure way to remove Johanna from the dangerous ground on which she was treading because of her foolish infatuation with the young doctor. Johanna was always drawn to the different, the out of the ordinary, the unusual. And Ross Davison certainly fit all those criteria.

If only Tennant hadn't given into Johanna's pleas not to be sent back to Miss Pomoroy's. Rebecca had been against it and yet had allowed herself to be persuaded. Privately she had decided Johanna was as "finished" as she need be. They could apply the saved fee to Cissy's turn to go next year. Rebecca had to admit that the thought of enjoying Johanna's company at home had influenced her decision. Now she regretted her quick capitulation.

How cleverly Johanna had managed to manipulate her parents for her own purpose. Rebecca could but wonder how she herself had been taken in by Johanna's persuasiveness. All Johanna had ever wanted was to stay in Hillsboro, near the young doctor. It's my own fault, Rebecca chided herself. I saw it on New Year's Day! They only had eyes for each other. Johanna attempted to hide it, but *he* was too honest to try. Rebecca sighed. Even then it was probably too late. It had gone too far by then.

But of course, this courtship was impossible. And now it was up to *her* to do something, Rebecca decided.

Quite unexpectedly she was handed the opportunity she had been searching for. She was brought back from her own troubling thoughts into the present when she heard Honey announce, "I'm planning to go to Winston with Jo when she returns home."

Winston! Of course! Rebecca thought immediately. Winston, where the McMillans lived, was a lovely place with two colleges and a seminary, a cultured atmosphere. It was a hospitable and friendly town. What a perfect solution! Get Johanna out of town. Her cousin had a wide circle of friends, most of whom had children Johanna's age who could introduce her into their lively social life. Johanna could accompany Honey on her trip. Honey adored Johanna, and if Johanna could be persuaded—

No, not persuaded—*told* she must go. Rebecca was through with indulging her. They would have to be firm. Johanna must be kept from a mistake that might ruin her life.

Rebecca decided to have a private word with Honey. As soon as Honey got up to leave, Rebecca quickly followed. Once outside walking together, she tucked her arm through her cousin's and outlined her plan, confiding the reasons she had not wanted to share with the others.

Honey was delighted with the idea. Encouraged by this response, Rebecca felt led to open up more about her concerns, about how unsuitable she felt Johanna's interest in Ross Davison was and how anxious she was to remove Johanna even temporarily from an impulsive attachment.

Honey looked doubtful. "Well, of course, I'm sure Jo will be happy to introduce Johanna and perhaps even give a party or two for her while we're there, but I've never seen parental interference do more than intensify a romance, sometimes even making it the reason to flourish."

"Be that as it may, Honey, it's a risk I shall have to take. You know how impulsive Johanna is, and I just cannot take the chance of her rushing headlong into something as disastrous as this match could be."

~❧~

Johanna had heard her mother leave and knew she would be gone several hours for the weekly quilting session. She could not remember at which auntie's house it was being held this week. It didn't matter. She knew that sooner or later her situation would be circulated on the family grapevine. Johanna expected this, anticipated it, both dreading and looking forward to the opinions they would express. All would be different, she was sure. She wasn't counting on allies because, despite their contrasting views, the cousins usually stood together on such things. All she could hope for was some understanding.

The house was empty. Now that the holidays were over, her sisters had started back to the dame school they attended in town, and she was alone.

It had been a horrible week. She had stubbornly refused to join the family for meals since the terrible scene with her parents two nights before. Johanna was not proud of the chaos she had brought into the usual harmonious atmosphere of the Shelby home. But they were being so unreasonable. They were refusing to even allow Ross to come and talk to them, ignoring all his fine qualities in an unyielding assertion that he was "unsuitable."

Her parents were giving her a studied silent treatment, maintaining a rare period of unity about the issue. That her father was as adamant as her mother was a bitter pill to swallow. Always before, he had been willing to let Johanna present her case, whatever it was. It especially hurt that this time he stuck with her mother, and her mother was entirely inflexible.

They had forced her to be deceitful, she justified, slipping out of the house on the chance that she would meet Ross as he went about making house calls in town. By some sort of unspoken agreement, they had found that the curved stone bridge near the churchyard was an easy place for their paths to cross by "happenstance." That's where she hurried on her way today. She felt a little uneasiness, a kind of nervous apprehension. She had not yet told him of her parents' reaction to telling them they were in love. She knew how deeply wounding it would be to his pride to learn they did not approve of him as a prospective husband for their daughter.

At the little bridge, Johanna looked anxiously for the familiar figure she hoped to see. She had only a few minutes to wait. Soon she saw Ross, his head bent against the wind, striding toward her.

As soon as she saw his expression, she knew something was very wrong. There were circles under his deep-set eyes, as if he had not slept. He looked drawn and there was a vulnerability about him she had never noticed before. Something had happened. Had someone in her family gone to him, told him they considered his courtship unacceptable? Her father? No, not him. Her mother? One of her uncles?

Perhaps they had even gone to Dr. Murrison? She had been foolish to think they could keep their love secret—not in *this* family, she thought with some bitterness. Not when everyone lived in everyone else's pockets. Her heart felt heavy and she felt almost sick. Ross's step slowed as he approached her, almost as if he were reluctant to see her, to tell her what she felt in her heart of hearts he had come to say.

Shivering with cold and nervousness, Johanna wasted no time. She had already broken so many rules of so-called ladylike deportment as related to him, it would be better to know at once what was the matter. It was too important. She had to know.

"What is it, Ross? You look so troubled."

"Johanna, we cannot go on meeting like this. Your parents would be angry if they knew. We must not see each other again."

"Not see each other? What do you mean? Not ever?" How did he know about her mother and father's disapproval? "Ross, why? Is this your idea? But you said—" She hesitated. Then she had no pride left and finished, "you said that you loved me."

"I shouldn't have, Johanna. It was wrong of me."

"*Wrong?* How is it wrong? You did say you loved me, didn't you? Or did I imagine it? Dream up the whole thing?" Her voice trembled, tears glistening in her eyes.

"No, of course not. I do love you, Johanna. Maybe I should never have told you, because it was wrong—"

"I don't understand." She shook her head.

"The fact is, Dr. Murrison himself has discouraged me from pursuing my courtship. He says I should never have spoken to you about love—or anything—without first speaking to your parents. Dr. Murrison pointed out that this was probably the first thing they hold against me. That I don't know the proper thing to do, that I don't have the manners or the right background for—"

"Oh, for pity's sake, Ross, has he threatened you? Would he dismiss you?"

"No, of course not. He just pointed out the simple truth. You come from a home, a family, a life, so different from mine or what I have to offer—"

"Does love mean nothing? That we love each other—did you tell him *that?*"

Looking abject, Ross slowly shook his head. "No, I didn't. Because in my heart, I know they're right."

"No, they're not. They're very, very wrong. I love you. I won't hear any more of this." Johanna placed her fingers on his lips to keep him from saying more.

Ross pulled them gently away from his mouth and went on speaking.

"We must be sensible, Johanna. What *do* I have to offer you? A doctor without a practice of my own. I'm going back this summer when my apprenticeship with Dr. Murrison is over. Back to the mountains—you don't know what living there would be like. There'll be hardly any money, because most of the folks I'll be caring for don't have any. They'll pay in potatoes or corn or firewood, most likely. Johanna, how can a man ask his wife—a girl like you, who's been used to so much more—"

"I don't care about that!" she protested.

"But *I* do. And if I were your father, I would. Dr. Murrison's right. He told me he worked years before he could get married. I have nothing to offer you—"

"That's not true, Ross. You have everything to offer me. Your life, your love, your whole heart—that's all I want, all I'll ever want."

She put her gloved hand on his arm. His head was turned from her, and she longed to see his face, to try to read what he was thinking in his eyes. "Look at me, Ross." Her voice was low, urgent, sweet to his ears. He turned, took both her hands in his, brought them to his chest, looked down into her upturned face.

"Oh, Johanna. I love you, but I want to do the right thing."

"This is the right thing," she whispered. "Let me talk to my parents. Surely they want me to be happy."

"I believe they want your happiness, but I also believe they don't think I would be part of the happiness they want for you."

"I think it was a surprise—even a shock—but when I tell them how I feel, how I really feel about you, I think they'll understand."

Ross did not look so sure. "I don't want you to be alienated from your parents, Johanna—" His voice deepened with determination. "I won't go against your parents' wishes. I respect them too much for that."

A shaft of wind blew Johanna's bonnet back, her hair about her face, and she pushed it back impatiently, tucking the strands behind her ears, then straightened her bonnet.

"I've always been able to convince my parents when I really and truly wanted something. *This* time it's the most important thing in my life." Johanna tried to sound convincing. However, Ross's expression, the uncertainty in his eyes, shook her confidence.

When they parted, she felt cold and a little afraid. It was beginning to get dark as she walked home. The damp, gusty wind blew wet leaves, scattering them, plastering them on gates and fences along the way. The glow of being with Ross, the warmth of his kiss on her lips, began to fade. She shivered. She had never before felt like this. The loving closeness of her family had always protected her, sheltered her. No one could understand how miserable she was, how desolate, how totally alone she felt. There was no one to comfort her, support her. She was in this by herself. It would take all her courage to see it through, to stand fast. Even Ross doubted the wisdom of what they were doing. He was even willing to give her up—for what? For people to whom wealth, privilege, and standing in society meant more than love?

Her mother was already home when Johanna returned red-eyed from her walk, hoping she could blame it on the cold wind. She halted briefly at the door of the parlor, made some comment about the weather to her mother, then went upstairs.

Johanna seemed oddly subdued, Rebecca thought. The suspicion that she might be hiding something confirmed her own decision. She had made the wise choice, done the right thing. The sooner Johanna was out of harm's way, the better.

In her room, Johanna paced agitatedly. She must get this over, get everything out into the open. The sooner, the better. She would wait until after supper, after both her younger sisters were in bed. Then when both parents were together, she would go to them. The only way she could hope to make her parents understand that she was serious was to tell them in clear, brave, simple language, "I love Ross Davison and intend to marry him." Over and over she rehearsed just what she would say. But she never got to say those fiercely independent words.

Johanna worked herself up to such hope that she never imagined she could fail to convince them. She did not take into account that her parents were just as determined not to let their daughter "throw herself away" on a penniless doctor from the hills.

Chapter Eight

The following evening during dinner, the atmosphere was strained. Even the two younger girls seemed affected by the hovering storm. Finally everyone finished and as Johanna rose, preparing to do her assigned job of clearing the table, Rebecca spoke, "Leave that, Johanna. Cissy and Elly can do it tonight. Your father and I want to speak to you in the parlor."

Johanna followed, half glad that although this was unexpected, it might be the chance she was waiting for. She drew a long breath and followed her parents across the hall.

Her mother stood at the door and closed it after Johanna entered. Rebecca moved to stand at her husband's side, and they both turned to face her. Johanna felt a premonition—of what, she wasn't quite sure. Then her mother spoke.

"We have been shocked and saddened by your rebellious spirit, your unfilial behavior, your unwillingness to obey us as your parents, who are wiser and far more competent to judge what is best for you. This unsuitable attachment must be ended at once. Since you do not see fit to obey us out of love and submission, we are sending you away from the occasion of your willful disregard of parental guidance until you come to your senses. Tomorrow you are leaving with Aunt Honey for an extended stay at Aunt Jo's in Winston. We hope this will give you the opportunity to examine your recent behavior, come to your senses, and once more trust that we know what is best for you."

Stunned, Johanna gasped. "You can't mean that! You wouldn't! How could you, Mama?" Her voice broke into a sob. "To send me away like this—like I've done something wicked! I don't deserve to be treated like a child!"

"You *are* little more than a child, Johanna—a foolish, stubborn one, we have to concede. However, you are still under our supervision, and we are responsible for your actions, certainly for your future. You will do as you are told."

"Papa, do you agree?" Johanna turned in desperation to her usual advocate. But Tennant's face was averted. He stared into the fire and did not turn to look at Johanna. But her mother spoke, drawing Johanna's attention back to the one who was the real originator of the idea to exile her.

"Your clothes and other things are packed, and you will leave first thing in the morning."

Unable to speak, blinded by tears, Johanna whirled around and ran out of the room, tripping on the hem of her dress as she stumbled up the stairs to her room. She let the door slam behind her, then stood there for a moment looking wildly around as if for some escape. Then her gaze found her small, humpbacked trunk at the foot of the poster bed. The lid was raised but it was neatly packed, just awaiting a few last minute belongings to be placed in the top layer.

A sob rose and caught in Johanna's throat. So it was true. They were sending her away. Well, if they thought that would make her forget Ross or change her mind about him—they were wrong. Johanna's jaw clenched.

❧❧

Later, coming upstairs, Rebecca paused on the landing. From behind Johanna's closed bedroom door, she heard muffled sounds. One hand gripped the banister. Her sobs were pathetic, heartrending to hear. Consciously Rebecca stiffened, stifling her maternal urge to go in, to comfort. Then her sensible nature took over. No, Johanna needed to learn that life wasn't simply a matter of choices. There was a reason. She could not allow her daughter to throw away her life, all she'd been groomed and trained for, on a nobody—a man from who knows what kind of family? Slowly Rebecca mounted the rest of the stairs and passed her daughter's door without stopping.

⚜

The next morning when Aunt Honey's coach was sent around for her, Johanna came downstairs to find her father had already left the house for his law office. Puzzled, she asked, "Didn't Papa even wait to tell me good-bye?"

"You have hurt your father deeply," Rebecca replied tightly.

Her words stung Johanna as much as if she had been slapped in the face. She stepped away from her mother, feeling both guilty to have caused her beloved father unhappiness and wounded by this rebuke. She knew she had behaved impulsively, spoken disrespectfully. Much she wished she could retract. She was remorseful and if he had been there, she might have begged her father's forgiveness. But to let her leave like this seemed too cruel a punishment.

"It's time to go, Johanna. Matthew and Honey want to get an early start, and you still have to pick up Aunt Jo."

Her mother turned a cool cheek for Johanna to kiss, and dutifully Johanna bid her good-bye. She prayed that someday all this hurt between them would be healed. She dearly wanted this, but not if it meant giving up Ross.

The night before, she had committed one last rebellious act. She had written to Ross, planning to post it somehow on the way. In her letter, she told him of her departure, adding,

Ross, I am doing what my parents wish by going to my aunt's without complaint, if only to prove that this imposed separation will not change my feelings toward you. In fact, I believe the old adage "Absence makes the heart grow fonder." I trust that you feel the same as I do. I trust that when you said you loved me, you meant it and are willing to wait and hope that this forced parting will have been worth it when my parents give their consent.

After writing those lines, Johanna had put her pen aside for a moment. She knew she had laid her heart bare and it may have been reckless to do so. But Johanna knew Ross was a man to trust—his word was his bond. He had told her he loved her, and that was enough for her. Both of them knew that the feeling between them was too strong to be denied. It wasn't as simple a matter as her parents thought. What was between her and Ross was deeper than that.

A future together seemed threatened, but Johanna felt that whatever the future held, she wanted to share it with Ross. No matter what price she had to pay. Otherwise, she foresaw for herself a life of bitter regret, a loss that nothing else would ever fill.

Now as she looked through the oval window in the back of Uncle Matthew's carriage and saw the house she had left grow smaller and smaller as they went down the lane, Johanna's heart was wrenched. Home, with all it implied, meant a great deal to Johanna. She had often been homesick when away at school, had longed to be back in the warm, harmonious atmosphere with her parents and sisters. But now it was almost a relief to be going. The strain between her and her parents had become unbearable. On the other hand, leaving Hillsboro meant that even a chance encounter with Ross was impossible.

Well, she would have to make the best of it. Ross would know she had not given up, and however long her exile would be, her parents would see it had not achieved its goal. When it was over and she came back, surely they could work things out.

Aunt Jo and Aunt Honey were companionable fellow travelers, and the daylong trip was not too arduous at all. Even though Johanna was sure her aunties had been advised of the reason she was accompanying them, they did not mention a word, and the day passed pleasantly. Uncle Matthew fell asleep almost as soon as they had passed the town limits, and he slept most of the way.

The McMillan's house was a rambling fieldstone-and-clapboard structure a little distance from town. Aunt Jo's husband, Mac, as everyone called him, came out on the porch to greet them heartily as the carriage came to a stop in front. His warm welcome was the key to the rest of Johanna's visit.

There was an assortment of relatives from odd branches of all the families that were merged with the Logan clans, and all of them outdid themselves to entertain the visiting cousins. Everyone contrived to make Johanna's visit pleasant. There were parties of all kinds, dancing, skating, suppers, and teas. Aunt Jo had many friends with sons and daughters Johanna's age. Most of the young men attended the local college and always came with two or three classmates to any sort of gathering to which they were invited. Johanna never lacked for dance partners at any of the events, even though she felt less like dancing and partying than she ever had. She missed Ross terribly. In the midst of any party, her thoughts would stray to the one person who wasn't there, and her vivaciousness would visibly fade, her attention span falter, her conversation become distracted.

The days passed, one after the other, until Johanna had been in Winston almost two weeks. One morning she woke up close to despair. She felt so helpless. If only she could do something instead of sit it out and drearily wait for her parents to alter their decision. She had no idea what her mother had arranged with Aunt Honey about how long she was to stay at Aunt Jo's. She was getting very weary of the seemingly endless round of Winston social life—it struck her as inconsequential and meaningless.

Her forced "exile," as Johanna privately termed her visit, did provide a chance for some rare introspection, something she had little time for at home. In Rebecca's well-run household, every chore was assigned, checked upon, every moment of the day accounted for. But here Johanna often lay awake at night after the rest of the house was quiet, its occupants asleep. Then most often her thoughts flew to Ross. She wondered what he was doing, tried to imagine him meeting with patients or perhaps sitting at his study table at night, his dark head bent over his huge medical books.

In the long nights before sleep overtook her, Johanna examined her reasons for her strong attraction for this man, who had come as a stranger into the town where *she* had grown up. Yet there had been an immediate bonding. It was as if heart spoke to heart, soul to soul, as if they had looked deeply into each other's eyes and found life's meaning there.

It must be unusual, it must not happen often. She readily understood why her parents found it bewildering. She did, too. Even though she didn't fully understand it herself, she knew it was real.

Johanna decided to confide in Aunt Honey. She had always been easy to talk to, quick to sympathize, ready to understand. There was a disarming innocence about her, maybe due in part to Uncle Matt's take-charge attitude toward her. He treated her with such caring affection, almost as if she were a child. But Honey was far from childish. She was a keen observer of and had a tolerance for human behavior, its foibles and failings. She never seemed critical nor surprised by anyone's failures.

One afternoon Johanna came into the parlor when Aunt Jo had gone riding, and she found Aunt Honey was alone. Her aunt raised her eyes from her knitting. "Well, dearie, are you enjoying your visit?"

Johanna walked over to the window, fiddled with the drapery tassel, staring disconsolately out the window for a few minutes. Then spinning around, she faced her aunt. "It's not working, you know," she said bluntly.

Honey surveyed her niece warily. "What do you mean, dearie?"

"Oh, I know you had to join in the conspiracy," Johanna blurted out. "And I don't blame *you*, Aunt Honey. I know my parents think they're doing the right thing, separating me from Ross. They think I'm going to change. But I'm not."

Aunt Honey lowered her knitting and looked at Johanna. "You think not, eh?"

"I know not!" replied Johanna firmly. "I love him and he loves me. And they should just accept that."

"Can't you try to see this from your parent's viewpoint?" Aunt Honey suggested mildly.

"I can't. How can I?"

"I suppose you're right, dear. How could anyone expect you to?"

"You do understand, don't you, Aunt Honey?" Johanna sighed. "It's so unfair. They won't even let him come to the house, let themselves get to know him." She paused, then turned to her aunt eagerly. "When we get back to Hillsboro, would you let Ross visit me at your house?"

Startled, Honey looked at Johanna, then slowly shook her head. "Johanna, dear, I couldn't possibly go against your parents' wishes. It would be wrong—"

"But it's wrong of *them* to keep us apart. All I want to do is be happy! Why don't they want me to be happy?"

"Don't be so harsh on your parents, Johanna. They *are* thinking of your happiness. They just don't think what you want to do will make you happy."

"Ross *will* make me happy."

Aunt Honey looked pensive. Her eyes rested thoughtfully on her niece.

"No other person can guarantee you happiness, Johanna. Much as you think they can. Life isn't a fairy tale with everyone's story having a happy ending."

But she saw that Johanna wasn't really listening. There was a bemused expression on her face, a faraway look in her eyes. She was gazing somewhere into the future, a future with Ross. Honey realized she might have been talking to a stone for all the good her warning was doing. A fairy-tale romance was what Johanna was living, what she wanted. All true love, glorious sunsets, moonlit nights, music, eternal bliss. Honey sighed, perhaps she'd better write a letter to her cousin Rebecca.

However, Honey procrastinated. Maybe it would just take more time. After all, Johanna seemed to be trying to enter into the social activities Jo arranged for her.

At least for another week or so. Then came a day when Johanna did not come down to breakfast. She complained of a headache. When her aunt took her up a tray of tea and toast, she found Johanna's eyes swollen from crying. The next day she remained in bed. She refused to eat, no matter what dainties or delicacies the McMillan's cook fixed for her. She grew pale and wan. The aunties became concerned, then worried.

"This won't do," Aunt Jo said severely to her cousin. "It won't do at all." So Honey sat down and wrote the letter she had put off writing to Rebecca and Tennant.

My Dear Cousins,

I hesitate to write this letter, but both Jo and I feel it is necessary to apprise you of the rather alarming decline in Johanna's physical condition, which causes a great deal of concern. We know the reason you felt a change of scene from Hillsboro would be beneficial (her interest in Ross Davison, whom you consider an unacceptable suitor). However, we must inform you that her interest in him has not diminished, nor has her determination wavered. Her symptoms would seem grave if we all did not know their source to be emotional. To put it quite plainly, Johanna is "heartsick" and fading fast like a flower deprived of sunlight. She is without energy, enthusiasm, takes little food or liquids—in other words, she is gravely depressed. We are really concerned that she may be moving into melancholia. She no longer takes any interest in the social life here in Winston, although she has been both welcomed and sought after by the young people of Jo's acquaintance. We therefore have come to the conclusion that it would be best if she came home, where she can have parental care.

Your devoted cousin,
Honey

Within a week word came back that Johanna was to return to Hillsboro on the next stagecoach.

Chapter Nine

Johanna arrived back home looking considerably thinner and quite pale. Her first look at her daughter gave Rebecca a start. Gone were the rosy cheeks, the sparkle in her eyes, the lilt in her voice. Even if Johanna were dramatizing herself, the result was effective. Determined not to soften her attitude to her recalcitrant daughter, Rebecca simply saw to it that she ate every bite of the nourishing food placed before her, got plenty of rest and a daily walk in fresh air.

For her part, Johanna was glad to be home, glad that her parents seemed reasonably happy to see her. Things settled back to the normal routine of life Johanna knew before she had disrupted it with her rebellion. Elly, of course, was delighted to have her adored older sister home, while Cissy seemed aloof. During Johanna's absence, she had strenuously played the dutiful daughter, in contrast to Johanna. It amused Johanna somewhat to see her sister take advantage of the situation. It also saddened her, because although no one spoke of it, she could tell her own place in the family was not quite what it had been.

Secretly Johanna was biding her time, trying to find some way to contact Ross or prevail on her parents to change their minds about allowing them to see each other.

Liddy Chalmers, her first visitor, seemed shocked at her appearance. "My goodness, Johanna! What's wrong? You look so thin and pale! Have you been ill? What has happened?"

Tears welled up in Johanna's eyes at the sympathy in Liddy's voice. "*Everything's* happened!" she wailed. "Everything in the world. My heart is breaking. I'm in love with Ross Davison, and I don't know what I'm going to do about it."

Liddy's eyes widened. "Ross Davison? *Really?* I mean, I noticed you only had eyes for each other at the taffy pull, but then you went away, and—"

Johanna poured out her heart. Liddy was titillated by the details of Johanna's description of her secret meetings with Ross, which to Liddy's imagination had all the elements of one of the romantic novels she devoured about star-crossed lovers. But sympathetic as she proved to be, Liddy still was shocked that Johanna had defied her parents. It just wasn't done. Not in their ordered world. Johanna soon sensed that her friend was not as supportive as she had hoped she might be and that it would be wiser to keep her own council rather than confide in her.

During the days after her homecoming, Johanna spent a great deal of time in her room. Ostensibly, she was working on her album quilt or otherwise putting her time to good use. Actually, she was doing much soul searching.

Johanna knew that her parents' purpose in sending her away to forget Ross had been a failure. It had confirmed her feelings for him, deepened her conviction that their two lives were meant to be joined.

Johanna felt that with Ross her life would take on new depth. None of the young men her parents deemed eligible had stirred her heart, her imagination, her spirit, as Ross Davison had done. Observing the lives of the women in her family, Johanna found them a tedious round of shallow pleasures and rigid duties, restricted by limiting social rules. Johanna desperately wanted something else. She wanted her life to have meaning, to have it matter that she even existed.

She believed strongly that by sharing Ross's life, she would find the meaning she was searching for in her own. Johanna was convinced this was her chance. She even dared to think it was God's purpose for her life, if she just had the courage to grasp it.

On the brink of despair, deep in her heart she believed that if they were *not* allowed to marry, the rest of her life would be lonely, dissatisfied, unfulfilled.

At length she came to the important decision to take matters into her own hands. She would send a note to Ross asking him to meet her at the bridge near the churchyard. That would be easily enough arranged, since her mother insisted on her daily "constitutional." Whether he answered or met her or not, Johanna would accept it as God's will. She was willing to risk leaving the result to God.

She wrote only a few lines.

My Dear Ross,

> *I am home again and must see you so we can talk. Please meet me at the bridge near the churchyard.*

Ever your Johanna

❧

A little before the hour she was to meet Ross, Johanna hurried past the steepled church and, winding through the graveyard, to the arched stone bridge. The day was gray and overcast, and the willows bending over the river were bare. Johanna arrived breathless with anticipation and anxiety. What if Ross did not come? Not showing up could be his way of telling her he was not going to defy her parents' disapproval. As she came in sight of the bridge, to her relief she saw Ross already there. She saw his tall figure, the shoulders hunched slightly, folded arms on the ledge, staring down into the rushing water below.

She ran the last few steps toward him. At the click of her boots on the bridge, he turned, and as he did, Johanna remembered how at their first meeting she'd had the strange sensation that they were being reunited again after a very long separation. What she had felt before was some kind of mysterious precognition. Only this time it was true. This time it was *really* happening.

Johanna halted and there were a few seconds of hesitation before either of them moved. Then simultaneously they both rushed forward. He caught her hands tightly in his. His gaze embraced her hungrily.

"Oh Ross, I missed you so!" Johanna cried.

Ross did not reply. His eyes said so much more. He simply drew her to him, holding her so close that she could feel the thud of his heart next to her own. Then, his arm around her waist, they walked down closer to the water.

"Johanna, was this wise? I feel so guilty deceiving your father and mother by meeting you. And Dr. Murrison too. But when I got your note, I couldn't *not* come. I never meant to cause such . . . trouble."

"It's not your fault, Ross. I had to see you. I had to be sure. . . ." Johanna paused and looked at him anxiously.

Ross shook his head sadly. "It's wrong to meet like this when your parents have made it clear that—"

"Ross, don't say that. Just listen. *Listen!*" she begged. "I love you. Nothing else matters if you love me, too. You *do* love me, don't you?"

"You know I do, Johanna, but I had no right to speak without first—"

"If you love me, Ross, I have no intention of forgetting you or giving you up. I shall go to my parents, tell them. And if they still—"

"No, Johanna." Ross's tone was firm, decisive. "That's not your place. It is mine. I have given this a great deal of thought. In fact, I have thought of scarce else since you went away. I will go to your father like any honorable man would do, ask him to give me, to my face, the reasons they consider me unworthy to ... court you." The corners of his mouth lifted slightly at the use of the old-fashioned word. "I love you, Johanna, and I intend to fight for you."

During the next few days, the March weather was as unpredictable as Johanna's emotional seesaw. One day she would awaken to gusty winds, rain dashing against the windows—the next morning sunshine would be drenching her bedroom. Johanna's mood vacillated from hope to despair. Had Ross acted as he had told her he intended to? Had he gone to see her father? Written him? Life in the Shelby household seemed to go on its usual smooth way, neither parent giving Johanna any indication that Ross had taken the step he had promised.

Then one late afternoon Johanna's father came home earlier than usual. He came to the door of the room where Rebecca sat at her quilting frame, beckoned her to follow him into his study, then closed the door.

Johanna had been in the room with Rebecca, dusting her mother's collection of porcelain figures. Evidently her father had not seen her. As her parents disappeared, Johanna put the Dresden shepherdess back on the mantelpiece and tiptoed across the hall. She paused briefly at the closed study door, straining to hear some of their conversation. But all she could hear was the steady flow of her father's deep voice, interrupted occasionally by her mother's. However, she could not tell anything from the tones of their voices.

Johanna's heart beat a staccato. She felt sure she and Ross were under discussion. Had there been a meeting? Had Ross been dismissed, his suit rejected? Had he been humiliated? No, her father was first and foremost a gentleman. He was also a compassionate, understanding man, a gentle father.

In an agony of uncertainty, Johanna crept past the closed room, up the stairway, and into her bedroom. There she flung herself on her knees and prayed. She tried to pray as she had been taught, a submissive, surrendered kind of prayer, the kind she had been told was most pleasing to God. However, such learned prayers were in conflict with the desperate ones of her heart. Even as she murmured, "If it be your will . . .," deep down it was *her* will she wanted done. Her stubborn, rash, reckless will to have Ross no matter what the cost.

Johanna was not sure how long she had prayed when there was a brisk knock at her bedroom door. Quickly she scrambled to her feet, just as Cissy poked her prim little face in, saying importantly, "Johanna, Mama and Papa want to see you right away." She delivered this message with the unspoken implication, *You're in trouble!*

～❧～

Johanna entered the room with a sinking feeling. Her mother was seated at her quilting frame and did not look up. Her father stood, his back to the door, staring into the fire blazing on the hearth. At her entrance he turned. His expression was unreadable.

"You wanted to see me, Papa?" Johanna asked in a voice that trembled slightly.

"Yes. Your mother and I want to talk with you, Johanna. Come in, please, and take a seat."

Johanna wasn't prepared for the gentleness in her father's voice. In fact, she had been half afraid they had discovered her secret meetings with Ross and she was about to receive a stern lecture on deceitfulness and disobedience. She came in and closed the door behind her and walked across the room to the chair he'd indicated.

Her knees were shaking, so she was glad to sit down. However, she perched on the edge of the chair, clasping her hands tightly together on her lap. Holding her breath, she looked from one to the other of her parents. Her mother continued stitching and did not meet her daughter's gaze. Johanna then looked toward her father expectantly. There was a tenseness in his posture unlike his usual relaxed attitude when at home.

"First, I want you to know, Johanna," he began in a rather lawyerly manner, "that we respect you, admire you even, for your courage to withstand our persuasion—yes, our attempts to influence you from making what we deem an unwise decision. It shows character—"

Her mother stirred as if in disagreement, and Mr. Shelby glanced over at her. He paused a few seconds before he continued, amending his statement. "At least a determination that, while perhaps misguided, is nevertheless commendable."

Johanna braced herself for whatever was forthcoming.

"As your parents, we feel it our responsibility to guide you in matters that your youth, inexperience, may not give you the wisdom to decide for yourself. When someone is young and in love, clarity is often blurred." He paused again. "Your mother and I have spent many hours in prayerful discussion of this situation." He spoke slowly and very deliberately. "We feel that as your parents, we should point out to you that with such a man as Ross Davison, his lifework, which he intends to pursue in a remote, very poor mountain community, will always come first. The needs of the people he serves will always be his priority. Much like that of a dedicated minister of the gospel. A wife and family will always have to take second place, even though that might not be his conscious choice. Do you understand what I mean?"

"Yes, sir, I think I do."

"You and this young man, Ross Davison, have very different backgrounds, as you must know. You have been reared in a comfortable home, provided with all the necessities—and what's more, some of the luxuries. You have been sheltered, privileged. From what I understand, he was raised in poverty, hardship, but through his own efforts and those of some who believed in him, he has managed to get an education and is now a skilled physician."

Mr. Shelby turned, picked up one of the fire tools from beside the hearth, poked at the logs. The sizzling hiss of a breaking log filled the temporarily silent room. It was a full minute before he began to speak again.

Johanna pressed her palms together in suspense. Where was all this leading?

Slowly her father turned back, and in a voice thick with emotion, he said, "We have met with our trusted friend Dr. Murrison, who told us that Dr. Davison is a man of unquestioned integrity and honor as well as being a fine doctor. The young man you have chosen and wish to marry is one of remarkable intelligence, character. Still, I feel I must tell you, Johanna, that if you marry this man, you will be going into a kind of life for which you have no preparation. It will be a hard life, a life of work, privation—" He halted, as though he felt it difficult to go on.

"Yes, Papa?" Johanna prodded breathlessly.

He looked at her and she saw on his face infinite resignation, sadness. Then he said, "We have agreed nothing is worth the stress and discord that have been constant in this household of late." He cleared his throat. "So we want you to know that if you truly believe that a marriage to Ross Davison will bring you fulfillment and happiness—then we consent to it."

Stunned, Johanna glanced at her mother, then back to her father.

"Oh, Papa, do you really mean it?"

"Yes, my dear. I would not say so if I did not. We give our consent." He shook his head. "That is not to say that we approve of it or have reconsidered the obstacles we see in such a marriage. What we are saying is that we give our permission for you and Dr. Davison to see one another and"— Mr. Shelby shrugged—"the rest is up to you."

Johanna jumped up and rushed over to him. "Oh Papa, thank you, thank you!" She spun around toward her mother. Rebecca held up a hand as if to ward off a hug.

"No, Johanna, don't thank *me*! You have had your way in this matter. Over my disapproval, my objections. I hope it won't bring you unhappiness."

Johanna was too relieved to let even her mother's coldness dampen her joy. "I'm sorry if I've hurt you, Mama, but I know it's the right thing." She paused. "May I have permission to let Ross know your decision?"

She glanced at her mother, whose mouth tightened as a flush of anger rose into her face. Johanna turned to her father for the answer.

"Dr. Davison has already been told. Through Dr. Murrison. It was Alec Murrison who came to see me at my office to plead the young man's cause. His arguments were valid, convincing. I told him he should have become a defense lawyer instead of a doctor." Mr. Shelby smiled but it was a tight, rather grim smile. "I'm sure Dr. Davison now knows he can pursue his . . . courtship."

Johanna moved to the parlor door. Tears of happiness sprang into her eyes. Her hand on the knob, she turned back into the room. "Thank you," she said again, then went out and started up the stairs. She saw her two sisters leaning over the balcony at the top of the stairway. She recognized by their guilty faces that they had been doing their best to eavesdrop on the conversation in the parlor. But too happy to be cross, she laughed. Running the rest of the way to the top, she grabbed each girl by one hand and spun them around, pulled them with her down the upstairs hall in a merry, exultant dance.

The next morning, in the cold light of day, her euphoria wore off.

She had dashed off a note to Ross informing him of her parents' decision, hoping he would call upon her that evening. That done, Johanna's soaring spirits had suddenly departed. The impact of what had taken place began to filter through her elation of the night before. Reality flooded Johanna.

The full impact of what her parents had done hit her. They were not forbidding her to see Ross. They were giving her the freedom to make up her own mind. It was to be her choice, her decision. It was overwhelming and a little frightening.

It was rather like, she remembered, how she had struggled with the doctrine of free will when she had attended confirmation classes. "But why did God give us free will when he knows we will sin and might lose heaven? I'd much rather God made us be good and be *sure* I was going," she had argued with the baffled young assistant minister who had taught the young applicants.

She had rushed headlong into this exciting experience of falling in love. Perhaps she had not thought long or far enough ahead. All she had been aware of was that she loved Ross, wanted to be with him, was thrilled he loved her.

106

Her parents had given her permission to exercise her free will and marry him. Now she could make her own choice. As she fully realized this, she felt some trepidation at being told she was responsible for her own life.

She had won her fight to have her own way. But what had she lost? Somehow Johanna had always known that she was her father's favorite, his chosen companion for walks in the woods, where he had pointed out to her the flora and fauna. Botany was one of his many interests. And he had a love of words, of Shakespeare's plays and poetry, which he shared with Johanna. However, in the past few months their old easy camaraderie had disappeared.

Johanna desperately wanted it back, wanted to be reconciled with her father. Yet truthfully she felt it was too late to regain what was lost. Ever since Ross had become an issue, Johanna's father had kept his distance from her. Certainly he'd been influenced by her mother's disapproval. But the look on his face the night before, even as he gave Johanna her "heart's desire," had been a mixture of sorrow, regret.

She hadn't meant to hurt anyone. Especially not her beloved father. Was there always a shadow side to happiness?

Within the week, Ross arrived at Holly Grove in the evening to begin what was to be his formal courtship of Johanna.

Johanna waited upstairs in her bedroom, its door half open, listening for the brass knocker on the front door to announce Ross's arrival. When it came, her heart echoed its clanging. Next she heard footsteps on the polished floor of the downstairs hall, the murmur of male voices, and knew Ross was being greeted by her father. Breathlessly she prayed, *Oh, dear Lord, let it go well.*

Then, at the rustle of taffeta skirts on the stairway, Johanna shut her bedroom door quietly, holding her breath until there came a tap and her mother appeared in the doorway. Her expression was bland. Whatever she was feeling, she concealed it well.

"Johanna, Dr. Davison is speaking with your father now. In ten minutes you may go down and join them."

Johanna nodded, smiling at her mother, a smile that was not returned. Rebecca left and Johanna stood, hands clasped against her breast, feeling the pounding of her heart. She went out into the hall and remained at the top of the steps, counting silently to herself until the clock struck ten minutes past the hour. Then she slowly walked down the stairway.

Her father held open the door to the parlor for her. Beyond him she saw Ross standing, his back to the fireplace.

"I'll leave you two now—I am sure you have much to say to each other," her father murmured and went across the hall to his study, leaving the door slightly ajar, as was only proper.

Johanna started toward Ross just as he took a few steps forward, holding out both his hands to her. "Johanna, Johanna—"

Tears of joy sprang into her eyes. Her tongue tried to form his name, but her throat was too tight to speak. They stood inches apart, simply looking at each other. Then Ross took one of her hands and kissed her fingertips. "At last, Johanna, at last," he whispered. "Your father has given us his permission." He did not say "his blessing," and Johanna wondered if Ross realized the difference. However, at the moment she was too consumed with happiness to pursue the thought. She had won—*they* had won—and that was all that was important for *now*.

She moved closer and lifted her face.

"I love you, Johanna," he said, almost in a sigh, then leaned down and kissed her softly.

With a small indrawn breath she returned his kiss. A sensation of pure joy swept over her. This was it, the answer to all her prayers, hopes, and dreams.

Each evening thereafter, unless some medical emergency prevented him, Ross appeared at the Shelby home to spend some time with Johanna. Johanna lived for those moments alone with him, albeit the parlor door was always discreetly left ajar.

One evening, Ross was delayed and Johanna waited impatiently for him to come. A family had come down with some kind of fever and he'd had to attend them, he explained when she rushed to welcome him. In the parlor, his arm around her waist, Ross led her over to the sofa. "I have something to show you, Johanna. Something I've had for a long time. Something I had made while you were in Winston, with only my faith that this time would come, that this would happen."

Ross held out his hand, and in its palm lay something round, shiny, a circlet of gold, her wedding ring!

"Look inside," he urged her. Johanna held the small band up to the light shining out from the glowing fire.

"Love, Fidelity, Forever. JS-RD," she read aloud.

She looked up at Ross with eyes glistening with tears. For a minute emotion made her unable to speak. She remembered Ross once saying, "What do I have to offer you, Johanna?"

Here lay the answer in the palm of her hand. A circle of love, embracing, enveloping, protecting love, that's what he was offering her now and forever, as long as they both should live and on afterward into eternity.

Chapter Ten

Once the aunties and other family members were told and her engagement was formally announced, Johanna—her heart's desire granted—became the daughter Rebecca had always dreamed of. She could not have been more docile, more open to suggestions, directives, plans. Johanna was ready to compromise on any detail. Rebecca found this new side of her oldest daughter remarkable. Though easier to deal with than the one that had balked at so much Rebecca had wanted in the past, it was a little difficult to get used to and somewhat unnerving.

The plans for Johanna's marriage to Ross went forward smoothly, at least on the surface. Rebecca was still given to moments of deep doubt. She would think that if she and Tennant had simply held out longer, not given in to Alec Murrison's championship for his young assistant nor to Johanna's alarming melancholy, perhaps—*perhaps*—it all might have eventually resolved itself. But Rebecca was too pragmatic to spend much time in vain self-reproach. There were too many details to be attended to, too much to be accomplished and completed to waste any time in useless regret.

The wedding was to be a quiet one, not in church but in the Shelby's parlor, with only the immediate family attending, which in their case made up quite a crowd. To Rebecca's secret relief, Ross informed her—without seeming embarrassment—that none of his family would be able to come. His mother never traveled, he told her, and his sisters were too young. Spring planting would keep his younger brother Merriman and his family from coming as well. Although Rebecca accepted his explanation and assured him she understood, privately she had not been sure if the Davisons would be comfortable among the Hillsboro people. Of course, they would have been welcomed graciously. Still, it was one less problem to worry about, she told herself complacently.

❧

Johanna could hardly wait to tell her best friend, and a few days following the Shelbys' acceptance of the inevitable, Liddy was invited over so that Johanna could share her news.

"Oh Johanna, are you *sure*?" Liddy's eyes were wide, marvels of ambiguity. She was both excited and sad. A romantic, she was thrilled at the happy ending of this star-crossed love story, and yet she felt uneasy about her friend's future.

"I've never been more sure of anything in my life!" declared Johanna. The two girls were sitting on Johanna's quilt-covered bed a few days after the Shelbys had given their consent to Ross's marriage request. "Ross is everything I ever dreamed of, Liddy, and so much more. I am beside myself with happiness." Johanna's smile and eyes radiated joy. Her whole expression glowed.

"But to go live up in the mountains, Johanna, miles away from everyone you know, from everything you're used to." Liddy's voice held doubt.

"I've been away from Hillsboro before, for goodness' sake, Liddy! Almost three years at Miss Pomoroy's. And if *that* wasn't different from what I'm used to, nothing is! I love Ross

111

and we're going to have a wonderful life together. And it will all work out. Don't worry about me." Johanna reached over and squeezed Liddy's arm.

"I don't know, Johanna. I heard Mama talking to one of your aunts, and—"

"I hope you didn't pay any attention to any of that? Who was it, Aunt Hannah? She always takes the gloomy side of everything."

"Well, Mama agreed with it, Johanna. She said when love is blind, there's a rude awakening."

"Oh, fiddle! That's one of those typical old wives' tales ladies say to each other when they don't agree about something. I just hope *I* never get old and narrow and view anything that is different as bad. Of course, Ross is different from most of the insipid men we know here, Liddy."

"Not all of them. Take Burton, for instance—"

"*You* take him, Liddy!" Johanna said indignantly, then giggled.

"I *would* if I could!" Liddy retorted snappishly. "The problem is, he's brokenhearted over *you*, miss!"

"I'm sorry, Liddy. I was teasing. Burton is a dear, lovable fellow. I just don't love him. Not all his persuading would ever change that. You can't just decide to love someone. It just happens. Like it did with Ross and me. Neither of us was expecting it or even looking for it. But we *knew* when it *did* happen, and that's what makes me so sure."

"Johanna, be serious for a minute, please. I just have to talk to you!" Liddy suddenly burst out. She began to sniff and her eyes filled. "It's all wrong. You must give it some more thought before you go and do something you'll regret for the rest of your life! I just hope you won't be sorry. As Mama agreed with your auntie, 'Marry in haste, repent in leisure.'"

Johanna looked at her, startled.

"Oh Johanna, he's just not right for you!"

"What do you mean, *not right?*" Johanna echoed, bewildered.

"I mean—well, it's not that he isn't fine, honorable, and a good doctor, but to *marry* him, Johanna, and go so far away to live, on the edge of nowhere, in the hills, with people you don't even know, will have nothing in common with.... Oh Johanna, you just *can't!*" Liddy's eyes filled with tears that began to stream down her face.

"I don't see what you mean, Liddy."

"That's because you're not willing to look, Johanna."

"Pish tush!" Johanna said scornfully. "You're a regular old lady, Liddy. Where's your sense of romance?" She teasingly tossed a small embroidered pillow at her friend.

Liddy tossed it back, pretending to pout. "Well, don't say you weren't warned."

"Not warned? No, I'd never say *that*. If you only knew how many times I've had to listen to the same sort of thing you've been saying. I think every one of the aunties, one way or another, have delivered such warnings." Johanna smiled. "And I'm going to prove them all wrong! So there!" She stuck out a small, pink tongue.

Her friend ignored Johanna's attempt at comedy. "Mama says Millscreek Gap is real backwoods, Johanna. You're not just going to move everything from your home up there like it was a paper cutout and fit it in there and everything will be the same. Don't you understand how *primitive* mountain people's lives are? You've never even met his folks, never been to his home, seen how they live—my goodness, some of those mountain people that come down to town to sell their baskets and chairs ... why, they're just not like *us*, Johanna. I mean, some of them don't even know how to read or write, Johanna, do you realize that?"

Indignantly Johanna stared at her. "I can't believe you're saying this, Liddy. You sound like Emily Archer! Place Ross beside any other man in all of Hillsboro, and he'd stand head and shoulders above them all. Ross is a *doctor,* an educated man. You should hear him discuss things—all sorts of things. Not just about medicine and all. Even Papa had to admit that he is very intelligent."

"Maybe. But that's a man's world, Johanna. You're going to miss things you don't even realize now."

"Like what?" Johanna demanded.

"Well, like things you take for granted. Things we all take for granted, everyday things as well as special things. Up in the hills, there are no shops or stores or theater or—"

"None of that matters." Johanna's eyes grew dreamy. "Don't you understand that, Liddy? Not when you're in love the way Ross and I are. The question isn't, Is he good enough for *me?* but, Am I good enough for *him?*"

"Johanna, will you just listen?" begged Liddy.

"No, I don't think I will," retorted Johanna, getting up from the bed on which the two had been seated. "I thought you were different, Liddy. I thought you would understand, be glad for me. Not come here talking to me as though I'm some half-wit that doesn't know what she's doing. Telling me that I'm making a mistake. What kind of a friend are you?" Johanna was getting choked up as the words rushed up on her. "I'm so lucky that Ross loves me. I have to pinch myself at times to make sure I'm not dreaming." Johanna turned her back on Liddy and went over and stood at the window, her shoulders stiff with anger.

At length the sound of sobbing caused her to turn back into the room. Liddy was bent over, her head in her hands, crying brokenheartedly. Johanna's soft heart melted. She went over to her weeping friend, put her arms around her.

"It's all right, Liddy. Don't cry anymore. I know you just said what you thought you should. But believe me, I'm going to be so happy."

"Oh Johanna, I'm sorry," Liddy sobbed, her arms tightening around Johanna. "I'm just going to miss you so terribly."

"And I will miss *you*! We've been friends *so* long! But you will be one of my bridesmaids, won't you? I'd ask you to be the maid of honor, but Mama says I must have Cissy—it's only proper for the sister of the bride and all that. But I do want you specially, so will you?"

"Of course!" Liddy said and the two girls hugged.

During the rest of the visit, the two girls discussed colors, material, and design of the bridesmaids dresses. By the time Liddy left, things had smoothed out between them. At least on the surface. But Liddy's criticism had wounded Johanna, and she knew that somehow their friendship would never be quite the same.

❧

One afternoon just a few days later Johanna had another visitor, an unexpected one. Bessie stuck her head in Johanna's bedroom door and announced, "Miss Johanna, dere's a young gemun to see you."

"Dr. Davison?" Johanna asked excitedly, jumping up from her desk and dropping the quill pen with which she was addressing wedding invitations.

"No'm, it's Mr. Lassiter."

"Oh, dear!" Johanna's exclamation was dismayed. She had not seen Burt since her engagement had become common knowledge in Hillsboro. She wasn't looking forward to this, she thought as she gave a quick peek in her mirror, smoothed her hair, and straightened her lace collar. But there was no help for it. She had to see him, even if it turned out to be unpleasant.

Burton had never made a secret of his feelings toward her, at least as much as she would allow him to. Johanna had consistently tried to avoid his getting serious. She knew it was only her efforts that had delayed his proposing. She knew Burton had planned to talk to her father as soon as he completed his year of reading law with his uncle. Well, it was all neither here nor there now, she sighed and went downstairs.

As she entered the parlor, Burton turned from where he stood staring moodily out the window. Johanna had no trouble reading his expression. His face was a mixture of disappointment and indignation.

"Johanna, how could you have done this? You hardly know the fellow. No one does!" were the first words out of his mouth.

This declaration immediately infuriated Johanna, and she lost no time indicating that to Burton.

"*I* know him. *Dr. Murrison* certainly knows him. And who are you to make such a statement?" She drew herself up, attempting to look both angry and dignified, a hard combination to achieve.

"But *I* love you, Johanna. I always have. I always intended to ask you to marry *me*! You must have known that."

"I'm sorry, Burton. I knew you were fond of me. Why, we've been friends since—since we were children almost. At least from the time we went to Mrs. Clemens's dancing classes. And we shall always be friends. But I never led you to believe there would be anything else between us. I certainly never *meant* to, if you somehow got that impression."

"That's beside the point, Johanna. We have everything to make a really good marriage. We have the same background, we grew up at the same time, we go to the same church, we know all the same people. I am my parents' only son, and I will get all the family silver, seventeen acres of land on which to build you a beautiful house, provide you with a home, a life that you're used to—there's no reason at all why you wouldn't accept my proposal."

"The most important reason of all, Burt," Johanna said softly. "I don't love you—not the way a woman should love the man she marries. I'm sorry, but that's the truth. Hard as that may be for you to accept."

Burton shook his head vigorously and went over to her.

"Johanna, you've got to listen to sense. This is a fool-hardy thing you're doing. Marrying a man who's practically a stranger, going off into the mountains, to who knows what kind of a life? It's ludicrous. Everyone agrees."

Anger rushed up in Johanna. The idea that Burton's family and, as he indicated, *everyone* in Hillsboro, were talking about her, discussing her decision, infuriated her.

"Burton, I'm sorry if you're hurt. I'm sorry if you think I'm making some kind of terrible mistake, but there it is. And despite what you or anybody else—*anybody* at all—has to say about it, I'm going to marry Ross Davison, and I'm more proud and happy about that than anything I've ever done in my entire life."

Burton looked crestfallen. He threw out his hands in a gesture of helplessness.

"I always knew you were stubborn, Johanna, but mark my words, what you're doing is beyond reason." His mouth tightened into a straight line. Then quite suddenly his expression changed into one of inconsolable regret. "I *know we* could have been happy, Johanna. If you'd just given me a chance...."

Johanna's sympathetic heart softened at the sheer dismay in his face, the sadness in his voice.

"Oh Burt, if it were as easy as that. Someday you'll understand. I mean, I genuinely hope that someday you'll find someone and feel the way I feel about Ross. You'll recognize it *then*. You'll understand what I'm saying and know you can't settle for anything less."

Burton shook his head again. "How can you be sure that isn't the way I already feel about *you*, Johanna?"

Johanna took a step back, moved toward the parlor door leading into the hallway. "I'm sorry, Burt, I truly am. I never meant to make you unhappy." She knew there was really nothing else to say. She wanted him to leave, to have this painful confrontation over.

Head down, Burton crossed the room and, without looking back, walked past Johanna into the front hall. There he picked up his hat and cloak, opened the door, and went out.

Johanna sighed. It had been a difficult half hour. But what else could she have said or done? Truthfully she did hope Burton would find someone to love. Someone he could love as much as he thought he did Johanna. As much as she loved Ross.

However, much as she tried to dismiss it, Burton's words hung like a shadow over her own happiness. He had said a great many things that she didn't want to agree with but knew were true. Of course, the conventional wisdom was that you married someone from a similar background, someone with whom you had much in common.

She and Ross *did* come from different worlds, but a strong love could bridge those differences. And the one thing of which Johanna was sure was that their love was strong enough.

~⚹~

Burton's emotional plea for her to reconsider her decision to marry Ross was not the only such experience Johanna had after her engagement was announced. A visit from her paternal grandmother proved even more difficult. The old lady had arrived one morning, earlier than she usually went out anywhere. Johanna was called down to the parlor to find her father's formidable mother seated by the fireplace, one hand clutching the top of her gold-headed cane. Her small, bright eyes pierced Johanna as she entered the room.

Hardly before Johanna had kissed her withered cheek and greeted her, Melissa Shelby demanded, "What's this I hear about you, young lady? I couldn't believe my ears when your father came to inform me that you were to be married to someone I never heard of!"

Johanna had tried to explain that Ross was Dr. Murrison's assistant and a doctor, but her grandmother waved her ringed hand in a dismissing gesture.

"Tut, tut. Alec Murrison, what does *he* know? I've known *him* since he was a lad, and never did think him too bright!" she had said sharply. "Being a doctor don't give him insight or the ability to make a good match." She shook her head, making the silver corkscrew curls under the black lace widow's cap bob. "*His* say-so don't make it the right thing for *you*." She glanced over at Rebecca. "Neither does your mother and father's *reluctant* approval of this engagement. In *my* day, daughters married whomever their parents picked out for them. Not just any Johnny-come-lately that happened along."

Patiently Johanna attempted to placate the indignant old lady. "Grandmother, I truly believe that if you met Ross, you'd change your mind."

The old lady's chin had risen disdainfully. "Well, young lady, I'd planned that you would have my Georgian silver tea set when you married, but I thought you would chose someone from one of the Hillsboro families I know. What's wrong with some young man from among your parents' friends?" She turned to Johanna's mother accusingly. "I just don't understand young people these days—or their parents, for that

119

matter. My papa ruled with an iron hand, and we all snapped to, I'll tell you." She tapped her cane sharply on the floor.

"We certainly intended to bring Johanna's young man to call on you, Mama-in-law," Rebecca had replied. "It did all come up rather unexpectedly. We thought—" She never got to finish what she might have said, because Melissa interrupted.

"*Intended*? What good does that do *now*? As I told my son, everyone knows what is paved with good *intentions*."

"I'm sorry," Rebecca had murmured, then sent Johanna an angry glance that said, Now, see what you've done?

Impulsively Johanna had gone over to her grandmother, knelt down in front of her, and looked up into the frowning face.

"You want me to be happy, don't you, Grandmother? I'm sure if you allowed yourself to know Ross, you'd see how very kind and good he is and you'd see that I was making a good choice, the *right* choice for *me*. Please, may I bring him over?"

Rebecca had looked at her daughter, mentally shaking her head. There she goes, turning on the charm. And she'll have her way. She always does! In front of her eyes, she saw her daughter wield the magic she had seen her use so often on her father.

In the end, Johanna had received a grudging invitation from Grandmother Shelby to bring Ross for tea the following Sunday afternoon.

~≈~

That evening while waiting for Ross's usual, often brief visit, Johanna wondered if all the opposition they were getting had made her more stubborn or strengthened her love. It was a tossup. The more people told her she was making a mistake, the more she dug her heels in, declaring they were wrong. Ross often seemed distracted, and she worried that he might have the same kind of doubts. They had stepped onto this path together, and there was no turning back now. The question was, Was it true love or pride? Johanna quickly dismissed these troublesome thoughts. Of course she loved Ross. Of course she wanted to marry him. When they were together, nothing like that entered her mind. She basked in the love she saw shining in his eyes. The clasp of his hand on hers, his kiss on her lips, thrilled her, and then she knew she wanted nothing more than to spend the rest of her life with him.

During the next few weeks, the Shelby household was as busy as the proverbial beehive. The local seamstress had all but moved in to work on Johanna's gown and the bridesmaids' dresses.

Concentrating on filling a suitable hope chest for Johanna, Rebecca often asked herself in frustration, What in the world would the girl need for a log cabin in the mountains? If Johanna were marrying a young man from Hillsboro and doing things properly, there would have been at least a six-month engagement and they would have spent a year embroidering and monogramming linens. Rebecca sighed. So much for that. What was expected of a bride in town had nothing to do with what her housekeeping requirements in Millscreek Gap might be.

Johanna did not appear at all troubled by whatever doubts others had with her marriage plans. As she basked in her love, her days passed in a kind of euphoric daze. She would soon have her heart's desire. However, she *was* sensitive enough to realize that Cissy was jealous of all the attention she was getting. For weeks the wedding had been the center of activity at Holly Grove, and Cissy's attitude had become increasingly noticeable. Johanna did not want her sister to be unhappy, even if only because her pouting face sometimes intruded on Johanna's own happiness. She decided to do something. One night at bedtime she crossed the hall, tapped gently at the door of the bedroom Cissy shared with Elly, and entered.

Elly was already asleep. Cissy was perched on the bed, brushing her hair their mother's required one hundred strokes. She looked up in surprise at Johanna's entrance. Cissy neither smiled nor gave Johanna an opening. Probably brooding over some imagined slight or something that had happened that made her feel neglected, Johanna thought. However, she continued with her intended mission. She held out her hand, in which she held a folded, lace-trimmed hankie.

"Cissy, I'll soon be gone and you'll be the oldest one," she began. Cissy gave her head a little "So what?" toss. Undaunted, Johanna continued, "And I want you to have something special to remember me. Here."

Cissy's eyes widened in surprise. "What is it?"

"Take it and see."

Looking cautious, Cissy took it into her own hands and slowly unfolded the dainty linen handkerchief. Lying within the folds was a pair of earrings, small garnet drops surrounded by tiny pearls.

"Oh, Johanna!" Cissy exclaimed. "Thank you. I've always loved these."

"I'm glad."

"Are you sure? I mean, do you really want *me* to have them?"

"Yes. And you're to wear them on my wedding day. They'll look perfect with your dress." Cissy's gown was to have pink draped puffs over rose taffeta.

Impulsively Cissy hugged her. "Thank you, Johanna!"

Suddenly Johanna felt sorry for all the spats, all the spiteful words they'd carelessly flung at each other in the midst of small tiffs and little arguments. She wished she and Cissy had been closer all these years. She wished she could have loved this sister as easily as she had Elly.

For now, anyway, their particular bridge of built-up resentment and disharmony had been crossed. Johanna was satisfied she'd responded to her inner nudging to make amends with her sister. She was going on to a new, wonderful life with Ross, and she didn't want to have any regrets about unmended fences left behind.

～❦～

The aunties had combined their talents and many hours to make their niece a beautiful quilt in record time, to give as a wedding present. Although Rebecca knew what they were doing and why they were meeting more frequently, she used the explanation that her demanding duties as mother of the bride-to-be prevented her from coming to the regular weekly sessions. This left her cousins free to discuss the situation regarding what was commonly agreed to be an "unsuitable" match.

"Johanna's marriage is a terrible blow to both Rebecca and Tennant," Hannah declared.

"If that's so, Rebecca is holding up very well under the circumstances," remarked Jo McMillan.

"Of course. Rebecca's got too much pride to admit it," snapped Hannah, bristling that her opinion would be contradicted.

"But I think Dr. Davison is a fine young man," Honey ventured mildly.

"If he's Johanna's choice, what difference should it make to anyone else?" demanded Jo McMillan.

"That's fine for *you* to say, Jo—*you* don't have a daughter. I'm sure Rebecca hoped Johanna would do her proud and make a prestigious marriage. That Lassiter boy, for example. Or Judd Sellers," persisted Hannah.

"'Love laughs at locksmiths in spite of parents' plans,' to misquote Shakespeare. Didn't Rebecca and Tennant try locking Johanna up, so to speak?" demanded Jo. "Wasn't that what the trip to visit us after Christmas was all about?"

Hannah pursed her lips. "Well, even if they gave in, it has still all happened too fast. A proper engagement should last at least one year." Hannah gave a definitive nod. "And as long as we're quoting or misquoting, 'Marry in haste, repent in leisure.' That's all I have to say."

Honey and Jo exchanged an amused look, sharing their doubt that it was all Hannah had to say.

"It's really not for us to judge. If Johanna is happy, what else matters? She's the one who will suffer if it's a mistake," commented Bee.

"I agree, and when you come right down to it, I've never seen anyone look happier. Why, Johanna's become quite beautiful in the last few weeks, haven't you noticed?" Josie asked.

"The two of them absolutely adore each other. He can't keep his eyes off her. The way he looks at her . . ." Bee's voice trailed off, and a dreamy expression passed over her plump, pink face. "Humph—" *was* all Hannah seemed to be able to say after that.

<hr />

The wedding was set for a Tuesday, the first week in June. It was a far cry from the wedding Rebecca had wished for her oldest daughter. It had always been her hope to put on an elaborate wedding reception appropriate for the Shelbys' standing in the community. But if Johanna noticed the lack of what would have been extravagant preparations had there been another type of celebration, another bridegroom, she was too blissful to care.

The ritual service would be read by Reverend Moresby, and the couple would respond standing in front of the fireplace, which was to be decorated with simple arrangements of flowers and candles. Afterward, cake and wine would be served to the company.

The morning promised as pretty a day as anyone could have wished for a June wedding. The first thing Johanna saw upon awakening was her gown, which was hanging on the pine armoire opposite her bed. It was of oyster white faille and, touched by the sunlight flooding in from the window, seemed to sparkle with iridescent light.

Elly was her first visitor. She came into Johanna's bedroom proudly bearing a tray with hot chocolate and biscuits. "Mama said I could bring you your breakfast this morning, Johanna," she announced. "See, I picked this myself for you." She pointed with one chubby finger to a single white rose, drops of dew still sparkling like diamonds on its velvety petals faintly blushed with pink.

They were soon interrupted by a quick tap on the door, and Cissy came in, her hair still wrapped in paper curlers, to sit beside Elly on the foot of the bed while Johanna sipped her cocoa.

Cissy had dropped the superior air she had maintained while Johanna was in their parents' disfavor. After Johanna's gift, she had changed and had entered into the wedding preparations helpfully and happily. She gloried in the position of being the maid of honor as well as in knowing that once Johanna had departed, *she* would be the oldest daughter in the home. Privately she intended to learn by her sister's folly and only have beaux her parents approved. In the meantime, there was no harm in being close to her sister again. In fact, down deep Cissy knew she would miss Johanna. Terribly. Throughout their childhood, Johanna had always been the lively center of fun games and merriment and mischief. Cissy realized that something sparkling and delightful would disappear out of all their lives with Johanna's departure from their home.

Elly too was caught up in the general prewedding excitement and anticipation, but Johanna had always been especially sweet to her little sister Elly, her pet. There was enough difference in their ages that there had never been any competitive rivalry between them as had existed between Cissy and Johanna, Cissy and Elly. When she realized that Johanna would actually be leaving them, going off to live with Ross far away, Elly felt very sad. And she was quite fond of the tall, gentle man who, Johanna had explained, was going to be her "brother." Having them both leave together would be hard for Elly to take.

The entrance of Rebecca soon sent the two younger girls scuttling to get dressed. "Hurry now. I'll be in later to tie your sashes," she told them. "And do your hair, Cissy." Cissy was the only one of the three who did not have natural curls.

When they had left, Rebecca turned to Johanna. "Come, Johanna, it's time," she said briskly. Her daughter's glowing eyes and radiant face brought sudden, unexpected tears stinging into Rebecca's eyes. To hide them, she quickly turned her back, went over to the armoire, making a pretense of smoothing the shimmering folds of the wedding dress.

When Johanna was bathed, her hair brushed, braided, and wound into a coronet, with four ringlets on either side, bunched and tied with white ribbon, Johanna stood in front of the mirror while her mother buttoned the twenty tiny buttons down the back of her bodice.

Where was Ross? Johanna wondered. Was he getting himself into a white shirt, uncomfortably submitting to the requisite fastening of a high, stiffly starched collar, a silk cravat, getting some last-minute advice from Dr. Murrison, who was to stand up with him at today's ceremony? Dear Ross, she thought with a tender sympathy—it will only be for a few hours. One can withstand anything for a few hours. And then—a lifetime of happiness together.

Johanna was so preoccupied by her own happy thoughts that she missed the expression on her mother's face reflected in the mirror as she stood behind her. Rebecca looked at her with a mingling of sadness and hopelessness. *If only . . . If only . . .* were the errant thoughts flowing restlessly through her mind.

But Johanna was unaware of such maternal regrets. Her heart was singing. At last! At last, all her dreams were coming true.

"Now the skirt, Johanna," her mother said, and the silk overskirt slid over her taffeta petticoat with a delightful whispering swish.

Throughout the morning, the aunties had arrived one by one, peeking their bonneted heads in the bedroom door, whispering, "Could I be of any help?" Only Aunt Honey's offer was accepted, as she had brought the bridal bouquet Johanna was to carry, lilies of the valley, picked fresh that very morning from Aunt Honey's garden, then encircled in a paper lace ruffle and tied with satin ribbons.

Cissy came in next, looking very grown-up in her maid of honor gown, gazing at herself in the mirror as she moved her head back and forth to make her new garnet earrings swing. Next Liddy and Elly were admitted, looking like two spring flower fairies in their pastel dresses, wreaths of fresh flowers on their heads. Finally Johanna was ready, just as there came a discreet knock on the door, and her father stood on the threshold.

When Johanna turned to greet him, she was caught off guard by what she saw in her father's eyes as he gazed upon her in her bridal gown. For perhaps the first time in her life, she grasped the intensity of his love. Mingled there also was something she could not quite discern. It was a moment filled with a depth of emotion she had never plumbed. Her instinct was to lighten it. Affecting a coyness she had often mimed on other occasions to amuse him, Johanna put her forefinger under her chin and curtsied, asking, "How do I look?"

Tennant cleared his throat, said huskily, "Beautiful, my dear." They had survived the emotional moment, and Johanna moved swiftly across the room and placed her hand on his arm. He patted her hand and asked, "Ready?" She nodded and together they went into the hall to the top of the stairway, then slowly descended the steps. At the bottom, they turned to enter the parlor, where the preacher and Johanna's bridegroom waited.

The familiar parlor had been transformed into a bower of fragrant loveliness. All the aunties had contributed the choicest flowers from their individual gardens, and arranged them in milk glass vases on the mantelpiece and in baskets fanning out from the fireplace.

For Johanna, who was seeing it all with starry eyes, the room shimmered with light from hundreds of candles, although actually there were only two four-branched candelabra behind Reverend Moresby, creating an angelic haloed aura around his head. Then her gaze met Ross's, and her breath was taken away by the impact. All nervousness left her. Never before in her life had she felt so calm, so confident, so sure, as she did going forward to take his outstretched hand.

All past tragedies were forgotten in that one triumphant moment. Having one's dream come true was a very satisfactory state of affairs.

As her father took her hand and placed it in Ross's extended one, Johanna felt the symbolism of the act, which signified a transfer of responsibility, protection, and caring between the two men. Up to this moment Tennant had been her "cover." From this day forward it would be Ross's duty to love, honor, and cherish her.

Johanna was fully aware that in the exchange of vows, she was not only giving herself into Ross's care but promising to hold him in esteem, give him reverence and obedience, "as long as you both shall live." It was the most solemn, sacred pledge she had ever taken, and she intended to carry it out with all her mind, soul, spirit.

She held her breath as the minister intoned the closing admonition of the marriage ritual. "The sacrifices you will be called upon to make, only love can make easy—perfect love can make them joy." *Sacrifices?* she thought, glancing up at Ross's serious profile. All she could think of was the *joy*.

A smile played at the corners of her mouth. Of course she promised to "love, honor, and obey." She pushed back the lace mitt on her third finger, left hand, so that Ross could slip on her wedding band. Then she heard the thrilling words before the benediction. "I now pronounce you man and wife."

A long moment of quiet followed that pronouncement, then suddenly it was broken by a rush of voices. Hugs, kisses, and congratulations followed as the assembled family crowded around the couple.

Soon after the ceremony, other guests began arriving for the reception. The Shelby parlor had been too small to accommodate all their acquaintances and friends for the actual ceremony. In a daze of pure happiness, Johanna took her place beside Ross and her parents to greet them.

As the guests came through the receiving line, Johanna read in their glances—although they were all too polite to say anything—a startling message. It was the same look that had puzzled her when she saw it in her father's eyes earlier.

Now she understood it clearly. *Pity!* She could almost hear the whispers of some of the wedding guests, the comments. "Imagine! A pretty, popular, accomplished young woman throwing herself away to marry a penniless doctor and go live in a remote mountain community."

Even as it made her furious, she felt a slight chill slide through her veins.

If she had not been so completely in love with Ross Davison, it might have caused her deep anger. Or worse still, fear. But just then she felt his hand clasp hers in a reassuring squeeze. Looking up at him, she saw in *his* eyes all that mattered—unabashed, unconditional, unswerving love.

❧

Auntie Bee, young in heart and a romantic, had offered her home for the newlyweds to stay in for the three days before they left for their home in the mountains. She and her husband, Radford, were leaving right after Johanna's wedding for a long-planned visit to her husband's ninety-four-year-old mother in Pennfield. Therefore their house would be empty and thus provide the young couple privacy for a short "honeymoon."

In a flurry of rice and rose petals, Johanna and Ross, hand in hand, left the reception in the buggy lent by Dr. Murrison, drove the short distance to the Breckenridge house. Auntie Bee's housekeeper of many years, Tulie, met them at the door.

"Evenin', Miss Johanna. Evenin', Doctor," she greeted them, her wrinkled brown face creased in a wide, toothless smile.

Tulie had known Johanna since she was a little girl, so the curtsey was in deference to Johanna's husband the doctor and her new status as a "married lady."

"Miss Bee and me got the guest room all ready," she told them. "And Miss Bee thought you-all would like to eat your supper on de balcony oberlookin' de garden."

"That sounds lovely, Tulie." Johanna smiled and, still holding Ross's hand, followed the old woman up the winding stairway to the second floor.

At the top, Tulie turned as if to be sure they were behind her, then waddled down the corridor to the end and opened a door, gesturing them to enter. They stepped inside the spacious, high-ceilinged room scented with lilac and rose pot-pourri, and the door clicked shut behind them, signaling Tulie's quiet departure.

Johanna had been in and out of her aunt's house dozens of times, she realized, but she had never been in the guest room. She looked around with pleasure. Everything—colors, fabrics, and furnishings—was in exquisite taste. In the white-paneled fireplace, a fire had been laid, ready for the touch of a match should the evening turn cool. A golden maple tester bed was covered by Auntie Bee's prize Double Wedding Ring quilt.

Johanna walked over and opened the French windows to the balcony, where a round table covered with white linen cloth and set with sparkling crystal goblets and fine china awaited them. To one side was a wheeled cart on which were placed several silver-domed serving dishes and a coffee urn.

"Come look, Ross," she called.

He followed her out and stood behind her.

"Isn't it perfect?" she said.

He slipped his arms around her waist, leaned down and kissed her cheek. "Yes, perfect," he whispered.

Johanna turned in his arms. Ross's hands smoothed over her ringleted curls, causing Johanna's ornamented hair combs to drop with a plink to the polished floor, loosening masses of lustrous hair to tumble onto her shoulders. She lifted her face for his kiss. This was the kiss they had waited for, the kiss that expressed a love they both knew would be forever.

❧

At Holly Grove, in the master bedroom, Rebecca stood at her window looking out into the moon-drenched night. A tumult of emotions had kept her awake. This was her daughter's wedding night. Oh, Johanna! Dear child, foolish child. Rebecca closed her eyes, twisted her hands together, and leaned her forehead against the glass.

Her heart was full of pain, yet hope mingled with anxiety, resignation with prayer. Could she have done anything more to prevent this marriage? That thought still anguished Rebecca's mind. Was the premonition she felt just imagination gone wild? Didn't Paul exhort his followers to bring vain imagination into captivity? She must not borrow trouble but hope the best for a marriage that, in her opinion, was doomed to bring unhappiness to her beloved daughter.

She heard a stirring in the bed behind her, then Tennant's concerned voice. "My dear, is anything wrong?"

She half turned toward him, shook her head. "No, nothing. Just couldn't sleep."

How could she tell him how her thoughts of the past had rushed over her, overwhelming her with echoes of another love—someone whom she had weighed and found wanting, contrasted to *him*? In Tennant Shelby she had seen what she wanted in life. Tennant had never known that Rebecca had made so difficult a choice. She had already met Tennant when this other young man entered her life, and love—spontaneous, impulsive, unexpected—had flamed up between them. But she had let him go. His last words, flung at her in anger, still haunted....

Rebecca shuddered, drew her shawl closer about her shoulders. There are two tragedies in life, the old Arabic proverb says. One is not getting what you wish for—the other is getting it.

Tennant's voice came again. "Come to bed, love. You must be exhausted. It's been quite a day. . . ."

Part Two

Chapter Eleven

❦

A second-day reception was held at Holly Grove for friends of the family who had not been invited the day of the ceremony. A glowing Johanna, in a dress of red-and-white dotted swiss, its eyelet-ruffled neckline edged with narrow red velvet ribbons, stood beside her new husband and her parents to receive guests. Her pride was apparent as she introduced Ross to those who had not yet met him. She was all smiles, sweetness, and gaiety.

Rebecca observing her, thought with mild irony, *Of course, now that you've got what you wanted, my girl, butter would melt in your mouth. Let's hope that it doesn't turn to sour cream.*

The aunties were in full force, darting here and there, seeing that the refreshment table and punch bowl were kept replenished, buzzing like happy bees, murmuring among themselves, nodding and smiling as they gazed fondly at the newlyweds.

Ross, never all that at ease at social occasions, was glad when it was over. While Johanna, her sisters, and relatives gathered to ooh and aah over the many wedding gifts, Ross sought the respite of the side porch.

It was approaching evening and the breeze was cool, refreshing on his hot cheeks. He had been acutely aware of the curiously speculative looks of the Shelbys' friends who were meeting him for the first time. He could guess some of the comments being made, such as "What can a girl like Johanna see in *him*?" or "What can the Shelbys be thinking of to let their daughter marry him?" Perhaps he was oversensitive. However, even as strongly as he loved Johanna, he'd had moments of deep uncertainty himself. He had been brought up to respect his elders, to listen to their advice, heed their warnings, which had often been right. He hoped, for Johanna's sake, he had not allowed good judgment to be swayed by his emotion. He hoped he could make her happy—even though he wasn't sure just how.

❦

Early the morning of the third day after the wedding, Ross and Johanna started out from Hillsboro for the mountains. The farewells to her parents and sisters were blessedly brief. Happy and excited as she was to begin her new life with the husband she adored, Johanna did not trust herself to say good-bye without tears. Leaving her childhood home was hard enough. Leaving her parents, knowing that the hurt and disappointment she had caused them had not completely healed, was even harder.

Saying good-bye to Cissy, who had already assumed her coveted role as the oldest Shelby daughter at home, amused Johanna more than it saddened her. However, when it came to Elly, the dam of tears broke. The little girl hugged Johanna tight around her waist, wailing, "Don't go, Johanna, or take me with you!"

Kissing the child's wet cheeks, Johanna cuddled her, saying in a choked whisper, "You can come visit me, honey, if Mama will let you! But I have to go with Ross now." Finally she had to almost pry the little girl's fingers away from her clinging hold. Rebecca stepped forward and took Elly by the shoulders.

"That will do, Elly. Shame for being such a crybaby. Johanna is married now and must go with her husband." Almost the same words Johanna had used, but they sounded so different in her mother's voice. Startled at the hard edge to Rebecca's usually melodious voice, for a moment Johanna looked at her mother. But her expression was composed, controlled. Johanna started to say something. Something foolish, like "Mama, do you love me?" But the words caught in her throat. She felt Ross's hand on her arm.

"Come, Johanna," he said gently. "We must get started if we want to get there before dark."

With another kiss and hug for Elly, Johanna put her hand through Ross's arm and turned to go.

To her surprise, at the last minute Cissy came running down the porch steps after them. "Wait, Johanna, wait!" she called. Johanna turned and Cissy flung herself into her arms. "Oh Johanna, we're going to miss you." Johanna could feel Cissy's tears against her cheek. Surprised at this show of emotion from the sister who usually kept her distance, Johanna hugged her hard and whispered back, "Take care of Elly. Be sweet to her, won't you?"

Cissy nodded. Then they heard their mother's voice. "Come, Cissy. Don't delay them. They must be on their way."

They would be riding on the two horses that were the McMillan's wedding gift to them. Some of Johanna's belongings had already been sent ahead to the cabin where they were to live in Millscreek Gap. Later Johanna's trunk and other belongings would follow in a wagon.

"Come, Johanna," Ross said again.

The sisters' embrace loosened. For one long minute they looked into each other's eyes. Johanna wished she had taken time to become closer to Cissy, tried to understand her better. But now it was too late. Her real parting with family had come.

"Good-bye," she said over the hard lump in her throat.

Ross handed her up into her sidesaddle and tightened the straps of her small traveling bag behind her, then mounted his own horse. With one last look and wave to the group standing on the veranda, Johanna turned her horse's head and followed Ross down the drive. They rode side by side but were silent as they passed through town. Johanna was dealing with a myriad of emotions that had suddenly rushed up inside her. Ross was sensitive enough to understand that she was saying good-bye to what she was leaving behind.

At the town limits, they took the narrow, rutted road that led through the dense woods and upward into the mountains. It was nearly a day's journey to reach Ross's homeland. Johanna had never seen the sky so blue. A rising mist shimmered with the golden sunlight. The farther they got up into the hills, the sweeter the air, which was fragrant with the mingled scents of wild honeysuckle, sunbaked pine needles on the trail, ferns, spicy spruce. All along the paths and deep into the forest that flanked them on both sides, were masses of mauve and purple rhododendron, orangey azalea, and delicate pink mountain laurel, more beautiful in their random profusion than the arranged bouquets in church.

The deeper they went, the more the silence surrounded them, yet it was alive with all sorts of sounds. They heard the rustle of meadowlarks rising out of the brush, startled by the noise of their horses' hooves, muffled as they were by the carpeted trail. There were butterflies hovering over the blue-purple violets, half hidden by the shiny-leafed galax on the forest floor. Graceful sprays of white flowers hung from the sourwood, with clusters resembling the more cultivated wisteria on her Grandmother Shelby's porch. High in the treetops, there came the song of birds and the humming of bees. The singing of the creek could be heard far below them as they climbed higher. It was June in the high country in all its glory. Ross turned in his saddle and smiled at her. Johanna felt her heart melt with happiness. After all this time, all this waiting, hoping, and praying, she and her husband were on their way to their own home high in the mountains—could anything be more wonderful?

Soon Johanna noticed a wooden board nailed to a tree, on which was crudely painted the words MILLSCREEK GAP with an arrow pointing north. A little farther along, they passed through what could only be described as a wide place in the trail. There on one side was a slightly listing wooden building with a sign over the door that read GENERAL STORE AND POST OFFICE.

Was this it? Johanna wondered. Was this all there was to the town of Millscreek? Had Liddy been right? Johanna remembered that her friend had called it something like the far side of nowhere.

Ross turned again and smilingly pointed to the sagging, weathered structure but didn't even bother to stop. Is that where she would come to buy supplies and get her mail? A small frisson of anxiety stirred in the pit of her stomach, but she quickly quelled it. Everything was going to be all right, everything was going to be fine. Just different, Johanna reassured herself.

The trail began to climb now, and every so often they would pass a weather-beaten, gray house perched on the side of a hill. Sometimes they would see a sunbonneted woman with a couple of children out in a garden. As they passed she would lean on her hoe for a few minutes, watching them go by. Ross would always shout, "Howdy!" and Johanna would wave tentatively. Rarely were these greetings acknowledged or returned, except by the children, who would run forward at the sight of the two on horseback, then stand staring, their fingers in their mouths. Perhaps they were shy of strangers. *Not that we will be strangers for long,* Johanna thought optimistically. *Once Ross takes his place here as the only, much-needed doctor, these people will lose their shyness and become my friends, too. I'll visit and they'll visit. . . .*

This was her first chance since the wedding to give serious thought to what her new life with him might be like. Of course, Ross had spoken about his family at length, told her about his stalwart father, killed felling a tree when Ross was only fourteen. His mother, Eliza, was left a widow with four children and forced to scratch a living on the small plot of land to provide food, clothing, for her family. Johanna could tell Ross was proud of how Eliza Davison had kept the small farm going, reared the four children by herself, with only young Ross to help.

His brother, Merriman, had been just twelve when Ross had gone to live with the schoolteacher in town and get his education. His mother had been fiercely insistent on this. "I was torn," Ross had confided to Johanna, "thinkin' I oughta stay and be the man of the family, but she wouldn't hear of it. She told me, 'Son, the Good Lord give you a brain, hands to heal, and it would be like throwing away a gift if you didn't take this chance Teacher Gibbs is offerin' you.' I was determined then and there to come back. I'd do what she expected me to do, then give Merriman his chance."

"And did he take it?" Johanna had asked.

A kind of sadness had come into Ross's expression at her question. "No, he's married now and got two young'uns. I reckon he knew what he wanted. Sis Jenny is a sweet girl, and they have a home and a farm just up the hill from Ma. Merriman still helps her as much as he can. I guess folks do what they think will make them happy. You can't give something to someone if they don't want to take it."

Johanna had sensed Ross's regret that his younger brother had passed up on the opportunity Ross had been prepared to give him. It had also probably left Ross feeling sort of lonely as the only member of the family who'd furthered himself, she thought. That left his two little sisters, Sue and Katie, now eight and ten, still at home.

Johanna was both looking forward to and dreading meeting them all. What kind of a mental picture did they have of *her*? she wondered.

They climbed steadily upward, twisting back and forth along the winding trail. The forest was silent, beautiful, but Johanna found it rather foreboding with its impenetrable shadows even on this sunny morning. Just then Ross turned and called back, "We're almost there, honey. Up over this next rise and Ma's cabin is right on the ridge."

At the prospect of meeting Ross's mother for the first time, Johanna felt slightly apprehensive. She knew Eliza Davison must be a woman of strength and courage to have reared such a man as Ross. How proud she must be that he'd become a doctor! Johanna wanted desperately for Ross's mother to accept her, to think she was worthy of her fine son. And Johanna wanted to be a loving daughter to *her*. Ross had tried to tell her not to expect too much show of emotion at this first meeting. "You know, mountain folk are different. Not that they aren't as hospitable as, say, people in Hillsboro are. Ma is as kindhearted and generous as you'd find anywhere. She's just not talkative." In spite of his reassurance that his mother was looking forward to her coming and would welcome her, Johanna felt a little ripple of nervousness as they approached the rambling, weathered log house.

Ross turned his horse under the shade of a drooping pine tree, tethered him to the rustic fence, then came over to lift Johanna down from her saddle. His hands spanned her waist and he held her for a minute, smiling down at her.

"Don't look so scared," he teased. "Nobody's gonna bite you."

"Don't tell *me* that! You said you were shaking in your boots when you went to see *my* parents for the first time. Anyway, who said I was nervous?" Johanna demanded with mock severity. "Do I look all right?" She adjusted the brim of her tricorne.

"You look just right," Ross grinned.

"Really?" Johanna tugged at her jacket and fluffed out the lacy jabot of her blouse. She hoped her blue, braid-trimmed riding habit didn't look too fancy.

Before Ross had a chance to reassure her again, a tall woman stepped out from the house and came to the edge of the porch and said, "Well, howdy!"

"Ma!" Ross waved one hand. "This is Johanna, Ma." Turning to Johanna, he held out his hand. "Come on, honey." They walked toward the porch. "This is my mother, Eliza."

"How do you do, Mrs. Davison. I'm so happy to be here."

Holding Ross's hand tightly, Johanna went with him up the steps. At the top, Johanna debated whether she should kiss her new mother-in-law or not.

Eliza Davison was thin as a reed, with dark hair heavily peppered with gray. Her calico dress was crisp, covered by a spotless cotton apron. Immediately Johanna saw Ross in his mother's strong features—the firm mouth and chin, the deep-set, slate gray eyes under dark, straight brows. Under their searching gaze, Johanna felt exposed, disconcerted. The woman seemed to be staring right into her, taking her measure. In spite of the sun on her back, Johanna felt chilled.

Face to face with Ross's mother, she wondered how Eliza Davison, born and raised in these mountains, *really* felt about her oldest son marrying a girl from town.

However, Eliza's greeting was warm and friendly enough. "Well, Johanna, I'm right pleased to meet you. My son has shure spoke highly of you. Now, do come inside and out of the day's heat."

Ross held the door so that Johanna could follow his mother into the house. The interior was dim and cool, smelled of wood shavings, soap, and some delicious cooking aromas emanating from the kitchen area at the far end of the room.

"These are Ross's sisters, Sue and our baby, Katie." Eliza gestured to two skinny little girls standing in the shadows. Both were dressed in starched calico dresses, the hems of which they were twisting. Their hair was plaited in tight braids, but Johanna could hardly see their faces, because they'd ducked their heads at her entrance.

"Sue, Katie. Come on over and meet your brother's wife," their mother beckoned them. Heads still down, they took a few steps forward, then stopped a few feet from Johanna, bare toes wiggling.

"Hello!" Johanna bent toward them, smiling. "I have two younger sisters, too," she said. "I hope we'll be great friends."

The two smiled shyly but didn't speak. Ross stepped over and swung one up in each arm, and they burst into giggles. Johanna could see at once that they adored their older brother. It made her feel a little more at ease to see how quickly he acted completely at home and didn't appear anxious or uneasy. It was as though he were trying to show her that this was a place where one could act naturally, not have to put on airs of any kind or be especially mannerly.

"You must be hungry, comin' sech a long way, startin' out 'fore dawn. Sit ye down." Eliza indicated the long, rectangular, scrubbed pine table, with half-sawn log benches on either side, their surface worn smooth. "I asked Merriman and Jenny to come for dinner, but he was gettin' his garden in and not shure he'd be done by supper. But I reckon they'll both be here 'fore too long. And bring their young'uns. They've two boys, Johanna. Three and five, and they're a handful." She shook her head and a slight smile touched her thin lips. She looked at Ross. "Puts me in mind of Ross and Merriman at their ages." Then she motioned to the two girls. "Come on, you two, help me put things on the table." Over her shoulder, she said to Ross, "Do you want to show Johanna where she can wash up?"

Johanna was glad to be taken to the side of the porch, where a basin of fresh water, a clean towel, and a cake of soap were set on a wooden table under a small mirror. She took off her hat and unwound the veil, smoothing back her hair, tightening the ribbon that held it. She rinsed her face and hands. Then, as it was getting very warm, she took off her snug jacket.

Ross was waiting by the front door. "Merriman and Jenny just came," he told her and led her back inside.

Merriman was a head shorter than Ross but had the same lean good looks. He was very tan, however, and the bronzed skin made his eyes seem very blue. His wife, Johanna decided, would have been exceptionally pretty if she weren't painfully thin and pale-skinned. Her light brown hair was drawn severely back from her face into a plain knot at the back of her head. She seemed very shy and kept her remarkably lovely eyes downcast. She mumbled her hello, then immediately scooted over to help Eliza in the kitchen area.

"All right now, gather round, folks. Everything's ready," Eliza said as she brought two large platters to the table, one of fried chicken, one of roasted ribs. Jenny and Sue followed with bowls of sweet potatoes, hominy, greens, and an apple pie. Jenny and Merriman's two small, towheaded boys scrambled up on the benches on either side of the long table just as their grandmother set a black iron skillet of cornbread from right off the stove onto the table.

Once everyone was seated, a silence fell. It lengthened. Johanna felt her stomach tense. No one moved or spoke. Was this a kind of silent grace? Like the Quakers', maybe? She had never thought to ask Ross. At home, the Shelbys held hands around the table while Papa said the blessing. Under lowered lashes, she looked around warily. To her surprise, both of Ross's little sisters were watching her gravely. Eliza's head was bowed. The silence seemed to stretch. Johanna stirred uncomfortably. She felt Ross's hand squeeze hers gently, and she raised her head cautiously. Eliza was looking at her and said quietly, "If you'll do the honors, Johanna." Suddenly she realized that as the guest at the table, *she* was supposed to say the blessing. She glanced at Ross for confirmation. He nodded, smiling slightly. Quickly she bowed her head, trying frantically to remember the one so often said at home. In a low voice that sounded more like a mumble, she recited it. A moment later plates were being passed, and she let out a breath of relief.

It took her a few moments to regain herself. She ventured two or three attempts to engage Jenny in conversation but failed. She did notice, however, that once or twice Merriman's wife glanced at her furtively. Actually, Jenny was looking at her blouse! Given the plain gray calico Jenny was wearing, Johanna understood. It was only natural. Jenny couldn't be more than nineteen. Like any young girl, she loved pretty things. Probably she had nothing of her own like Johanna's Cluny lace-trimmed blouse.

Johanna tried hard to think of some comment to make, but all she could think of was to compliment Eliza on the food. It seemed insane. She had never before felt so tongue-tied. She wanted to please Ross by being friendly to his family, but everything she said seemed to fall flat. She ended up being quiet while Ross and Merriman talked about mutual friends, the crops planted, the weather. Maybe the Davisons didn't talk much at meals, unlike her own family, who always entered into a lively discussion at mealtimes. She should stop trying so hard, she decided. It wasn't that Ross's family disliked her, she assured herself. *It's just that I'm a stranger, an outsider, that I don't belong here yet. It will take time for them to get to know me, for me to know them.*

Johanna had heard somewhere that to find out what kind of a husband a man would be, watch how he treats his mother. She was touched by the gentle way Ross spoke to Eliza, the respect he showed her.

Johanna was relieved when Ross got to his feet, saying they must go if they were to reach their own home before dark. Johanna thanked Eliza, said good-bye to Merriman and Jenny, urging her new sister-in-law and brother-in-law to come see them as soon as they were settled. She gave the little girls a special invitation to come up and visit. Ross kissed his mother's cheek, hugged his sisters, then brought the horses around and helped Johanna mount, and they started back up the hillside.

In spite of the fact that she had wanted it so much, that first meeting, brief as it was, put Johanna off slightly, put her on her guard. Although she had not known exactly what to expect, it had not been the welcoming she had hoped for.

Ahead of them the mountains loomed, clouds, wreathing the summits, or opened to reveal peaks crowned with a glorious golden light. The path zigzagged upward. In the clear evening light, the mountain was bathed in sunlit isolation. "There it is, honey." Ross pointed and Johanna saw the peaked roof of a log cabin with a wide stone chimney just ahead. "That's *our* place."

Johanna's heart lifted. "Our place," Ross had said. The place where they would live as husband and wife. After all these months of longing and waiting, here at last they would begin their life together.

When she stepped inside the cabin, it seemed dark after coming in from the brilliant sunset. She looked around. One large room with a stone fireplace at one end. Ross was behind her, waiting for her reaction. He had spent the previous week getting it ready for her. Then she saw the rocking chair. She walked over to it, admiring its smooth finish.

"It's a wedding present from Uncle Tanner," Ross said. He gave it a gentle push and stood there smiling as it moved back and forth without a sound, without a creak. His hand smoothed the gleaming arms caressingly.

"Who is Uncle Tanner?" Johanna asked.

Ross smiled. "You'll find out soon enough. I reckon they'll be by to visit 'fore too long. He and Aunt Bertie—"

"Your aunt and uncle?" Johanna was curious because she'd never heard Ross mention them.

"Not really, but we've always called them 'Aunt and Uncle.' I think actually they're Ma's cousins."

"Oh, I see, like my 'aunties' are my mother's first cousins."

"That's right," Ross agreed, then said, "Now I'll show you the spring." He took her hand and led her outside. He guided her up a little rise to a clump of poplar trees, over to a ledge, and pointed, "There it is." Johanna looked to see a natural bowl of water standing clear as glass, surrounded on three sides with a ledge of rock and a tangled web of roots. Around the spring and beside the stream that flowed from it were beds of moss, and galax, and vines of other plants that bloom in summer. On the far side, overhanging the spring, were a dozen wild blackberry stalks. As they drew nearer, Ross said, "This is the lifeblood of our place, Johanna. The purest, sweetest water you'll ever taste." He reached down and picked up a dipper lying on the stone, filled it, and handed it to her to drink. It was just as he said, icy, delicious. She closed her eyes as she swallowed, and then she felt his lips warm on hers.

He took the dipper from her, laid it back on the stone, put his arm around her waist, and together they walked back down the path.

On the porch, Ross turned and pointed. "Look there, Johanna." A summer moon was rising slowly over them. Arms around each other, waiting, they watched until it hung, a great silver dollar, above the trees. It was so exquisitely beautiful, Johanna drew in her breath.

Then Ross swung her up into his arms and carried her into the house, saying softly, "Welcome home, Johanna."

Chapter Twelve

❦

Johanna stirred slowly out of sleep. Not fully awake, without quite opening her eyes, she was aware of brightness under her closed lids. She felt warmth. Sunlight. *It's morning*, she thought drowsily. She felt a floating sensation, almost like flying. *This is happiness! What I'm feeling is real, true, and it's me and I'm happy!*

She stretched and reached out to the pillow next to hers. She opened her eyes, blinking. The bed beside her was empty. Raising herself on her elbows, she looked around.

From the alcoved bed, she could see across the center room into the kitchen. She smelled the unmistakable aroma of freshly made coffee. Ross, she smiled. He must have got up early and made it. Just then the cabin door opened and he walked in.

He looked over at the bed and, seeing her, asked, "Sleep well?"

"Perfect!"

He came over and stood at the foot of the bed. "I love you, Mrs. Davison."

She held out her arms to him. "Say that again."

"Which? I love you? Or Mrs. Davison?"

"Both!"

He laughed, came over to the side of the bed, and took her into his arms. He buried his face in her tangled curls, and for a moment they just held on to each other. Then Johanna leaned back and smiled up at him.

"What shall we do today?"

"We could go pay Aunt Bertie a visit," Ross suggested as Johanna threw back the covers and got out of bed. "I saw Uncle Tanner yesterday when I went down to Ma's, and he asked me if the 'honey was still on the moon.'" He grinned. "Folks figure a new couple need a few weeks alone to get used to each other or find out they've made a mistake."

"Mistake?" Johanna pretended indignation. "Well, at least not *me*." She tossed her head. "I don't know whether your kin think *you're* the one that might have made one."

She slid her bare feet into the small velvet slippers, reached for her dressing gown. Ross held it for her to put on, then wrapped his arms around her.

"No, ma'am, no mistake. Best thing that ever happened to me." He leaned down, kissed her cheek, her neck, until she wiggled around laughing and turned, hugged him.

"Oh Ross, I'm so happy!" she sighed.

"Well, so am I."

Aunt Bertie and Uncle Tanner's cabin was nestled among shaggy rhododendron bushes as big as trees, and shadowed by balsams. Aunt Bertie was a treat. Just as Ross had told her, Johanna liked her right away. Who could not?

She was spare, straight backed, her movement as brisk as a much younger woman. Daily use of hoe, shears, washboard, and skillet had made her hands strong. Her wrinkled face had a rosy tan, and her snapping dark eyes held a twinkle. There was a youthful lilt in her voice. Cocking her head to one side like an inquisitive bird, she asked Johanna, "How old do you take me for?"

Afraid to offend if she guessed wrong, Johanna hesitated, and Aunt Bertie laughed, "Goin' onto seventy-nine next January. I 'spect to go on jest as I've been doin' 'til the Good Lord takes me home. I been working a garden and spinning wheel since I was eight years old. My mama had a passel of young'uns, and I was the oldest girl, so I took over a lot of the chores. I've been workin' all my life, and I don't want to end my days in a rockin' chair, although Tanner makes the best ones." She pointed to the two on the porch and urged Johanna, "Sit over there and try it."

"Uncle Tanner made one for us, Aunt Bertie," Ross said. "It was sitting in our cabin when we came. Figured it was a wedding present."

"Of course it were! I plum forgot. When he heard you were gittin' married, Ross, he started on it." She fixed Johanna with bright eyes. "Don't it rock nice and smooth?"

"Yes, ma'am. It's beautiful."

"Now, you-all sit down and we'll have a nice visit. Ross, Tanner's out there gittin' his cider press cleaned up, ready for when our apples are ripe." She glanced at Johanna. "Wait 'til you taste Tanner's sweet cider. But first you gotta try my pie," she chuckled. She bustled into the cabin.

Ross gave Johanna a "Didn't I tell you?" look just as a tall man came from around the house.

"Reckon I heard voices," the man said.

Ross went down the steps and greeted him. "Uncle Tanner, we just wanted to pay you and Aunt Bertie a call, thank you for the chair. Come meet my bride."

"Don't mind if I do," Uncle Tanner said, a grin cracking his weathered, tan face. He was thin as a whip, rather stooped in the shoulders, but moved with a lively gait. If Aunt Bertie was almost eighty, Johanna thought, Uncle Tanner must be that old or maybe older.

Uncle Tanner took the steps spryly. "Mahty pleased to meet you. Looks like Ross got not only what he needed and wanted but somethin' fine and purty, too," he chuckled and held out his hand to Johanna.

Johanna extended her own, and the old man grasped it and gave it a good, strong shake. Under his steady gaze, she felt herself weighed, measured, and not found wanting.

Johanna was pleased to feel she'd passed muster of someone she knew her new husband held in high regard.

Aunt Bertie appeared at the door. "Y'all come on in now." After the three of them were seated at the scrubbed pine table, Aunt Bertie came in from the kitchen, carrying a pie plate in one hand and a jar of honey in the other. She put the pie on the table and the jug of honey beside it, then started cutting generous wedges, lifting them one by one onto the plain, cream-colored pottery plates beside the tin.

"Now, if you want something tasty, spread some of this here honey over the top," she said as she handed around the plates. The pie was hot and its flaky crust a golden brown. The honey looked like clear liquid sunshine. Hesitantly but afraid she might offend Aunt Bertie if she didn't follow her suggestion, Johanna tentatively drizzled the honey over the top of her piece of pie.

A smile twitched Aunt Bertie's lips. "Never tried that before, I reckon?" Watching Johanna take a bite, Aunt Bertie said, "See? Good, ain't it?" With satisfaction, she turned to Ross. "How about you, Ross? You ever tried it?"

"No, ma'am, not that I can remember."

Aunt Bertie looked shocked. "You're funnin' me, ain't you? Can't believe you've lived this long and never had apple pie with honey."

When Johanna and Ross left, nothing would do but that they carry away with them a willow basket loaded with goodies from Aunt Bertie's larder—jars of strawberry jam, peach preserves, apple butter. "My apple butter's known in these parts," she told Johanna. "Come fall when the apple crop is in, I'll teach you how to make it with my recipe," she promised.

❧

"So what do you think of Aunt Bertie and Uncle Tanner?" Ross asked.

"I think they're wonderful!" Johanna answered.

"Good." Ross seemed satisfied. "I could tell *they* liked *you*."

What Johanna didn't say, afraid she might be misunderstood, was what she had found so surprising and so refreshing—their lack of artifice of any kind. They spoke, acted, responded, in such a natural, unaffected way. Johanna found it utterly charming. She was used to society's polite shallowness, especially in a first meeting with someone, when people tended to be somewhat formal. Aunt Bertie and Uncle Tanner had just taken her in, showing her the same warmth they bestowed upon Ross, whom they'd known all his life. Of course, she was sure they would have welcomed her just because she was Ross's wife. Still, Johanna hoped to win her own place within his family circle before too long.

Chapter Thirteen

❧❧

Johanna woke up and even before she opened her eyes, she knew she was alone. The cabin was quiet. Ross must have already left. She sat up feeling somehow bereft, deserted, even though she'd known this day was coming. She recalled their conversation of the night before, while Ross had been packing his medicine bag.

"Well, darlin' mine, I have to be about my doctoring. I've got people who've been waiting for me, and I had a whole passel of messages passed on to me—the Henson's baby has colic, Molly Renner needs a tonic, Tobias's leg is actin' up again, all kinds of ailments to see to up and down the mountainside."

Johanna had sighed, "I guess so. That's what we came up here for, wasn't it? For you to be a doctor and for me to be your wife! But what shall *I* do without you all day?"

"I don't know." Ross had looked puzzled. "Ma always found something that needed doing."

Johanna had felt somehow rebuked and said no more. As they kissed good night, Ross told her, "I'll be up and off at the crack of dawn, most probably. Got a lot of mountain to cover tomorrow."

Still, Johanna wished he had wakened her so that she could have fixed him breakfast, seen him off like a proper wife. She got up and looked around the small cabin. Here there were not the kind of household tasks she had been assigned at home—polishing silver, arranging flowers, or practicing her music. Or the social calls or visits from friends for tea in the afternoon, such as there had been in Hillsboro.

The long day stretched ahead of her emptily. Oh, there were chores enough to do, but Johanna did not feel like tackling any of them. She longed for—what?

She did not even want to admit that what she missed was the very thing she had run away from. Used to the activity of her busy home, Johanna was not accustomed to spending a great deal of time alone. Even at Miss Pomoroy's, there had been her classmates and the set pattern of the day.

There wasn't even anything really to do. Housekeeping, with no mahogany furniture to dust or polish, no brass candlesticks to shine, was simple.

When they arrived here, Johanna had found their shelves stocked with home-canned fruits and vegetables, deer jerky, and there had been a cured ham, a side of bacon, fresh eggs, butter, and milk in the springhouse. At the foot of the bed, a cedar box had been supplied with coarse sheets, homespun blankets.

Johanna's own belongings, her trunk of clothes, boxes of wedding presents, and her hope chest had not yet come. Perhaps when they did, she would have more to do, placing them, arranging things, putting her own touch on their home.

She poured herself a cup of the coffee Ross had made and left on the stove, then went over to stand at the open front door, looking out. An unwanted thought came into her mind. What would she do with the rest of her life, here on this isolated hillside with no family, no friends? Surely the novelty of marriage or coming here had not worn off so quickly.

Their cabin was surrounded by the tall pines, and suddenly she had a feeling of being closed in. Frightened, she turned back into the room. Maybe she should go down and visit Ross's mother. That would probably be a good thing to do, get better acquainted. Getting out in the open in the fresh air and sunshine would ease that strange feeling of being up here by herself, cut off from the world.

Johanna put on a fresh dress and did up her hair. She felt a little shy about just showing up at Eliza's with no invitation. But wasn't that foolish? She was sure that mountain folk didn't stand on any sort of ceremony, especially not among family members. As Ross's wife, Eliza's daughter-in-law, *she* was family now, wasn't she? She tied on a wide-brimmed straw hat and set out. She thought she remembered the way, although the last two times they had been there, they were on horseback. She had only to follow the path, and she would soon be at Eliza's house. However, the path had several forks winding in different directions, some quite overgrown with brush, laurel bushes, sweeping pine branches. Soon Johanna became confused and wondered if somehow she had taken a wrong turn.

At a little clearing she stopped, trying to orient herself. Suddenly she heard the sound of childish voices. Within a few minutes two little girls came into sight. Sue and Katie, Ross's sisters! Recognizing them, Johanna was filled with relief. They would show her the way, of course, even take her there themselves. "Good morning! I'm so glad to see you," she began, waving her hand to them. But their reaction stunned her. Immediately their smiles disappeared. The smaller of the two slipped behind the older, her finger in her mouth, while the other girl looked startled.

Knowing they were shy, Johanna smiled and took a few steps toward them, saying, "I'm on my way down to see your mother. Am I on the right path? I felt lost."

They stared back at her, eyes wide, but said nothing. Johanna tried again. "Is this the right way?"

They nodded in unison and then spun around and ran, stumbling over their bare feet in their hurry to get away, running back the way they had come. Left so unceremoniously, Johanna felt bewildered and hurt. Was it just shyness or didn't they like her? She had always been good with children. Elly adored her and so did all her little friends. Johanna sighed. She probably had a lot to learn about mountain people, children as well as grownups.

All desire to visit with her mother-in-law vanished. She was unsure of her welcome in the middle of the day, when Eliza might be busy with many chores and wonder why *she* wasn't similarly occupied. It might be an interruption or, worse still, an intrusion. Not willing to risk another rejection, Johanna turned around and retraced her steps back up to their own cabin.

That evening when she told Ross about her encounter with his sisters, he brushed it off casually. "They're just shy. Not used to talking to strangers."

"*Strangers?* I'm their sister-in-law," she protested.

Seeing Johanna's expression, Ross quickly said, "You won't always be a stranger, honey. But right now they don't know you, and to them you *are* a stranger. It'll work out in time. You'll see."

In spite of his reassurance, Johanna still felt uncertain. Day after day, she kept putting off going down to see Eliza. That is, until Ross brought up the subject himself, saying, "I stopped by Ma's on my way home today, Johanna, and she was wonderin' if you were poorly? I said, 'No, she's fit as a fiddle.' I think that was her way of asking why you hadn't been down to see her. Better go tomorrow, honey. Else she might feel slighted."

The next day, Johanna went down to see Ross's mother, and it was a pleasant enough visit, although she still found Eliza rather standoffish. That too could be shyness—or was it wariness of *strangers*? However, it made Johanna determined to win her over. She wanted desperately for Ross's mother to love her.

The weeks of summer went by. Still Johanna had to fight the feeling of being an outsider. She did not know how to break through the wall they had put up. She was longing to be friends. She couldn't summon the courage to bring up the subject again to Ross. At length she decided that all she could do was be herself, whatever the mixture was that made her who she was. Whether his family liked it or not, liked *her* or not, Ross had found that mixture exciting, desirable. Certainly enough to stand up to her father and, against all odds, ask for her hand in marriage.

Sometimes Johanna would stand on the porch of their cabin after Ross had left for the day and look down into the valley. She saw plumes of thin blue smoke rising over the treetops and knew they came from the piled stone chimneys in the dozens of log cabins scattered all along the way, up and down the hillside. Each of those cabins had people, families, women who would possibly be her friends. All she had to do was reach out. It was a new experience. Johanna had always been open to people, had always had friends. Why not now? Was she *really* that different that they didn't want to know her? As the weeks passed, she became even more reluctant to try.

One day, she saw Ross's little sisters come by on the trail below the cabin, carrying buckets. Johanna ran out onto the porch and invited them to come in. However, they shyly shook their heads. Sue, the older of the two, said, "No'm, we cain't. It's blackberry-pickin' time. Ma's goin' to make jelly, and we best get on with pickin'." She held up her bucket. "Ma don't like us gone too long."

Johanna was tempted to offer them some cookies and lemonade, cool from the springhouse, but then decided she wouldn't. Watching them go on down the path with their buckets, Johanna realized she missed her own sisters. More than she expected to, more than she had when she was away at school. The fact was that there were more and more times during the day when Johanna's thoughts flew home to Hillsboro.

⤎⋰⋱⤏

The tiny twinge of homesickness Johanna had consciously tried to push away surfaced when her trunks finally arrived. They were brought up the hill by mule, delivered by the taciturn Jake Robbins, the postmaster in charge of the small post office in back of the general store. As soon as he deposited them with the few words Johanna could wrest from him, she eagerly started to unpack them.

The first trunk contained the wedding presents that, before the ceremony, Johanna had been too excited to really appreciate. She put those beside the gifts of linen and china to wait so that she and Ross could look at them and enjoy them together. It was unpacking the second trunk that caused her first excitement and delight to vanish. An unexpected depression swept over her when she saw the contents. Her mother had seemingly emptied her bedroom of all traces of *her.* As if she had never lived there at all! Her books, vases, throw pillows, knickknacks. Her mother had sent Johanna her childhood, her girlhood, her life at home! As though she were never coming back! The emotional blow was stunning. It cut a deep wound. Johanna sank to the floor, her knees having suddenly gone weak.

Holding a small pair of blue Delft candlesticks that had once graced the little fireplace in her room, Johanna felt as though she had been cut adrift from everything dear and

161

familiar. She glanced around the cabin. Where would these go? Where would any of these things fit into her new environment, these surroundings? For the first time since she had come with Ross to the mountains, Johanna felt a sense of loss, a void that nothing came quickly to fill. Had she cut herself off from home, family, as completely as it seemed?

Chapter Fourteen

~≈≈~

*B*y the end of the summer, Johanna had organized herself to accomplish certain everyday chores, although there were still ones she hadn't got the hang of yet. Johanna realized she had a lot to learn about housekeeping.

She had no one to teach her the considerable skills necessary for her to learn if she was to keep house properly here, make a home for Ross. She wanted it to be a haven of warmth, comfort, and peace after a long day on horseback visiting the sick.

She was hesitant to ask Eliza, fearing that her mother-in-law would be scornful of her inadequacy. She didn't want to impose on Aunt Bertie, who had already been more than friendly and who was always busy and never seemed to know an idle minute. Why, Aunt Bertie would think Johanna plum daft not to be able to find enough to do to fill her days.

What Johanna did not understand was that far from being unfriendly, the mountain people were hesitant to intrude on someone they considered smarter, more accomplished than themselves. They would never offer help or advice that wasn't requested.

Ironically, Johanna discovered that among the books her mother had packed in her trunk was the well-thumbed dictionary her father had given her when she was ten. There was a needlepoint marker in the P's, the last section in which she had looked up a word, memorized the definition. She smiled, a trifle nostalgically. Her father's admonition was still a good one. She would continue to learn a new word every day, even if there was no one to test her on it.

"Perseverance," "persistence," "patience," were all good goals to pursue in this new life she had taken on. She needed them all as she tried to "perfect" her wifely skills. All had been badly employed as she groaned over lumpy rice, burned biscuits, scorched cornbread.

But Johanna was determined she would learn. And slowly, gradually, painfully, she did.

─────※─────

Johanna's inner doubts were transitory, usually lasting only the length of a long day spent alone when Ross was late coming home from "doctoring." She *was* happy, Johanna told herself over and over. She loved Ross and she tried to keep her moments of melancholy well hidden from him.

One night Ross was out very late. He'd been called to tend the children of the storekeeper, who all had bad earaches. The Millscreek Gap store also housed the post office, and while there, Ross had been given a letter addressed to Johanna.

When he got home, he found Johanna asleep in the rocker by the fire. Ross placed the letter on the mantelpiece, then gently wakened Johanna and carried her to bed. She sleepily acknowledged his presence but went right back to sleep. It wasn't until morning that he told her about the letter.

For some reason, she waited until Ross left to open it. She recognized her mother's fine penmanship and opened the letter at once. As she read it, she felt a rush of unexpected emotion. Pictures of Holly Grove flooded into her mind. She could almost smell the scent of potpourri, flowers from her mother's garden, the mingled smells of polished wood, baking apples, and beeswax candles. Turning page after page, other familiar images came. Things she hadn't realized she cared much about or missed, now became cherished memories. Johanna had left all of this happily for "love and the world well lost." A dear, familiar world, as it turned out.

Johanna read on.

> Cissy is growing into a very pretty young woman and is agreeable in every way. We had a length of silk, striped in pale blue and cerise, made into a lovely gown for her to wear to the Pettigrew's party, at which she was quite the belle of the ball.

Impatiently Johanna put the letter down for a minute. She could just imagine how Cissy was "toeing the mark" to her mother's satisfaction. She could read between the lines her mother had written, could almost hear all the same things her parents had tried to tell her. If she had listened . . .

Johanna got up and walked restlessly around the room. Why should news of the social life in Hillsboro bother her now? She didn't really miss it, *did* she?

When she had first come to the mountains, the possibility of unhappiness had seemed *impossible*, but now . . .

Suddenly the cabin door opened and Ross stood there. Startled, Johanna winked back her tears and got to her feet.

"Why, Ross! What are you doing back?"

He remained standing there for a full minute, then said, "I'm not sure, Johanna. I just thought maybe you might need me."

Johanna's heart lurched. She dropped the letter as she ran to him.

"Oh, Ross!" She flung herself into his outstretched arms. As they closed around her, she rejoiced in their strength, in the safety and security she felt in his embrace. Why should she ever regret anything? She could not stop the tears, but now they were not tears of self-pity but of thankfulness. How lucky she was to have this love. How ungrateful to ever question it or doubt that it was meant to be.

It frightened her that even for a little while, she had allowed herself to waver as to whether she had made the right decision. Ross was real, not the romantic myth they had tried to describe him as. He was the reason she had resisted all attempts to persuade her to give him up.

That night, the mountains echoed with the first summer storm. It began slowly, with big raindrops pattering on the roof then quickly becoming a deafening thudding. Thunder boomed, echoing through the ridges and valleys of the mountains that surrounded the cabin. Great jagged forks of lightning crackled in the darkened sky. Awakened, Johanna moved closer to Ross, who slept on, as if used to this kind of nature's noise. He was of these mountains, Johanna thought, born and raised here. Nothing about them disturbed or frightened him. Without waking, he drew her close. His nearness thrust away the uncertainties and doubts she'd had that day. Fear brought on by the storm disappeared as she moved closer to Ross, felt his lean, warm body. A warmth, a sense of security, took its place. This wonderful man who loved her, who understood her, to whom she was important, was her protection against foolish regrets. Here in his arms was safety, tenderness. She must value them, know how richly she was blessed.

Ross was her life now. She would prove her parents wrong.

Johanna knew she needed something to help her cope with her new life. She didn't know what. She had not thought beyond marrying Ross, getting her heart's desire. She had not anticipated the standoffishness she had encountered in Millscreek. Other than Aunt Bertie, none of the women she had met had invited her to visit nor taken her up on her invitations. Not even Merriman's wife, Jenny. Every time they were all at Eliza's house, Johanna had asked her. Jenny seemed even shyer than the little girls.

Johanna's feelings about Ross's mother troubled her most of all. She did not feel Eliza really accepted her. No matter how hard she tried, Ross's mother maintained an aloofness that Johanna could not seem to bridge.

Help for her anxious heart came from two unexpected sources. The first was from Uncle Tanner, who happened to drop in at the worst possible time. Johanna was crying tears of frustration over a batch of burned biscuits when his knock at the door and his friendly "Howdy, anybody home?" came.

Johanna hastily wiped her eyes, banged down the tin, and hurried out onto the porch to greet him. She invited him in but he said, "I reckon just some water will do me, as Bertie's expecting me home right quick." Johanna walked with him up the stone path to the spring. While Uncle Tanner helped himself to two dipperfuls, Johanna's expression must have told him something, because he said gently, "I gotta 'spicion you're feelin' some sorriness. Anythin' I kin do might help?"

"Oh, it probably sounds silly, Uncle Tanner. I just burned a whole batch of biscuits." Tears filled her eyes again. "Sometimes it seems I can't do anything right, and"—before she knew it, she was unloading to him—"and nobody seems to like me here!"

"Now, girly, let me give you a piece of advice. Go slow. Mountain folk don't make up to strangers easy, but once they take you in, nobody in the world could have kinder kin. You mark my words. Eliza will come 'round. My Bertie'll show the way, but you'll see. You're one of the family now—"

Uncle Tanner's soft-spoken voice fell like soothing balm. She had longed for just such comfort. His words were as much a gift of love as the beautifully crafted rocker. His genuine warmth, his smile, and his gentle way touched her deeply. As she waved him off, she felt much better. She went back inside, tossed out the "burned offering," and started mixing up another batch of biscuits.

One morning not long after Uncle Tanner's visit, Johanna was out weeding in the small vegetable garden Ross had started for her, when she heard the sound of horse's hooves plodding up the hill. She sat back on her heels, one hand shading her eyes, and looked to see who her visitor might be.

A stocky man in a shabby swallow-tailed coat, battered hat, and dusty boots dismounted and nodded toward Johanna. He had a scruffy red beard, prominent nose, but twinkly, bright blue eyes. He took off his hat, showing a balding head, then grinned and greeted her. "Howdy, ma'am. A good day to you and praise the Lord! Nathan Tomlin here. I'm the circuit preacher. Come to pay you a call."

Johanna got to her feet, aware of the skirt she had tucked up, the sunbonnet that had fallen back from her perspiring face. Self-consciously she wiped her dirty hands on her apron.

"Good morning." She tried to sound welcoming. Meanwhile she was hoping she had left the kitchen tidy before coming outside, and wondering what-on-earth refreshment she could offer him.

"Mighty pleased to meet you, ma'am. I knowed Ross from the time he were knee-high to a grasshopper. Growed up to be a doctor!" Preacher Tomlin shook his head as if in amazement. "Eliza told me he had hisself a peart wife, now. So I come up to see if it were true," he chuckled, "and to make your acquaintance."

"Please, won't you come inside?" Johanna asked, feeling flustered. She should be better prepared for company, she told herself, even if she rarely had any. Her mother was always prepared, serving without seeming fuss a dainty tea tray, whether it was a neighbor or their minister making a pastoral call.

"Thanky kindly, ma'am." He took out a red bandanna and made a swipe at his perspiring forehead. "Mighty hot morning, and something to wet my whistle would go down mighty fine."

Johanna untied her sunbonnet, stuffed it into the deep pocket of her apron, patted her hair, then ushered the preacher into the house. Inside, a quick look around assured her it didn't look bad. The floor was swept, the place neat. She was happy she had picked a bunch of wildflowers earlier and set them into a glazed pottery jug on the table.

Johanna picked up the kettle to heat water for tea, but Reverend Tomlin held up his hand. "Don't trouble yourself, ma'am. I got a passel of visits to make this day, so I can't stay long. Just a dipper of your spring water is all I need."

"You're sure?" she asked.

"Yes ma'am, thanky kindly," he nodded.

As she took out a tumbler and started to fill it, she saw his gaze sweep the room as if looking for something. After he took the glass of water she handed him, drained it, and returned it to her, he commented, "No Bible, young lady?" His eyes were kind, if curious. "In most mountain homes, it's in a place of honor, like yonder on the mantelpiece, or at the table so's it can be read mornin' and night."

At the mild reproach in his tone, Johanna blushed. Quickly she pointed to her small leather New Testament she'd had since school days, beside her prayer book on the hutch.

Preacher Tomlin shook his head and said gently, "That ain't enuf. Not by a long shot. Gotta have the *whole* Word, read it every day! The Prophets, the Psalms, and Proverbs. Next time I ride by, I'll bring you one," he promised, then he moved toward the door. "Now I'll bid you good day. Got places to go, people to see," he laughed. "Didn't mean to admonish you, but remember, 'Who the Lord loveth, he chastiseth.' The woman is the heart of the home, you know. Ross needs to hear the Scriptures every day to give him the strength he needs in his chosen work. You need to provide that for him."

Johanna stood on the porch and watched Preacher Tomlin mount his horse, turn around, and start down the mountainside. She felt strangely sobered by his visit.

As much a surprise to *her* as it might have been to Nathan Tomlin, a verse came into her mind just then—"Be not forgetful to entertain strangers, for thereby some have entertained angels unaware." Johanna almost had to smile in astonishment. Surely *that* was from Scripture! But from whatever unknown memory source it had come, Johanna knew it was important. However, she had no idea at the time how it would affect her life.

⚜

Johanna had never been what people call "religious"— she was certainly not "pious," as Aunt Hannah was—but there was a deep core of spiritual longing that she had never been quite so aware of as she was now. Although she had attended church with her family regularly every Sunday, whatever the subject of the sermon was, it was quickly forgotten. Johanna had never thought deeply about spiritual things. Lately, however, surrounded by the natural beauty of God's creation wherever she looked, Johanna was filled with awe and reverence. There had been no channel for it, no way she'd found to express it. Ross said a perfunctory blessing over their evening meal, but he was usually so tired when he finally got home that it was short. Often he hardly got through supper before his eyelids would droop, and not long after the meal ended he would kiss her good night and go to bed, exhausted by the rigors of his day. Many nights, Johanna sat by the fire long afterward, gazing into the flickering flames until they burned into glowing embers. It was at times like this when she most felt the emptiness within.

After Preacher Tomlin's call, Johanna felt chastened. She did not know exactly what to do about it. However, a few days later, true to his promise, he stopped by and brought her a Bible.

"You're goin' to find God's very close up here in the mountains, little lady," he told her before he rode off. Johanna soon discovered that as untaught as the disheveled-looking preacher seemed, as much as he altered the King's English, there was a goodness of heart, a genuineness, that she had never encountered before.

In the Bible he gave her, there were dog-eared pages, notations in the margins, verses underlined. She began to read it daily. First, the marked chapters, out of curiosity as to what Preacher Tomlin might feel was important. Then more and more she found her own favorites. On warm afternoons, she would sit on the small porch of the cabin, in the sunshine, the Bible on her lap. Gradually some of the verses became familiar, and she began to say them softly to herself, memorize them. Quickly Psalm 121 became a favorite. "I will lift mine eyes unto the hills—From whence cometh my help? My help comes from the Lord, the maker of heaven and earth." Johanna felt she needed help badly—to adjust to the loneliness of her new life, to become a good wife to Ross, the helpmeet he needed. She loved him more than ever, and she never wanted him to be sorry he had married someone not up to the challenge of being the wife of a mountain doctor. She often recalled Aunt Hannah saying, "You can't live on love, my girl." Well, *without* love it would have been impossible.

⁓≈❧≈⁓

Church was only held if Preacher Tomlin was in the neighborhood over a Sunday. The announcement that he was going to conduct a meeting would be circulated by word of mouth up and down the mountain. Ross usually brought home the news, but if there was sickness or a baby to be delivered, he could not accompany Johanna that Sunday.

The service was informal. No set ritual seemed to be observed, and it did not have a certain time that it was over. People brought their children, went up for healing prayers, commented with "amens" during Reverend Tomlin's sermons, which were apt to ramble and get diverted when his eye found someone in the congregation he wanted to address. Often he would break off in the middle of a sentence to say, "Good to see you, Sister Anna. How's your rheumatiz? Do say? Well, come up for prayer." Although this rather startled her the first time she attended, Johanna began to regard it as a real, down-to-earth way of reaching people—perhaps even the way Jesus might have done it when folks gathered around him and he talked, touched, and taught them. The hymns were sung without benefit of an organ. Someone would start and others would join in. The same verse might be sung over and over, and finally just fade away. "On Jordan's stormy banks I stand / And cast a wishful eye / To Canaan's fair and happy land / Where my pos-

172

sessions lie" or "O brother, it's how will you stand / And it's how you will stand on that day?" or "Sowing on the mountain / Reaping in the valley / You're going to reap just what you sow."

Johanna could not help but compare the services here with the formal services of the Hillsboro church she had always attended. There an air of solemnity reigned—the measured tones of the organ, the ritual that never deviated for that particular day of the church calendar designated by the prayer book. Here the small, frame church rang with hands clapping, feet tapping, spontaneous "hallelujahs," and joyously sung hymns. When Johanna looked around at the smiling faces, even the little children swaying to the rhythms, she thought that as different as the forms of worship were, maybe both were equally pleasing to God.

One Sunday when she and Ross had gone to church together, outside afterward Aunt Bertie had urged, "You-all come along home with us." Johanna always enjoyed being with the old lady, who she found was a fount of wisdom, humor, and good advice.

Ross went outside with Uncle Tanner to his apple press. It was soon going to be time to make cider and for Aunt Bertie to make her apple butter. The smell of biscuits baking and sausage frying crisply filled the cabin with delicious odor. "Can I do anything to help?" Johanna asked.

"No, thanky kindly, not this mawnin', but come time for me to make my apple butter, I might need some help a-stir-rin'. You see, it's a daylong job. Them apples gotta be stirred every single minute. If a body don't stand right over the iron pot and keep that paddle moving, the apples'd burn and the apple butter would be plum ruined. A heap of folks ruin their apple butter by not doing so. There's nothin worst than scorched apple butter."

Aunt Bertie went to the door and called out to Uncle Tanner and Ross to come in and eat. Coming back to the table, she said to Johanna, "Apple butter makin's not for a lazy-body or a weakly person. That's what I meant by mebbe you could come help me the day I do mine. Take turns a-stirrin."

Johanna said, "I'd be glad to, Aunt Bertie," having no idea what she had let herself in for.

Chapter Fifteen

❧❧❧

One evening when Johanna stepped out on the porch to hang up the dishpan, she called to Ross, "Come out here and see this!" She pointed to a new moon, a pale, thin crescent in the dark cobalt sky. "Have you ever seen anything so beautiful?" Standing behind her, he put his arms around her waist, bent his cheek against hers.

"Yes ma'am, many a time," he said softly. "Mountain moons are the prettiest, and I'm glad you're beginning to appreciate them."

"Oh, but I do! Did you think I wouldn't?"

"I guess I thought that come fall, you might miss all those parties, dancing, and taffy pulls." There was a hint of laughter in his tone.

"Not when I have *you* and the moon," she smiled in the darkness, snuggling against him. "It's very romantic."

He laughed. Then, stifling a yawn, he murmured, "I'm off to bed, darlin'. Must've rode a hundred miles up and down the mountain today." He kissed her cheek and went back inside. For the tiniest moment Johanna felt deserted. But she realized his days were long, arduous. He would be up before dawn, upon his horse, and on to making his calls. He needed his sleep. Still, it was so lovely out here, not a bit cold, and the moon was so beautiful. She didn't want to go back inside. But such beauty ought to be shared. It was the kind of night to be with someone you loved, maybe quoting poetry to each other....

Johanna sighed. Suddenly she felt a little lonely. Her thoughts wandered. What were they doing at home tonight? Was Cissy getting ready to go to a party? Or were they all playing a parlor game together—snap-rattle or charades? Irrationally she wished she were there—and then, almost immediately, she knew she didn't want to be. That part of her life was over. She had what she wanted. It was just that there was a void that nothing here had quite filled for her yet. Not that Ross wasn't enough. He was everything to her. It was just that a girl needed a friend. Someone her own age. Another girl to laugh with, someone to share secrets with, someone to talk to....

Ross was completely at home here. He moved confidently where she felt so strange. She remembered how only a short time ago *he* had sometimes seemed awkward where she was so at ease. It was that very awkwardness that somehow had seemed so endearing to her, made her want to reach out to him, make him comfortable. His shyness and inarticulateness around her parents only made her love him more, made her feel protective. Her thoughts grew tender as she thought of her husband. His gentleness undergirded his strength and skill. He'd gone away to learn "doctoring," but he still belonged—he'd come home to heal and help them. She had seen the looks of awed affection that followed him, the respect in the eyes of people as they greeted him with "Howdy, Doc."

Now it was *she* who was in a different environment. What was that Scripture verse? Hadn't the captive Israelites complained that they couldn't sing in a strange land? That's how she felt sometimes, "a stranger in a strange land." She wanted so much to be liked, to be understood. Would it ever happen?

One sunny morning early in September, Johanna had taken her mug of coffee out onto the porch steps to drink in the sunshine. Ross had left before daybreak and had not wakened her. Since he usually returned at night exhausted from the long, work-filled days, mornings before he set out were the only real time they had together. Johanna cherished that time, and today they had missed that. A long day alone stretched out before her.

Suddenly a piercing scream caused her to jump up, spilling her coffee. She looked around to see where it was coming from. Then, stumbling out of the brush, Ross's sister Sue came running. "Oh ma'am, ma'am, Miss Johanna, ma'am!" she called when she saw Johanna.

Johanna set down the mug and hurried to meet the little girl rushing breathlessly toward her. "Oh ma'am, it's Katie. She's—" Sue stopped a few feet from Johanna, panting. "She's—she's—oh, please come help her!"

"Of course! Where is she? What's happened?"

Sue was sobbing. Her small, freckled face was flushed, tear-stained. She gulped and tugged at Johanna's apron. "Please, ma'am, come. Up yonder!" She pointed to the craggy hillside above their cabin. "We wuz out pickin' berries and started to crost the creek, over a log that had fell, and I got to the other side, but Katie, she—she got skeered, I reckon. Anyhow, she couldn't move no more. She jest sit down and started a-yellin'. I tried to git her to come. But she jest kept lookin' down at the water rushin' over the rocks, and—" She halted, gulping. "She cain't move!"

All the time Sue was talking, she was pulling Johanna by the hand up the hill. It was steep and rocky, and Johanna's own breath was coming fast and hard. From what Sue told her, she had a mental picture of what had happened. But she had no idea how bad the situation was until they reached the

177

top. There she saw how high above the rushing mountain stream was the log where the little girl was stranded.

She had stopped screaming and was clinging to the rough bark of the log with both thin little hands. Johanna saw that the child's eyes were glazed and staring, a look of stark terror on her face.

"Why in the world did you try to cross there?" she asked Sue in a hushed voice. The child shook her head. "Dint know it was so high, I reckon. 'Til I got on it—then I knew I had to go on, but Katie got skeered and couldn't."

Sue, older by two years and having long, skinny legs, had probably made it across on sheer pluck. The younger, smaller Katie probably made the mistake of looking down, got dizzy, and panicked.

However it had come about, the situation was dangerous. Johanna tried to figure out how deep the water was, how she could get to the child to rescue her. First she had to calm her so she wouldn't get more frightened, lose her grip on the log, and fall off. The current was fast, the stream full of huge rocks. If Katie fell, she could hit her head on one of the jutting stones or be swept away in the swift waters. Johanna knew she had to act quickly.

"Don't worry, Katie," she called. "Don't be afraid. I'm coming to get you!"

She sat down on a large rock on the bank and untied her boots. She'd have to wade out to the middle, reach up, grab the child, and pull her into her arms, then carry her to shore. She had to do it fast, before Katie got dizzy, lost consciousness, tumbled into the water. From things Ross had told her, Johanna knew most accidents happened because people panicked.

Johanna's heart thundered. Her hands trembled as she loosened her laces, pulled off her boots and stockings. Standing up, she lifted her skirt, unbuttoned the waistband of her petticoat. Letting it drop, she stepped out of it and tossed it aside. Then, gathering up her skirt, she tucked it into her belt. The less she had on, the less chance that the water would soak it, weigh her down, drag her into the current.

Behind her she heard Sue sobbing, but she had no time to stop and comfort her. She had to save her little sister.

The first shock of the icy water on her bare feet made Johanna gasp. She would have to move quickly so that its freezing temperature would not hamper her progress. Hard rocks under the tender soles of her feet made her steps torturous. The cold water rose to her ankles and calves as she plunged forward. It was deeper than she thought and the current stronger. What if the water was even deeper in the middle, at the point on the log where Katie sat motionless, dazed with fear? Now she felt the water rushing around her knees, the edge of her turned-up skirt. Clenching her teeth against the onslaught of icy water, she pushed on. Nearing the fallen log, she almost lost her footing in a sudden drop of the riverbed.

"I'm coming, Katie. Hold on, honey," she called through her chattering teeth.

The water had reached her thighs, and she could feel the wet cloth of her soaked pantaloons chillingly against her skin. The rush of the swirling water made it hard to get a foothold. She stretched out one hand. The scaly bark scraped her palms. Gripping it desperately, she inched her way closer to Katie. *Please, God, help!* she prayed. At last she was just below Katie. In a voice that shook, she said, "Now, Katie, I want you to let go of the log, lean down, and put your arms around my neck. I'll hold you—just come slow and easy." Johanna put up one arm toward the child, holding on to the side of the log with her other hand to steady herself against the current.

"I cain't, I'm skeered!" wailed the little girl weakly.

"Yes, you can, Katie. Come on, honey. I'm here and I'll catch hold of you. Just let go."

Every minute the child hesitated was agony. Johanna knew she had to get through to the child, who was now numb with cold and fear. Time was of importance, the situation desperate. Johanna was losing the feeling in her legs from the freezing water, and she still had to make it back to the bank safely with Katie.

"Katie, come on!" she cried.

All of a sudden she felt the child throw herself forward onto her. The thin little arms went around her neck in a choking hold. Katie's trembling little body pressing against her nearly unbalanced Johanna. *Dear God, help us!* Words of Scripture Johanna didn't even know she'd memorized came pouring into her mind.

I have called thee by name, thou art mine. When thou passeth through the waters, I will be with thee and through the rivers, they shall not overflow thee.

Struggling with the added weight of Katie, Johanna turned, the strong current pressing against her, and made her way painfully back across the sharp stones, through the cold, rushing water, toward the bank. Finally, gasping for breath, her feet cut and bruised, she stumbled onto the grassy bank and fell on her knees, still holding the shivering Katie.

Sue hunkered down beside them, alternately sobbing and sniffling, "Oh, thanky, ma'am. Thanky." Then Katie began to sob. Johanna felt salty tears roll down her own cheeks. Then she started laughing. Both girls looked at her, startled, then gradually they too began to laugh. Johanna knew it was mostly hysterical. But it didn't matter. She'd rescued Katie. That was the important thing.

At last, breathless from laughter, she wiped her tears away, scrambled up. Her bare feet were beginning to have some feeling again. In fact, they felt hot and tingling. She picked up her stockings and boots, slung them over one shoulder by the laces, and threw her discarded petticoat over one arm. "Come on," she said, reaching out a hand to each of the girls. "Let's go back to my place and get dry and have a treat."

Johanna thought of the tin of powdered chocolate her mother had sent in her last box from Hillsboro. She guessed maybe Sue and Katie had never tasted it. She'd make some hot cocoa and wrap Katie up in a quilt, and they'd all feel better.

Without even realizing it at the moment, Johanna had crossed over whatever line Ross's family had placed between them. By coming to Katie's aid that day, she had definitely won over Sue and Katie. The very next day, Eliza came up the mountain to thank her personally, after hearing the children's story of Johanna's rescue. She brought a rhubarb-and-berry pie and shyly told Johanna that if she wanted the recipe, it was one of Ross's favorites. On a deeper level, something even more significant happened to Johanna after the day she rescued Katie. She realized that the Bible reading she had been doing lately had taken hold. She was not even sure from which chapter, what verse, she had drawn that passage she'd remembered. In the midst of panic but still with faith that she would be heard, Johanna had cried out for help. "I called on the Lord in distress, the Lord answered me and set me in a broad place." As Preacher Tomlin told her, "He does what he promises to do."

Chapter Sixteen

◈◈

The whisper of autumn fell like a soft melody on the mountains. The air had a crispness in the mornings, a tart sweetness like a ripe apple in the afternoons. The hills were russet touched with gold, asters blue-gray swayed in the wind, goldenrod nodded on the banks of the winding road up to their cabin. In the October mornings, mist veiled blue hills, frost sparkled on the sumac in roadside thickets, hickory log smoke curled up from stone chimneys within the log cabins that hopscotched down into the valley, as breakfast fires burned on hearths inside.

Aunt Bertie sent word that she was going to start her apple butter. "You're to be there at dawn," Ross told her, his mouth twitching slightly, his eyes mischievous. Johanna's eyes widened. "Uncle Tanner gets the fire going before the sun peeks over the ridge. She's spent the last two days peeling and paring the choicest apples, and she'll be ready to start by sunup."

By the time Johanna ate a hasty breakfast and made her way down the hillside to their cottage, Aunt Bertie stood with a wooden paddle, stirring the boiling apples in a big black iron pot over the hickory fire. Uncle Tanner was sitting on a bench nearby, whittling. They both greeted Johanna cheerily.

"You come in good time, girly. My arm gets wore out a lot sooner than it used to, so I'd take it kindly if you'd spell me once in a while."

"Of course, Aunt Bertie. Now?"

"Not yet. Look at this and I'll show you what's next." Aunt Bertie motioned her closer with her free hand. Johanna bent and looked into the pot, where the apples were boiling, bobbing and making little popping sounds. "I've poured in a jug of Tanner's fresh cider, and now it's 'bout time to put in sugar and spices," Aunt Bertie said. "You can take over, Johanna, whilst I add it in."

Johanna had never imagined it would be such hard work. After Aunt Bertie had poured in the sugar and spices, Johanna took the paddle and slowly began stirring. The sun climbed into the sky, time passed, and still the apples kept boiling, puffing and popping like soap bubbles. Wood smoke got in her eyes, and she shifted arms for stirring, wiping her forehead with the back of her arm and pushing back her perspiration-dampened hair. Still, it seemed, the apples weren't ready.

Uncle Tanner kept feeding the fire, and he insisted on taking a turn stirring, because as the liquid got redder and stickier, the stirring got harder and harder. When Aunt Bertie protested, he gently but firmly told her, "Now, Bertie, don't fuss. I do my share of eatin' your apple butter—'tis only fair I pitch in on the makin'."

Johanna knew it was his way of giving Aunt Bertie a needed rest. She herself found the stirring very tiring and wondered when this famous apple butter would ever be called "done and ready."

She soon offered to do her spell of stirring, and it was hard going. The wind rose and a cool breeze blew on Johanna's red, hot face. It seemed an age before Aunt Bertie came to her side, peered into the pot, took the paddle from

Johanna, then said to Uncle Tanner, "It's done. Lookahere, it's so nice and thick, you could cut it with a knife. Come on, you can move the pot offen the fire."

Aunt Bertie gave a couple of extra stirs, then lifted the paddle, tapped it on the side of the iron kettle. Holding it in one hand, she swiped some of the apple butter onto her finger and stuck her finger in her mouth. Her eyes brightened as she tasted it, then smacked her lips. "Umhmmm!"

"How is it?" Johanna asked eagerly, feeling she'd had some small part in making it.

"It'll do," was all Aunt Bertie said. "Right tasty. Not a bit burned. Try some?"

When Johanna got a sample, she knew that Aunt Bertie's comment was a vast understatement. It was absolutely the most delicious apple butter she had ever tasted.

~⚹~

A week later Uncle Tanner stopped one day to bring Johanna several jars of the product. Johanna felt a particular pride to have helped make it. "Won't you come in?" she invited.

"No, thanky kindly, but can't stay. Too much to do. Firewood to cut and store. Winter's a-comin', rhododendron leaves is rolled up tight as a tobacco leaf. Soon it'll be November, and the frost in the mornin's means cold weather ahead," he predicted. Then he went on his way.

Johanna stood on the porch for a moment, her arms holding a basket filled with Aunt Bertie's bounty, and watched gray squirrels rattle in the leaves under the hickory trees, stopping every once in a while, shoe button black eyes darting back and forth, bushy tails quivering, then scrambling up the oak tree. Shivering, Johanna went back into the house. Uncle Tanner was probably right, she thought. October was fast slipping away, and now in the mornings, the wind rustled the tree branches and whistled down the chimneys.

Very early the next morning, she was awakened to the delicate patter of rain. She raised herself on her elbow and sleepily looked out the window. She saw silver needles of rain falling steadily. She cuddled back down into the quilts and went back to sleep. By the time she woke up for the second time, it was raining hard. Afterward, she wondered if she had experienced some kind of premonition. For some reason, she felt reluctant to get up and start her day. It was as if somehow it held something to dread. However, it was a fleeting feeling, and she soon was out in the kitchen, where Ross had a blazing fire going and had made coffee. As he poured her a cup, he said, "I'm riding down to Hayfork to the store to see if the medicine I ordered has come in yet."

"On such a bad morning?" Johanna asked with a worried frown.

"Ain't goin' git no better," he told her, grinning. Sometimes when he was teasing her, Ross deliberately lapsed into "mountain speech."

After he left, Johanna got busy with her chores. But to her surprise, only a short time later she heard the sound of his horse outside. She hadn't expected him home before late afternoon. Puzzled, she turned from the stove just as he came in the door. He was dripping rain from the brim of his wide hat, the shoulders of his slicker. There was something about his face that should have warned her. But it didn't. At least, not until he brought a letter out from under his coat, held it out to her. "It's from your mother—addressed to both of us. So I opened it, and—"

Somehow Johanna knew even before he spoke the words.

"I'm sorry, darlin'—" Ross's voice wavered slightly. "Your father is dead."

Unable to speak, Johanna moved stiffly toward him, then went into his arms, closing her eyes against the awfulness of those words, leaning against him.

"No," she murmured. "No. *No!*"

They stood holding each other wordlessly for a long time.

Then Johanna looked up at him, asking numbly. "How? What happened?"

His expression was one of infinite tenderness, pity. "He was only ill a few days. They didn't think it was serious, or they would have sent for you—he went very quickly."

Before he could say anything more, Johanna burst into tears. She gasped, "It's my fault. I caused it. If I hadn't disobeyed . . . If I hadn't left home . . ."

"Oh Johanna, you mustn't say that. Don't. Don't blame yourself." His voice broke and he just held her tighter, unable to find anything to stop the pain she was inflicting upon herself. It was a pain she had not known nor understood nor even knew existed, one she did not think she could endure.

Throughout that long, cold night, Ross held her. Outside, the wind howled around the house, moaned through the tall pine trees, sighing like the keening sound of mourners. Johanna shivered and he drew her closer. She felt the deeply buried aching, the longing, rise within her. *I want to go home. I must go home.* She lay awake through most of the night, unable to stop thinking. When the gray light of dawn crept through the windows, she eased herself out of bed, crouched in front of the hearth, where the one remaining log left burning when they had gone to bed glowed red, making a whispering sound. She felt cold clear through. Her hands were icy, and she held them out to the fire to try to warm them. Johanna's eyes burned watching it and filled up with tears again.

She heard movement behind her, and Ross was beside her, holding her in his arms, rocking her like a baby while she sobbed on his shoulder. After a while he carried her back to bed.

When she awoke, Ross's place beside her was empty. She heard him moving around in the kitchen. A fire already blazed in the hearth, and she heard the clink of pottery, smelled the scent of boiling chicory. After a while he came to the foot of the bed. "I let you sleep. You needed the rest. But I'm taking you to your mother's today. You must see your father buried."

The rain had stopped and there was the smell of wood smoke in the air, which had a touch of frost. They rode down to his mother's house to tell them they would be gone to Hillsboro for the funeral, to spend some time with Johanna's grieving family.

While Ross explained, Johanna sat huddled on a bench and stared into the fire, her mind pain-paralyzed. She was unable to speak. Eliza's voice was gentle as she said, "Of course you must go. Your ma needs you."

Johanna did not answer. She started to say something, tell the truth. Her mother did not need her. Her mother had never *needed* her. The truth was, *she* needed her mother. Or at least everything her mother symbolized—comfort, safety, childhood.

She felt Ross's tender gaze upon her, saw him exchange a glance with his mother, a bid for understanding. Johanna made an effort to speak very politely. She longed for sympathy but could not seem to respond to it. Eliza poured a mug of tea and placed it in Johanna's numb hands. "Drink this afore you go. It'll help," she said softly.

~≈≈~

During the long, jogging journey along the trail that zigzagged down the mountain, Johanna was racked by grief and burdened by guilt. Was her stubborn, rebellious behavior in some way the cause of her father's death? Her mother had often mentioned in her letters,

> Your father is often downcast and without his old cheerfulness. He misses you, Johanna, always having relied on your special companionship.

Could such a thing have brought on a depression leading to illness? It didn't seem possible—her father had always been hearty and vigorous.

I deserve everything I'm feeling, Johanna thought bleakly. But even in her misery, she was reminded of Preacher Tomlin's exhortation—"Condemnation is not from God. In Christ Jesus there is no condemnation." She wanted to believe that. Why then did she *feel* so guilty? But could God forgive her if she couldn't forgive herself?

At last they came into Hillsboro. It was raining here as well. The roads were wet. On walkways, sodden clumps of leaves were piled under the dripping branches of the bare trees. As they rode through the familiar streets, past the familiar houses, out the familiar road that led to Holly Grove, Johanna felt as if she had been gone forever, much longer than five months.

On their way down the mountain, several times Ross had drawn his horse up beside Johanna's, asked anxiously if she wanted to stop, take a short rest. She had shaken her head. Her only thought was to get home.

At last they saw the road, fenced with split rails, that led up to Holly Grove. In the curving driveway were several buggies and one carriage drawn up in front of the house. At first that startled Johanna, until she realized that of course the aunties would all have gathered to do all the things caring relatives did in times of sorrow. She could just imagine them flocking there in proper mourning attire, like so many blackbirds.

Drenched in spite of her wool cape, and saddle weary, Johanna put her hands on Ross's shoulders and let him lift her down.

"I'll see to the horses later. I want to get you inside," he told her. His arm supported her as they went up the steps of the porch. Before they reached the top, the front door flew open, and Elly flung herself into Johanna's arms.

"Oh Johanna, you've come! I *knew* you would! I've been waiting and waiting. Oh Johanna, poor Papa—" And she burst into heartbroken sobs.

Johanna leaned over her, smoothing back the silken curls from the small, tear-streaked face, murmuring comfortingly, "Hush, sweetie. I know, I know."

"Do come in. You're chilling the whole house," spoke another voice with a trace of irritation. Johanna looked up and over Elly's head and saw her other sister standing there, holding the door open.

Cissy looked different, more grown-up even than a few months ago. She was dressed in black taffeta, her hair held back by a wide black velvet band. However, it was her expression that puzzled Johanna. She had a fleeting impression that her sister was not all happy to see her. Quickly Johanna dismissed that thought. She was probably wrong. Her cool attitude must be Cissy's way of handling her grief, Johanna thought, and she went forward to embrace her.

"Where's Mama?" Johanna asked. The words were no sooner spoken than Aunt Honey and Aunt Cady appeared from the parlor, followed by Aunt Hannah. Immediately Johanna was smothered with hugs and sympathy. Ross was taken in hand and led to the dining room, where, as Johanna knew it would be, food was spread out in abundance.

"I must go see Mama." Johanna extricated herself from the lilac-scented embrace of Aunt Cady, who was handsome in an elegant mourning ensemble.

"Of course you must, my dear. I'll bring up some tea for both of you," Aunt Honey promised, and Johanna shed her hooded cloak and went swiftly up the stairway.

❦

Johanna opened her parents' bedroom door quietly. Her mother, dressed in a wide-skirted black dress, was sitting in the wing chair by the window, her chin resting on one graceful hand. At the sound of the door opening, she turned her head. In that brief moment, Johanna thought again how beautiful her mother was. Her dark hair rose from a distinct widow's peak. When she saw who was standing there, Rebecca gave a little cry, "Oh, my dear!" and held out her arms, and Johanna went into them.

For a long moment, mother and daughter clung to each other. Rebecca was the first to let go. Drawing back, she regarded Johanna thoughtfully.

"He loved you so, Johanna . . . so very much." In those few softly spoken words, Johanna sensed something else. A reprimand, an accusation, a judgment? Without actually saying so, her mother had deepened Johanna's own feelings of guilt. It was almost as if she had said, "If you hadn't gone away, this would not have happened."

There was no time to think that through, because Rebecca gestured for her to sit on the tufted hassock beside her chair.

Rebecca was unusually pale yet composed and as exquisitely groomed as always, onyx pendant earrings set in silver filigree swung from her ears, and an onyx cameo was pinned at the throat.

"Oh Mama, I'm so—"Johanna's voice broke. Her sense of loss and sadness was too deep for her to express. Her mother patted her hand. "I know, dear, I know."

"How did it happen? Was he sick long? Was it a heart attack, what?"

Still holding her daughter's hand, Rebecca began, "He came home one evening, chilled. There had been a cold drizzle all day that turned to a freezing rain. He was thoroughly soaked, not having taken an umbrella with him. He refused my suggestion to change and get to bed immediately to ward off any possible effect. He wouldn't hear of it—just took off his boots and had dinner with us as usual. But the next morning—" Rebecca shook her head, her eyes moistened. "He awoke with a rasping cough, pains in his chest. I sent for Dr. Murrison, but he was out delivering a baby in the countryside and did not come calling until that evening—"

Johanna clasped her mother's hand. "Oh Mama, how dreadful—did he suffer much?"

"You know your father, Johanna, how he always makes—*made*," she corrected herself, "light of any physical problem he might have—" She paused. "I don't think any of us realized how serious it was. He did agree to stay in bed that day, however. He asked me to bring his writing tray, some papers from his desk. Although I protested he should rest, he insisted. He worked for some time, then said he felt tired and would sleep for a while. But by the time Alec—Dr. Murrison—came by, he was already far gone—the congestion had gone into his lungs, and he had a high fever. Dr. Murrison thought he might be able to fight it." Rebecca sighed. "But he never really rallied. Spoke only a few mostly incoherent words, then—slipped into unconsciousness."

"Oh, Mama." Johanna felt as if her heart were breaking. Tears rolled unchecked down her face. She put her head on her mother's lap, felt Rebecca's hand laid lightly upon it.

After a few minutes, Rebecca said, "I must go downstairs now, Johanna. People will be calling. People have been kindness itself, and I must receive them. That's what your father would want me to do." With a rustle of taffeta, she rose to her feet, then said to Johanna, "You don't have to come, not just yet, anyway. Tomorrow after the funeral, there will be those who will want to see you." Rebecca moved over to her bureau, peered briefly into the mirror to check her appearance. She lifted one of the two boxes on top, took out an envelope, then turned and held it out to Johanna. "He wrote you a letter."

Johanna got up and walked over to where her mother stood, and took it. Her mother was watching her with appraising eyes, the ones Johanna had always felt could see and judge beneath the outer shell of a person. Rebecca seemed to hesitate, as if to wait for Johanna to open it and read it while she was there. But Johanna simply stared down at the familiar handwriting, the classic swirls and loops of her father's Spenserian script. Her finger traced the wax seal imprinted with the familiar crest of her father's signet ring. Torn by wanting to read it and somehow dreading what her father might have written to her, Johanna hesitated. Rebecca waited only a few seconds before going out the door, saying over her shoulder, "We've put you and Ross in Elly's room, Johanna. Cissy took yours when you left, and Elly can sleep with her while you're here."

Those words sent a chill through Johanna that her mother surely could not have guessed or intended. Although Johanna had relinquished her privileged place as the oldest daughter at home to Cissy before she left, the fact that Cissy had taken over the room *she'd* had since she was born made Johanna realize that things had truly changed in this regard.

That explained the enigmatic look on her sister's face upon their arrival. It was the unspoken fear that by Johanna's coming, she might be displaced. The old instinctive rivalry. Johanna smiled ruefully. It was *she* who felt displaced.

Leaving her mother's room, she walked down the hall and opened the door to Elly's room, went in, and closed the door. She went over to the window, then with hands that shook broke the seal on her father's letter and drew out two folded pages and began to read.

My Dearest Daughter . . .

In the months that were to come, Johanna would read that letter again and again. Its pages became stained from the tears that fell as she read what her father had written. In these lines, Johanna discovered the parent's heart she had never known. His love, his dreams for her, his hopes, his disappointment, his loneliness for her. In spite of what had happened to cause their estrangement, her willful insistence on making her own marriage choice, his love for her had never changed. Now that it was too late, she understood it was that very love that had seemed so strangely cruel to her. This letter, written when he was so ill, perhaps when he knew it was a mortal illness, was undertaken to release her from any remorse or guilt. It was his last will and testament to a beloved child.

※

On the day of Tennant Shelby's funeral, the sky was overcast. In the church, Johanna sat in the family pew, beside Rebecca on one side, her sisters on the other. Behind them were all the aunties, their husbands. Johanna's eyes, swollen from all her weeping, were hidden behind the veil that one of the aunties had hastily sewn onto her bonnet the night before because Johanna had been too shocked to come prepared with the mourning attire expected to be worn by members of the family. Tears blurred the print as Johanna tried to read the words of the service in her prayer book.

The church was filled. Tennant Shelby had been an outstanding man of the community, revered for his integrity. However, none had known him as Johanna remembered—a kind, gentle, loving father. Why had she not appreciated him more? She had taken his sheltering care, his indulgence, his concern, for granted. She had stubbornly resisted his counsel, his advice. Johanna thought of the times she had turned away as he had tried to embrace her during those awful months when he had opposed her marriage.

If only she could go back—do it over. Not that she would have loved or wanted Ross less, but she could have been less selfish, tried to see her parents' side more.

Winter sunlight shone weakly through the arched window behind the altar but soon faded, leaving the interior of the church gray, full of shadows. Johanna shuddered. Elly, sitting beside her, glanced at her worriedly and slipped a small hand, wearing a black kid glove, into hers. Johanna gave it a reassuring squeeze. She must be strong and brave for Elly's sake, for Cissy's too. At least *she* had Ross, while her sisters were left without a wise father, a protector.

The service ended and Johanna, with the rest of the family, followed the pallbearers carrying the casket out of the church to the adjoining cemetery.

The aunties were all appropriately draped in crepe veiling, which flowed from their bonnets in the November wind. With their caped shoulders and black-gloved, folded hands, they looked like a flock of black-winged sparrows hovering around their cousin, the widow.

Johanna tried to concentrate on the minister's words.

The minister began reading the final words over the casket before it was lowered into the newly dug grave. "In the midst of life, we are in death. . . ."

Standing among the granite crosses, the engraved headstones, the flowers and wreaths, Johanna knew a sense of intolerable loss, of terrible aloneness. Frightened, she glanced around and still felt apart.

She looked over at Ross for reassurance. But his head was bowed. She felt separated from him too. *I am a stranger here. Among my own people.* Involuntarily she shivered. She must pay attention. She clenched her hands. She felt as if she might faint and stiffened her body, willing herself not to.

The minister's words came again, intoning the words of commitment, consigning her father to his heavenly rest. "Most merciful Father, who has been pleased to take unto thyself the soul of this thy servant, grant unto us who are still in our pilgrimage and who walk as yet by faith . . ."

Something in Johanna's heart refused to be comforted. Inside she was wrenched with a terrible need for her father. She didn't want to let him go. *Not yet. I don't want you to go. I have so much I want to say to you, so much to explain. . . .*

It began to sprinkle, large drops falling slowly. Umbrellas opened up. The mourners huddled closer together, and the minister's voice picked up speed.

"Thou knowest, Lord, the secrets of our hearts. Shut not thy ears to our prayers but spare us, Lord by thy gracious mercy. . . ." He hurried to the last part of the service. "The Lord be with thy spirit. And so we say together, Our Father, who art in heaven, hallowed be . . ."

The assembled mourners joined in the Lord's Prayer as the rain began to come harder, the wind stronger. Johanna's throat thickened and she could not get past the hard, painful lump lodged there, to repeat the familiar words. "Forgive us our debts . . ."

Back at the house, the aunties bustled about, setting out the dishes, the cakes, pies, and other things they'd baked and brought for the funereal feast. *Feast!* What a name, Johanna thought bleakly. She sipped the tea Auntie Bee urged upon her, wrapping her icy hands around the cup, trying to warm them. She accepted condolences from family friends, nodding, murmuring thanks. All she could think of was her father out in the graveyard in the rain.

The afternoon lengthened painfully. Toward dusk, the last of the guests began to straggle to the door with last-minute expressions of sympathy, platitudes of solace, offering to provide whatever the grief-stricken family needed. Soon the aunties began gathering up their assorted dishes and containers, promising to replenish or refill them before they too departed.

Ross came to Johanna and led her into the small alcove off the dining room.

"I'm going over to Dr. Murrison's tonight, Johanna. I've already spoken to him. As a matter of fact, he came over to me at the funeral, asked me to come. I'll have to leave early in the morning to go back, anyway. As you know, I've got a lot of sick folks in Millscreek that need me. If I'm over there with him, my leaving won't disturb your family." His eyes showed concern. "You look exhausted, Johanna. You *all* need your rest. It's been a long, sorrowful day. But I think you'll be a real comfort to your mother if you stay here a few days. Whenever you feel you can leave her, just send me word and I'll come for you."

Johanna was a little taken aback by Ross's decision. Truthfully, she had made no plans. She had not even thought as far as the next day. However, she could see that his was the wisest course. Perhaps he was right—maybe her mother did need her, more than she had thought.

He held her for a long time, kissing her gently before he left. When she realized he was actually going, she felt suddenly bereft. Perhaps, in a part of her mind, she had thought how comforting it would be to be in his arms tonight—where he would kiss away the tears that all day had been near the surface.

But he was already putting on his coat, slinging a knitted scarf around his neck, reaching for his hat. It was too late to ask him to stay.

However, that evening her mother, accompanied by Cissy, retired earlier than usual, and Johanna found herself alone. Elly, worn out, had gone to bed before the company had all departed. In Elly's borrowed bedroom, Johanna found she was restless, too upset to sleep. She wished she had not agreed to Ross's leaving. She missed the feel of his arms enfolding her, comforting her.

The events of the day, and her father's letter, had been emotionally wrenching. Before long, Johanna began weeping uncontrollably, trying to smother the sound in her pillows.

The squeaking of the bedroom door startled her. She sat up in time to see a small, white-gowned figure, like a little ghost, slip into the room and with a rush of bare feet run to the bedside and jump up.

"Oh Johanna, I woke up and thought about Papa. I couldn't go back to sleep. Can I come in with you?" Elly whispered urgently.

"Of course!" Johanna said and threw back the covers. The two sisters clasped each other and, close in each other's arms, wept together for all they had loved and lost.

～∾⋐∿～

One day followed the next. Soon Johanna realized she had been at Holly Grove for over a week and had not sent word to Ross. The flow of visitors continued, because Tennant Shelby, a man of wide acquaintance, had been well liked, respected, held in affectionate regard by a number of people. Johanna took it upon herself to act as hostess in her mother's place, greeting guests. This became sometimes tedious and stressful, given her own emotions, yet Johanna considered it a labor of love, deeply appreciating the esteem in which her father had been held. In spite of their shared grief, Cissy's attitude toward her remained guarded. Employing newly gained sensitivity and tact, Johanna tried to ease the tension between them, to show her in small ways that her coming home did not threaten her sister's place. Gradually Cissy softened. The two older daughters were able to divide the many varied tasks in the wake of Tennant Shelby's death.

There was much to be done. There were thank-you notes to write for all the gifts of flowers, food, and visits from neighbors, friends, and acquaintances. Their father's office had to be closed with all the moving of books, papers, files. There were meetings with his law partners, arrangements to be made, and matters to be decided concerning disposition of property.

With all this to deal with, two more weeks passed before Johanna realized that she had moved back into the rhythm of life at Holly Grove. Her life with Ross in the mountains seemed to have faded into the background.

It wasn't until she had been there four weeks that the full truth of this came to her. Dr. Murrison was called to the house because of Elly's earache. Johanna had been taking care of her sister and was in the bedroom with her when Dr. Murrison arrived. He looked surprised to see her. "You *still* here, Johanna?"

After he finished examining Elly, he left a small bottle of oil on the bedside table with instructions on how to administer it. "Heat it slightly and put two or three drops in each ear every few hours." Then he turned to Johanna and gave her a sharp look. "So when will Ross be down to fetch you back *home*?"

The blunt question and almost accusatory tone startled Johanna. Her cheeks got hot under his appraising glance. Busying herself smoothing Elly's coverlet, she replied defensively, "Soon, I suppose. Right now I'm needed here."

"Oh? Is that right?" was the doctor's only comment as he repacked his medical bag, patted Elly's hand, saying, "You'll soon be up and around, young lady. Won't need any more of your sister's fussin' and coddlin', I expect." With another glance at Johanna, he departed, leaving her indignant and confused.

Johanna spent another few minutes plumping Elly's pillow, then went to refill her water jug. Why had she let Dr. Murrison's remarks upset her? Wasn't she doing what she *should* be doing? Didn't her mother *need* her during this terrible time? After all, her mother had lost the husband on whom she had depended for over twenty years. Didn't Dr. Murrison realize she needed support, comforting? Maybe he was just not sensitive to such things.

Later, still bothered by what the crusty old physician had implied, Johanna knocked at her mother's door. At her answering call, she went in.

"Can I do anything for you, Mama?"

Rebecca was seated at her escritoire, writing replies to the many condolence notes she had received. She looked up at her daughter's entrance. For a moment, she studied the slim figure standing in the doorway. Johanna seemed fragile, vulnerable somehow—Rebecca had not missed her roughened hands. And she was thin, too thin. What had she been doing all these months to bring about these physical changes?

Rebecca bit her lower lip. Was her new life as the wife of a hill doctor in that primitive backwoods community too hard for her? Johanna was still lovely looking, the prettiest of all her daughters. But youth and beauty were fleeting, and a life of deprivation and hard physical work could age a woman too soon. Rebecca curbed her inclination to say something—something she might regret, something that might bring pain or, worse, remorse. Besides, there were other things she had noticed, all to the good—a patience, a gentleness, a genuine sweetness in Johanna that had not been there before.

Life teaches hard lessons. Evidently, Johanna was learning this. Rebecca sighed, then answered Johanna's question. "Nothing, thank you, dear." She went back to the note she was writing.

Johanna remained standing there. "You're sure?"

Rebecca signed her name to one of the black-edged note cards she was writing. "Quite sure."

Johanna still hesitated.

Rebecca looked up again. There was something in Johanna's expression that Rebecca had never seen there before. An uncertainty—a pleading in her eyes. Ever since she had returned to Holly Grove, there had been something about Johanna that puzzled Rebecca. It was utterly unlike Johanna. She had been at Rebecca's beck and call, interpreting a gesture, a glance, a word, anticipating her slightest wish, volunteering to fetch a shawl, a footstool, seeking to please, anxious to help.

"Wouldn't you like a cup of tea?"

All at once Rebecca understood. Johanna was "doing penance" for what she perceived was her guilt. Somehow she blamed herself for her father's death. As if her being here would have changed anything!

Rebecca knew in her soul that she had often been jealous of Tennant's closeness to Johanna. She had sometimes been stricter, perhaps, to counteract his indulgence.

Things had always come so easily to Johanna—love, popularity, happiness. Rebecca had told herself she didn't want her to be spoiled. But was it more than that? Had she wanted the intimacy Johanna shared with her father for herself?

With sudden clarity, she saw that it was possible for her to have what she had always longed for from her oldest daughter—closeness, companionship, dependency even. In this moment, Rebecca knew it was in her power to bind Johanna to her more closely than she had ever been with her father. It would be easy, because Johanna wanted it, too. She could keep Johanna here, keep her from returning to where she had never wanted her to go in the first place. It would be so easy—*too* easy.

Then came an image of the tall, young, awkward man who loved her daughter. In her mind, Rebecca saw his compassionate expression, his thoughtful eyes, the way he looked at Johanna with unselfish love.

Pain slashed Rebecca's heart. That kind of love was no longer *hers*, but it was Johanna's. And she could not rob her of it. Johanna was a married woman, with duties that took precedence over any need her mother might have. Johanna must be made to see that. Johanna must go home to a husband who loved her, missed her, longed for her, wanted her *home*. The home he had made for her, the home that was theirs to live in together! It would be dreadfully wrong of Rebecca to delay Johanna any longer here at Holly Grove.

"Mama?" Johanna ventured hopefully. "Isn't there *anything* I can do for you?"

"No, dear, nothing," Rebecca said firmly and turned away from the eagerness in Johanna's eyes, back to her correspondence.

"Don't you need help with your notes?" Johanna persisted.

"I'm almost finished." Rebecca tapped the pile of black-rimmed envelopes with one finger. "Besides, Cissy can help me if there are any more."

Her mother's tone was definite. Of course Cissy was here to help her with anything that might come up, Johanna thought. Why hadn't she realized that? Johanna went out of the room, closing the door quietly behind her.

≈∽≈

At the click of the door being shut, Rebecca's hand clenched compulsively and a blob of ink dropped from the point of her quill pen onto the neatly written note. With a stifled exclamation of annoyance, she crumpled it up and tossed it into the wastebasket by the desk.

Rebecca knew she had hurt Johanna. However, she had deliberately sent her away. She also knew that when she was gone, she would miss her daughter dreadfully. Even with Cissy and Elly still at home, Rebecca knew she would be alone in a way she had never been before. Rebecca winced, placing her fists against her eyes.

Johanna was the child of her heart, the way the others were not. However, she had done the right thing—she had "freed" Johanna. A mother's sacrifices never end.

≈∽≈

Outside her mother's closed door, Johanna stood for a few minutes. Slowly the myth of her mother's need for her dissolved. The truth of her mother's self-sufficiency was obvious. Rebecca Shelby had not been prostrated, become unable to function, or fallen into a melancholic depression with her husband's death. She did not need Johanna here any longer. The household at Holly Grove hummed along as it always did, even without Tennant Shelby. Especially, it did not need Johanna to see that things ran properly.

The truth was, she had stayed longer than necessary, deceiving herself into believing that she was needed. The truth was that *she* had been the needy one. She had welcomed sliding back into the ease and comfort of her old home. Meals appeared on the table without her lifting a finger, hot water was brought upstairs for her morning bath by Bessie, fresh sheets appeared on her bed, and clean towels were there like magic when she needed them.

Why had she not seen what was happening? It had taken bluff old Dr. Murrison's words to turn the key. He had unlocked this truth in her mind by asking her when Ross was coming to take her *home*.

Hillsboro and Holly Grove were no longer her home. Home was with Ross, in the mountains, his beloved mountains—*her* beloved mountains. In her heart, understanding burst like a bud opening into a beautiful blossom.

That very day she wrote a letter to be sent in the next day's post. That night she packed her things.

When at the end of the week Ross came, no word was spoken. None was needed. They rushed into each others arms as if it were the first or the last time they ever embraced.

When Johanna caught sight of the cabin, her heart gave a lurch. It stood there as if waiting for her return. *What an imaginative ninny I am*, she said laughingly to herself. Then she turned to smile at Ross, who was looking at her as if anxious to see her reaction.

"I'll take the horses down to the barn, rub them down, and feed them, then I'll be in directly," Ross said as he helped her out of her saddle.

When Johanna walked up the porch steps, she saw firewood neatly stacked at the far end. Often people paid Ross back with such things—suddenly there would be split logs piled beside the barn, with no clue as to who had left it there in payment. Or jugs of cider would be left outside the door. It was the mountain folks' way. No money but too proud to accept charity. These evidences of how much Ross was appreciated touched Johanna. She wished her relatives in Hillsboro who still thought she'd married beneath her could know this.

Opening the door, she walked inside the cabin. Immediately she breathed in mingled delicious smells—pumpkin pie, apple, cinnamon. Over the stove hung strings of red peppers, dried onions, pods of okra, striped gourds, rainbow-colored Indian corn.

"Aunt Bertie's doings, I expect," she said to Ross when he came inside.

"And Ma's too," Ross said quietly.

Johanna felt stricken that she hadn't thought of Eliza first. Ross's mother had not been nearly as forthcoming and friendly to her as Aunt Bertie.

"When she heard I was going down to bring you home," Ross added, "she said she'd bring up supper so you wouldn't have to cook when we got back. She knew you'd be tired. I think there's beans and ham and bread. Probably other things as well."

"How kind," Johanna murmured, making a mental resolution to make a real effort to get to know her mother-in-law better.

Chapter Seventeen

❧❦❧

That winter seemed long and cold and lonely to Johanna. Although Ross had suggested she might want to spend Christmas with her family in Hillsboro, Johanna felt a strange reluctance. Without her father's jovial presence, there would be a terrible void.

As it turned out, there were heavy snows, and with the mountain trails impassable, traveling was out of the question. It was hard enough for Ross to trek to the isolated homes in Millscreek Gap to make necessary sick calls. There was a great deal of illness that year—children with whooping cough, the older people with severe rheumatism and colds. Ross came home late most evenings, exhausted, too tired and chilled to do more than eat and fall into bed.

The snow kept away even her rare visits from Aunt Bertie and Uncle Tanner, as well as Sue and Katie, who had become frequent visitors since the rescue. Left much alone, Johanna experienced some melancholy about her father, thinking about what she might have said or done differently. She thought of the letter she had procrastinated about writing to him after her marriage, a letter expressing her love, her sorrow at having hurt him, her assurances that her choice had been the right one. She wished she had told her father that Ross was a good and loving husband. However, she had put it off time and again, not sure of exactly what to say. Now it was too late.

Little by little, Johanna gained peace of mind. With her newfound faith, she believed her father *did* know.

With the coming of spring, the mountains burst into glorious beauty. The air was filled with lovely smells—damp moss, sweet clover. There were warm, lovely days, longer afternoons, lavender evenings.

It was in these first weeks of April 1841 that Johanna knew she was going to have a baby.

After her first excitement at the prospect, Johanna had most of the same nagging little worries of any about-to-be mother. Tears came and went like April rain. *I'm as bad as we used to tease Elly about,* she admonished herself, *crying at the drop of a hat!* She knew it was the early stages of her condition. She had heard that expecting a baby sometimes made a woman fanciful and silly. After those first few weeks, a marvelous calm overcame Johanna, and with it a lovely glow.

Ross was deeply happy and proud and couldn't wait to tell everyone. Johanna wanted to wait to first share the news with his mother. Johanna felt somewhat shy about confiding some of her qualms about her approaching motherhood. Eliza was so strong and capable, she probably wouldn't be very understanding. After all, she had birthed four of her own with no seeming problem. However, Johanna instinctively felt it was the right thing to do to tell her mother-in-law first, before Ross, in his own happy pride, blurted out the information to someone else.

The path down to her mother-in-law's house was steep, winding its way precariously between the dark woods on one side, the rocky cliff on the other, with a sheer drop down to the glistening river snaking through the cove below.

Eliza's thin, lined face broke into a wide smile at the news Johanna shyly confided.

"I'm right pleased for you, Johanna. Havin' a baby, becomin' a mama—why, I reckon it's one of the happiest times in a woman's life. I 'spect Ross is beside hisself, ain't he?" Eliza nodded. "He'll make a fine daddy. He was always so good with the younger ones. Patient, kind to 'em. Even Merriman, who could be ornery," she chuckled. "He's got all that from *his* pa, and that's what makes him such a good doctor, I reckon."

In that afternoon she spent with Eliza was the first time Johanna began to feel close to her mother-in-law. Telling her about the coming baby seemed to have narrowed the gap between them.

"Now, of course, you're going to have to have quilts for the young'un. And it'll pass your waitin' time to be makin' some."

"I'm ashamed that I don't really know how to put one together," Johanna confessed. "I guess I was too impatient, too restless, always wanting to be doing something else."

"Well, you'll be sittin' plenty in the next few months and the further along you git. It's a nice, peaceful thing to do, sittin', dreamin' 'bout the baby to come. It was fer me. I musta made a half dozen each time I was expectin'."

Eliza went over to the blanket box and opened the lid. The smell of cedar rose as she did so. Inside were neatly folded quilts. She brought one out, smoothed it with her gnarled, work-worn hands, then unfolded it to show it to Johanna. "This here is one like I'd made for Jenny's last little 'un. I had some pieces left over, and I dunno why, I jest made up another one. It was even 'fore you and Ross got married. Mebbe even 'fore I knew about you."

"Oh, it's beautiful—*Ma*," Johanna said softly, using the name for the first time, then reaching out a hand tentatively to touch the quilt.

"You gotta be right careful about what pattern you use for a baby cradle," Eliza went on, warming to her subject. "It's just not the color or a pretty design you're lookin' for. There are some old tales about quilt patterns. Not to say I believe all of 'em. . . ." She shrugged. "I've always called this here one Turkey Tracks, that's the way it was taught to me. But some of the old women say it used to be called Wandering Foot, and nobody would use it for a child's bed."

"Why ever not?" Johanna was curious.

Eliza shook her head. "Oh, there's lots of old stories about it—things like iffen a child sleeps under it, it'll grow up discontent or with a roaming mind. You hear lots of things like that. Not that I pay a lot of mind to them. But there's lots of other pretty patterns to pick from."

"My mother quilts and so do all my aunties."

Eliza looked somewhat taken aback. "Then mebbe when they know about the baby, they'll all be sending you one they'll make up special. You won't need this 'un." She started folding the quilt up, as though to put it back in the cedar box.

"Oh, please no, Ma. I *want* this one," Johanna protested, then added shyly, "I think for our baby's first quilt—it should come from his daddy's ma."

For a minute Eliza almost seemed startled. Her eyes glistened and she turned her head quickly. "Well now, iffen that's what you want—"

"Yes, it is," Johanna assured her, then hesitantly asked, "Ma, would you teach *me* how to quilt?"

"You really don't know how?"

"Not really. I was never much interested, I'm afraid. I've made a few patches but never put together a whole quilt."

"Well, now." Eliza sat back on her heels, her expression thoughtful. "I've got a pattern—," she said slowly. "Made up a few patches but haven't got 'round to finishing it. Mebbe you could start on it. It's simple enough for a beginner." She leaned over the cedar chest again and brought up a brown paper package and slowly unwrapped it. Inside were layers of folded cloth, some cutout patterns, and other pieces of material. On top were two or three finished blocks on cream-colored cotton, each banded with deep pink. In the center of each block was appliquéd three stylized, pink-petaled flowers accented with green stems and leaves.

Johanna smoothed her hand over the delicately sewn pieces. She imagined Eliza bent over her quilting frame, taking the tiny stitches painstakingly by firelight after all her chores were done. It was a thing of simple beauty, crafted out of the creativity within her that needed expression.

"Oh Ma, it's truly beautiful," Johanna said softly. "What do you call this pattern?"

"Hit don't have any right name. I jest always admired the mountain lilies that bloom along in July. I didn't have a pattern—I just drew it off on paper from looking at it, then used that to cut out my material."

"Mountain lilies, of course," Johanna smiled. "Carolina Mountain Lily. That's what we'll call it."

She slipped her hand over Eliza's worn, rough one, awed that it could make something so exquisite as well as chop wood, churn butter, hoe corn.

On her way back up the mountain, the package containing the quilt pattern and materials strapped behind her saddle, Johanna felt excited, as if she were launching into a whole new phase of her life. It was funny, actually. Back at Holly Grove she'd had to practically be dragged to the quilting frame, constantly be made to pull out her indifferent stitches and do her part over. Now she was looking forward to learning how to make a quilt of her own. For the first time,

Johanna felt a real bonding to Ross's mother and to the mountain community that was now her home.

～✳～

The news spread fast among the extended Davison family up and down the mountain. Aunt Bertie and Uncle Tanner were the first to come visit and congratulate them, bringing a cradle made by Tanner's own skilled hands. As Ross and Johanna stood around it admiringly, Bertie told them, "Tanner's cradles are the best. Made out of buckeye log. He worked on it like he was makin' something fit for a king. He likes buckeye 'cause it's light and hollows out so easy and it's a pretty wood. He pegged it with oak pins to two hickory rockers, curved just so. His rockers never creep. It's somethin' I never saw in no other cradle." She gave the cradle a gentle press of her foot. "See there, it jest rocks so nice and easy. I always called Tanner's cradles a lullaby of buckeye."

Trying to look indifferent, Uncle Tanner beamed at his wife's praise.

Later the men went up to check the few apple trees on the hillside, and Johanna brought sassafras tea for Auntie Bertie and herself to drink out on the sunny front porch.

"When your time comes, honey, Tassie Rector's the one," Aunt Bertie said. "She's been bringin' babies for nigh on forty years, I reckon. Never lost a baby nor a mother in all that time. Iffen I wuz you, I'd go make her acquaintance, let her know you'll be needin' her," Aunt Bertie advised.

"But Ross is a doctor, Aunt Bertie. He knows all about babies. He's already delivered dozens since we came back up here," Johanna said.

"Doctor or not, he's a man, ain't he? I think you'd be glad if you go see Tassie and talk to *her*. A woman needs another woman at a time like that."

"I'm sure Ross's mother, Eliza, will come," Johanna said tentatively, wondering if maybe there was more to having a baby than she realized. She had a sudden longing for her own mother or Aunt Honey.

"You jest take my advice, Johanna, and go see Tassie," was Aunt Bertie's last word to her before she and Uncle Tanner took off.

⟞≽⧫≼⟝

One Sunday after service, outside church Ross got into a conversation with Merriman, and Johanna was left standing with Jenny. She had always felt a little awkward with her sister-in-law. Jenny was one of the few people her own age—at least, one of the few girls—whom Johanna had not been able to win as a friend. She didn't know what made her feel so awkward around Jenny. She never seemed to be able to bring up a subject Jenny would respond to. Although Johanna told herself the girl was probably just shy, she had begun to feel that somehow Jenny disliked or resented her. This made it almost impossible whenever they were in each other's company. Most of the time, that was when they were all together at Eliza's. Then there was always so much to do, helping set food on the table or doing the clearing away or washing up. But sometimes, like now, Johanna found herself with a blank mind and a silent tongue.

Jenny seemed just as ill at ease as Johanna. Shaded by the broad-brimmed sunbonnet, her eyes were cast down, and her thin mouth worked nervously. At home, her father used to tease Johanna that she "couldn't stand a moment's silence," and this proved true at this awkward instant. Johanna surprised herself by impulsively bursting out, "Jenny, I'm really pretty scared about having this baby. You've had two—I wish you'd come up to visit me one day

211

and talk to me about it. It would really help to talk to someone else—I mean, someone my own age."

Jenny's face flushed and she looked startled. She opened her mouth and started to say something, then swallowed and seemed too taken aback to go on.

"Please, Jenny, I mean it. I'd really like you to come. Will you?"

"Yes, yes. Shure I will," Jenny finally murmured.

Just then the two brothers sauntered up to where their wives were standing. Ross smiled at them both. "What're you two ladies gossiping about?" he asked teasingly.

"Babies!" Johanna laughed and glanced over at Jenny merrily. To her surprise, Jenny had blushed beet red. Belatedly Johanna realized that maybe mountain women didn't talk openly about such things, even in front of their husbands, even when one of them was a doctor. She was sorry if she embarrassed Jenny, and she leaned toward her and gave her a reassuring touch on her arm, saying, "Now don't forget, Jenny—I'm looking forward to your visit."

Two days later Jenny did come, still shy, still pretty untalkative. She did, however, bring a gift of a beautiful little knitted baby shawl. She also endorsed Aunt Bertie's recommendation that Johanna go see Tassie.

"She helped brung both my boys," Jenny told her. "None better in all the mountainside."

❦

Some weeks later Johanna decided to follow both Jenny's and Aunt Bertie's suggestion. On a beautiful early fall morning, she saddled her horse and went down the mountain. The air was clear, with a definite sharpness to it. There was the smell of ripening apples, burning leaves, and she noticed the sharp-tanged fragrance of chokeberries.

"Tassie's home is easy to find," Aunt Bertie had told her. "If you get lost, ask anyone you see. Everyone knows her, will tell you how to get there." She was right, and soon Johanna came in sight of a weathered frame house on the side of the hill. As she got off her horse, leading him by his reins up the rest of the steep path, Johanna saw a woman sitting on the porch on a rush-seat rocking chair.

"Howdy," the woman called.

Johanna gave an answering wave. "I'm Johanna Davison," she said as she walked up to the porch. When she came closer, she saw the woman's strong, sensitive face, wreathed in wrinkles and a welcoming smile, and her deep-set, kind eyes.

"Well, I'm right happy to meet you. Doc's wife, ain't ye? Come and sit a spell."

For the next hour or so, Johanna felt as though she had been warmly hugged and comforted by this dear lady.

At once offered refreshment and the other rocker, Johanna was soon hearing the story of Tassie's life. "Was born right here, only a stone's throw from where we're sittin'. Married at twenty and had ten young'uns, all healthy, alive to this day. Now have thirty grandchildren and eight great-grands and brought 'em all into the world." She rocked and smiled with satisfaction. "I began midwifin' while my own was still little. It jest seem to be my callin' in life." She nodded. "We all come into this world with a mission. The Lord saw fit to give me this one, and so he was present with me all the time, at every birthin'. God give me the talent to bring babies safely, and that's what I've tried to do. I take no credit myself, you understand? I've had no real trainin' but what God give me. I jest always put my trust in him, and as Scripture says, "My grace is sufficient.""

When the sun was getting low, Johanna stood up, ready to leave. Tassie said, "I know your man is a doctor, and from what I heard, a fine one. But if you want me, jest send word and I'll be on my way."

"That's very kind of you," Johanna said as she tied her sunbonnet strings. She didn't think she'd really need Tassie, not with Ross there, but she didn't want to hurt the old lady's feelings.

On her way back up the mountain, Johanna wished she'd paid more attention when she still lived in Hillsboro, wished she'd listened when the aunties were discussing some friend's confinement or a birth in their circle of acquaintances. Then marriage and motherhood had seemed something in the distant future. Now that it was soon to be her own experience, she realized she knew next to nothing about it. Of course, Ross would be with her and certainly knew what to do when the time came. He was well trained and capable. And Eliza would also be on hand. She wouldn't have to rely on a backwoods midwife, thank goodness.

❦

Eliza helped Johanna begin her quilt. Uncle Tanner willingly made her a frame to set up. Once she got started, Johanna discovered she actually enjoyed doing it. She liked arranging the pieces of bright calico material and pinning them into the design more than the actual stitching. However, gradually and with Eliza's patient instruction, her stitches got smaller, neater, and after Ross moved the frame up to their own cabin, she found she could work while daydreaming about how life would be once their baby arrived. Being pregnant made her less active, and often Johanna found herself getting sleepy after only a half hour or more at her quilting frame, so it went slowly. She would often have to lie down and take a nap on the long afternoons as fall turned into winter and the wind blew around the cabin corners, sending the cedar boughs sighing against the windows, making the sound almost of a lullaby.

Chapter Eighteen

~❧~

Johanna felt her shoulder shaken gently and heard Ross whisper, "I've got a nice fire going, honey, but you stay in bed until the house gets good and warm. I've got a few visits to make, but I should be home early afternoon."

Johanna murmured something drowsily, felt Ross kiss her cheek, his hand smooth her hair, then she snuggled deeper into the quilts and went back to sleep.

She wasn't sure how much later she woke up. A fire was burning brightly but low in the big stone fireplace. Slowly she roused herself, pulled on her voluminous flowered flannel robe, got awkwardly out of the high bed. Six more weeks and she wouldn't be able to sleep in late like this, she thought with a smile. Neither would she have all this extra weight to carry around with her. She slipped her feet into slippers and went to the window. Outside the sky was a chalky gray. Snow? The edges around the glass pane were frosted slightly.

The kettle Ross had left hanging on the crane over the fire was sizzling. Johanna put a few spoonfuls of herb tea into a mug, poured in water, and stirred it into a fragrant brew. As she leaned over to replace the kettle, she felt a strange sensation in her back. Straightening up, one hand went to the curve of her spine. Had she imagined it? Probably pulled a muscle slightly when she reached for the kettle, she thought. Her body wasn't familiar to her anymore. She had all sorts of queer aches and pains now, in places she could never have imagined before. Sitting down at the table, she cupped her hands around the steaming mug, inhaling the spicy aroma of the tea. The room was pleasantly warm, the tea delicious. Johanna glanced around, thinking how happy and content she had felt in recent weeks.

Everything about the little cabin pleased her—the polished gourds on the mantel, the blue and white dishes on the pine hutch, the rocking chair, which she had enjoyed more and more these last months. Then her gaze rested on the cradle and the quilt folded over its side. Soon their precious baby would be nested within that. *Their* child, hers and Ross's. She didn't care whether it was a boy or girl, either way she would love it.

She looked out the window again. To her surprise, she saw a few snowflakes floating lazily down. If it snowed, it would be the first of the season. Autumn—or Indian summer, as they called it here—had lingered longer than usual in the mountains this year. It wasn't until way into November that the mornings had become really frosty and the evenings chilly.

Johanna got up from the table to go over to the window, when a quick, darting pain traveled down the back of both her legs. She gasped, clutched onto the edge of the table. What in the world? Had she slept in a cramped position so that her muscles were stiff? A fleeting worry passed through her mind. It couldn't be anything to do with the baby. Or could it? She took a deep breath. She put her weight back on her feet and straightened up. Nothing happened. It was all right. Just a twinge of some kind. Nothing more.

She walked over to the window, leaned on the sill, and watched the snow fall slowy, as if it were not in any hurry. Still, it was sticking, she saw, watching the steadily falling snow cover the ground with a light powder.

It looked beautiful. The sweeping branches of the pines and hemlocks that rimmed their property were dark green under the fluffy fringe of white, the rail fence like dark rickrack against the drifting snow.

Johanna moved back over to the stove, where the oatmeal she had set on the back burner the night before was now thickened, ready to eat. She started to dish herself out a bowl, when she again felt another strange little clutch in the middle of her back. This one lasted longer than the first one. She frowned. She waited a full minute. Nothing happened. She filled her bowl, poured milk and honey over her oatmeal, and went to sit by the fire and eat.

She hoped Ross would get home before the snow got any deeper. It was hard enough traveling the narrow ridges on the mountain to out-of-the-way cabins in good weather.

Finishing her breakfast, Johanna decided to work some on the quilt she was making for the baby. Then she wouldn't worry about Ross. Eliza had been right—making the quilt was a pleasant, "mind easin'" experience. Johanna enjoyed it more than she ever imagined. Wouldn't her mother and aunties be amazed? It used to seem a pointless occupation back when she would rather have been doing something else. Now, anticipating a baby, Johanna found it enjoyable. Working on the quilt, she dreamed of all sorts of happy things. With the baby, she felt that the life she and Ross shared would become even happier, more complete.

Johanna shifted her position. She seemed to become uncomfortable sooner than usual as she sat in the straight-backed chair at the quilting frame. She started to get up to get a pillow to wedge behind her back, when a sudden pain struck her. It was longer and stronger than either of the others. This time it traveled swiftly from the middle of her back down the length of her legs, causing her knees to cramp. She sat down quickly, holding on to the chair arms.

For a long while she remained absolutely still. What was going on? It *couldn't* be the baby. *Could* it? The last time Tassie stopped by, she had looked Johanna over with a practiced eye, declaring she had a good six weeks yet to go. Over a month.

Alarm coursed through Johanna. Was something wrong, then? Oh, if only Ross were there. She waited tensely but nothing else happened. Reassured, she got up and walked over to the window again. It was now near noon. The snow was coming down with a driving force. The ground was covered and the wind was blowing the snow in drifts along the fence and against the windowsills. Johanna put her hand on the pane and felt the cold.

Where was Ross? He'd better get home before it snowed any harder. She watched with increasing anxiety as the snow continued falling steadily.

Restless and unable to go back to her quilting, she felt suddenly chilly. She went over to the wood box, got a few smaller logs out, and threw them on the fire, sending up a spiral of sparks. She got down her shawl and wrapped it around her shoulders. Drawing the rocker closer, she sat down near the fireplace.

Suddenly a grinding sort of pain gripped her. She gave a startled cry. Was that the kind of pain that signaled the start of labor? Oh, no! Surely it was too soon. It couldn't be happening. Not now! When she was there alone! It couldn't be starting, could it? Please, God, no. A deep shudder went all through Johanna. She knew that once it started, there was no stopping it. What was it Tassie had said? "When a baby's ready to come, it comes!" Could this be how it begins? Slowly, so that you're not sure, then more often, harder, with sensations unlike anything else you've ever felt?

Holding the shawl close about her, she made her halting way back over to the window. The day was darkening quickly, clouds heavy with still more snow hovered, the boughs of the pines and hemlocks surrounding the cabin were now burdened with clumps of snow, and the wind-blown snow was now banked along the rustic fence along the horse trail down the mountainside.

Ross had better get home soon, or the way would be impassable. Fear stirred in the pit of her stomach, tightening her throat. If this *was* the baby coming, she couldn't go through it all by herself. She *couldn't*—dear God, she just couldn't! She felt her eyes fill with tears of fear and frustration. It just couldn't happen like this. Her body seemed almost apart from her mind, which became surprisingly clear. If this *was* the baby—and she was getting to the point where she *knew* it was—she should do something, get ready somehow to handle this alone, if she had to.

Before she could move or turn around, another slow pain clutched her, making her bend over and cling to the window sill, causing an involuntary groan. There was no mistaking it. This was it!

She closed her eyes for a minute, prayed frantically. *Please, God, make me brave, show me what to do. But please send someone! Bring Ross home!*

Boil water! That somehow tugged at her memory as something to do. She wasn't sure quite why, but she filled the kettle anyway and hung it over the fire. The fire was roaring, crackling, and the smell of apple wood was pungent as it burned. Still, Johanna could not get warm. She shivered and braced herself for another pain.

It came and she held her breath until it passed. Fifteen minutes later another one began. Between pains, Johanna heard the ticktock of the clock. She counted the time, clenching her hands on the arms of the rocker, waiting for the pain she knew would soon overtake her. Between those times, she prayed, *Please, someone come.* Outside the steady, silent snow continued.

The wind howled around the cabin, sounding like a hundred screeching owls. Johanna gritted her teeth, set her jaw, shuddered. How could this have happened to her? To the pampered daughter of well-to-do town folk? To be up here all alone in an isolated log cabin in a snowstorm that was gradually shutting her off from any help? At a time like this, she should be surrounded by loving, comforting, caring people—people who, for heaven's sake, knew what to do!

Panic set her heart to pounding. She hugged herself and moved closer to the fireplace, shivering in spite of its warmth.

She thought of the day Liddy Chalmers had come to see her before she got married, begged her to reconsider marrying Ross. "You *can't*, Johanna, you just can't!" Liddy had cried. Johanna thought of that scene in detail now. "To go so far away, to live on the edge of nowhere," Liddy had said.

Well, that's exactly what she *had* done. If she'd gone to Hillsboro months ago to have the baby there, as her mother had written to suggest, she wouldn't be in this awful situation. But Johanna had refused. *This* was her home now, she'd insisted in her letter back to her mother. Was she now paying for her stubbornness, her self-will, her pride?

Johanna imagined how it would have been for her now if she'd accepted her mother's invitation. A picture came to her of her own bedroom, with its slanted ceiling, the dormer windows looking out onto the garden, the four-poster bed, her little desk and white-paneled fireplace, her bedside table with her favorite books. She remembered how when she had some slight childhood illness, trays were brought up to her with cinnamon toast or lemon pudding, and if she had a fever, her mother's cool hand would be on her forehead. Ruefully she knew she'd never appreciated it enough.

Just then another wave of pain swept over her. Johanna clamped her teeth together, accidentally biting her tongue. Tears rushed into her eyes. Finally the pain passed and again Johanna made her way haltingly over to the window, peering out. Snow piled up on the window ledge and around the small panes shut off any view. Johanna saw that the trail was almost obliterated by the drifts. And it was still snowing. There was little hope that Ross would come now. He might be caught somewhere up the mountain. Perhaps he'd stayed too long at some remote cabin with a patient. Ironically, maybe even to deliver a baby!

First babies often took a long time, Tassie had told her. On the other hand, she'd said, some babies were in a hurry. What this baby would do, Johanna had no idea. She bit her lower lip as a strong spasm gripped her again.

She tried not to think of some of the horror stories she'd heard whispered among the girls at boarding school. Of course, none of them *really* knew anything about it. All they circulated were old wives' tales passed from one ignorant girl to the next. However, she *did* know that sometimes women died having babies. What if she died here all by herself? What if they came and found her dead, and the baby too?

If she died, how sad everyone would be. Even Cissy. The idea struck her that when people died, they always left a will. To distract herself from the next pain, which she knew would be coming soon, Johanna thought of what she would bequeath to her sisters in her nonexistent will. She really should have made a will, she thought. Facing what she was now, there was always the possibility of dying. If she *were* to make a will, she'd leave Cissy the cameo pin Grandmother Shelby had given *her* on her sixteenth birthday. Cissy had been really put out about that. She had always admired the delicate Grecian profile carved in ivory on a pale lavender background, framed in gold, circled with seed pearls. And Elly. What could she leave to her youngest sister. What would Elly want of hers?

That was as far as Johanna got in her melancholy thoughts. She perked up suddenly. Didn't she hear something? Above the wind, beyond the pattering of the icy snow against the windows—was that the sound of voices? Oh, dear God, was someone actually coming? She got up from her crouched position, staggered to the door. It *was*! She heard shouts! It wasn't her imagination. Someone was actually coming. Thank God.

Pressing her face to the window, wiping away the frost that veiled her view, she looked out. Stumbling through the blowing snow, the piled-up drifts, were two bundled figures, hanging on to each other, making their way toward the cabin.

With all her strength, Johanna slid back the wooden bars on the door. The wind pushed against it, and she was hard pressed to hold the door open enough for the two people to come inside.

Woolen mufflers around their heads hid their faces, and Johanna could only see their eyes, which were fringed by snow-crusted lashes. The tips of their noses were red with cold. Heavy shawls stiff with frozen snow were wrapped around them, disguising their shapes. Then as they began unwinding the long knitted scarves, she saw who they were. The first face revealed was Tassie's, the second that of Ross's mother, Eliza.

"Oh Ma, I'm so glad you came," Johanna gasped, clutching Eliza's arm. "I think the baby's on its way! But how did you know to come?"

"Tassie come by, told me she'd seen Ross up on the ridge near the Coltons' cabin early in the day. She heard tell that

Milt had broke his leg felling a tree, and thought Ross might have trouble gettin' down the mountain agin iffen it kept snowin' so heavy. We both decided you shouldn't be up here alone in case—well, just in case. So we come."

"Thank God you did!" Johanna said fervently. "But what about Sue and Katie?"

"They'll be fine. Took them over to Jenny and Merriman's 'fore I set out," Eliza told her. "Now, don't you worry 'bout nuthin' but bringin' this here baby into the world."

Even as her mother-in-law spoke, Johanna felt another pain coming. She nodded and braced herself. Her fingers clutched Eliza's arm. Immediately she felt the swift support of both women holding her firmly. When the pain had passed, Johanna let Eliza help her over to bed. There quilts were tucked around her, pillows piled beneath her head, shoulders, back. She could hear Tassie moving around in the cabin. Soon she brought Johanna a mug of steaming herbal tea, a mixture of red raspberry and chamomile. "Here, you sip on this, honey. It'll ease you and make you feel better."

After that, things became blurred. There was the rhythm of pain, each one closer and harder. Always in the background were the comforting voices of the two women, who held her hand, rubbed her back, soothed her with quiet, calm instructions.

Outside the day darkened. Between pains, Johanna asked, "Ross? Is Ross here?"

"Not yet, honey. Now, you jest quiet yourself. Everything's goin' fine. Your baby'll be here 'fore long."

Johanna couldn't remember just when she lost track of time—possibly hours passed. Everything centered on the cycle of ever-increasing pressure, Tassie's encouraging voice. Then she heard the slam of the cabin door as it was thrust open and banged against the wall. The next thing she knew, her hand was covered by two large ones, her name whispered. "Johanna, darling, I'm here."

She opened her eyes. Ross's face bent over her, his keen eyes worried. His cold cheek pressed against hers, and he said huskily, "It won't be long now, honey."

Relieved, reassured, Johanna clung tightly to his hand and gave herself up to the business of giving birth, feeling safe, secure, and completely comforted by his presence.

It seemed endless. Then, as if from a long distance off, Johanna heard the strong, unmistakable sound of a baby's cry! It was over. She'd had her baby. She fell back against the pillows, filled with a tremendous joy, a sense of accomplishment.

◦◦◦◦◦◦

Johanna awakened to the sweet aroma of spice wood tea boiling, then the stirring of the little bundle tucked into the bed beside her. Her baby! she realized in dreamy surprise.

She looked down into the pink, crumpled little face. The baby's eyes were closed. Gently she touched the downy crest of hair on the small, round head, let her finger trace the cheek. How sweet, how dear. She was in awe of this perfection. This is what she had waited for all these months, their child. Johanna felt an emotion new and deep move within her. "Thank you, God," she whispered.

Slowly she became aware of other movement in the room, and then she saw Eliza come to the side of her bed, holding a cup from which a spiral of fragrant steam arose.

"You're awake, Johanna. Let's see if we can sit you up some so's you can sip this tea. It'll give you strength, then mebbe later you can eat somethin'." She paused, then asked hesitantly, "Kin I hold the baby for you?"

Johanna smiled up at Eliza, turning back the edge of the blanket so she could see the little face better. "Isn't she beautiful?"

Eliza beamed. "Yes, she shure is a right peart little'un," she replied, nodding her head. "Ross sez you're namin' her Johanna—that's the custom in your family for a first girl."

"Yes ma'am, but we're going to call her JoBeth—Johanna *Elizabeth*."

Johanna watched as her mother-in-law's face underwent a change of expression, from a startled look to a softness she had never seen there before.

"'Lizabeth?" Eliza repeated softly.

"Yes ma'am, after *you*." Johanna said.

Eliza struggled not to show her emotion, but her eyes brightened suspiciously and her lips worked as if trying to say something. At length, not being able to express what she was feeling, she simply lifted Johanna's fingers and pressed them to her cheek. "I—well—thanky," she managed to say at last.

Chapter Nineteen

❦

Johanna's third September in the mountains seemed particularly beautiful to her. Coming out onto the porch one afternoon, she lingered. High in the tall trees surrounding their cabin, the wind sang. Listening to its music, Johanna realized it was a melody she had learned to hear and love. She felt a part of all this now—these hills, the scent of wildflowers, wood smoke, the special light in summer evenings, the sweet scent of honeysuckle, the clean smell of freshly cut pine. She felt the satisfaction of belonging. A feeling that had been long coming.

Sometimes, Hillsboro and her own girlhood seemed a hundred years away. Her life now was centered here in the mountains, on the baby, and on Ross.

After her father's death, Ross had been her strength, her comfort. She had never before realized the depth of his love, the generosity of his soul, the strength of his devotion, the selflessness of his being. Johanna felt sure her father would be glad to know how beloved she was, how cherished, protected.

The baby was napping and Johanna was tempted to stay, enjoying the sunshine, but there were still chores to be done. She sighed and reluctantly went inside.

Her glance fell on the quilting frame Uncle Tanner had made for her before the baby was born. There was an unfinished quilt stretched upon it. She hadn't worked on it for weeks. Somehow there was always something else that needed doing. Besides, this one wasn't coming out as she had planned. Maybe she was too impatient, or maybe she didn't have the skill—it didn't seem to have a theme. Johanna went over to it, stood looking down at it. Shouldn't a quilt have some sort of theme, a message—shouldn't it represent something? Something was missing. Something was wrong. The colors? The pattern? The pieces she had selected? It was a daily reminder of something lacking in her—the will to continue, to complete. Whatever the problem, somehow it didn't please her. Something seemed to be missing, but she didn't know just what.

Johanna had finished two smaller ones for the baby. Eliza had sewed the tops to the matting and flannel backing, and JoBeth slept sweetly and soundly, wrapped up in their warmth. This quilt was supposed to be Johanna's showpiece, to exhibit the skills she had learned through much struggle, much ripping out and redoing, a masterful work to be displayed proudly. And yet it wasn't right. Why? Not feeling inclined to work on it, she went on to do other chores.

She still had trouble juggling everything there was to do. The baby took up most of her time. Johanna found her a source of endless delight. She knew she neglected other things to spend time with her baby.

JoBeth was a daily miracle to her. Everything about her seemed extraordinary to Johanna. She could hardly put her down or stop watching her. She loved caring for her, cuddling, feeding, rocking, admiring the rosebud mouth, the startlingly blue eyes, the way her silky dark hair was beginning to curl around her forehead and shell-like ears.

Hearing the sound of stirring from the cradle, Johanna hurried over and, greeting JoBeth with soft, cooing sounds, she lifted the baby. It was just too pretty to stay inside, Johanna decided. Then, taking one of the quilts Eliza had given her, she carried her outside. Spreading the quilt on the grass in the mellow gold of the autumn sunshine, she placed JoBeth on it. The baby was just about ready to crawl. She would get up on her fat little hands and knees and rock back and forth, as if she hadn't quite figured out just how yet.

Johanna never tired of watching her. She felt that time with her baby was precious, and she didn't want to miss a minute.

The afternoon lengthened. JoBeth had now been placed on her back, kicking her little legs, waving her arms. Her round, blue eyes watched a cluster of birds flying back and forth between the oak tree overhead and the fence nearby.

Above them, purple-shadowed mountains arched against the sky. Johanna realized how much she had come to love them. They no longer seemed threatening or ready to close her in, isolate her, but instead seemed to protect and surround her with love.

The light began to change, the wind began to stir the pine boughs. Ross should be coming home soon. Johanna picked the baby up and walked to the fence overlooking the trail, peered down to see if Ross might be making his way up. At a long distance on the mountainside, she saw him coming. Her heart lifted with a little thrill she astonishingly recognized as being much the same as the very first time she had seen him at the Chalmerses' Christmas party.

He sat somewhat slouched forward in his saddle, his shoulders bent as though he'd had a tiring day, his hands easy on the reins. Johanna felt a rush of tenderness.

Coming near, he saw her and waved one hand.

"'Evenin', honey," he called, then smiled at the baby. "Evenin', Miss Johanna Elizabeth."

At the top of the hill he dismounted. Taking off the horse's bridle, then the saddle, he placed them on the top of the fence, opened the gate, and turned the animal into the pasture.

Ross walked toward Johanna and held out his arms for the baby and placed her against his shoulder. Then he put his other arm around Johanna, and together the three of them went into the house. Inside, Ross leaned down, gave Johanna a long, slow kiss, then sighed, "It's good to be home."

Joy surfaced in Johanna. It *was* good to be home. *Their* home. She remembered hearing it said, "Home is where the heart is, where your treasure is." *Her* treasure was Ross and the baby. She felt a deep thankfulness for all that was there and for all the years ahead of them.

Johanna glanced at the quilt on the frame. She went over, stared down at it critically. Suddenly she began to see its design. She saw the pieces all coming together in a harmonious pattern. What she wanted it to represent was her life here with Ross and the baby. All the things home meant to her—love, laughter, devotion, belonging.

All at once Johanna knew what she wanted her quilt to say. There was still much of their life that was yet to come, just like the quilt. There was more to work on, more to bring forth. But the pattern was there underneath. Nothing was missing—not from her quilt nor from her life.

American Quilts Series Bonus Section:

❧❧

Dear Reader:

This bonus section is our special gift to those who have enjoyed reading Jane Peart's *The Pattern* as much as we, the editors and publisher, have enjoyed bringing it to you. This section contains the "Prologue" to Jane Peart's next book, *The Pledge*, which is the sequel to *The Pattern*. It continues the story of Johanna and her family.

Also included is a brief outline of how to make your own American quilt, based on the Carolina Lily, the pattern discussed in this book.

Thank you again for reading this book. Zondervan and Jane Peart take pride in bringing you wholesome historical novels that can be read by people of all ages. If you have enjoyed this volume and the other volumes of the American Quilts Series, then be sure to read Jane Peart's other two outstanding series: The Brides of Montclair Series and the Westward Dreams Series. The twelve volumes of Brides of

Montclair Series tell the epic story of a single Virginia family from before the American War of Independence to the twentieth century. The Westward Dreams Series contains four books, all of which portray independent-minded women from the East who travel to the Western territories in the nineteenth century to find new lives for themselves and, of course, romance.

Happy reading.
The Editors of Zondervan Publishing House

Prologue to The Pledge

❦

*J*ohanna Elizabeth Davison sat at the small maple desk in her bedroom writing a letter to Wes when she heard her aunt's voice calling,

"JoBeth come down here at once! Harvell's brigade is marching by. Do hurry!"

She tucked a stray dark curl back behind her ear then put her pen back in the inkwell. Before getting up she slid the half-written letter under the blotter. Letters to Wes had to be hidden. Hurrying into the hallway she met her mother, Johanna, just coming from her sewing room. They exchanged glances. Although full of understanding, her mother's eyes held a message JoBeth dared not ignore. JoBeth nodded and together they went down the winding stairway to the hall where Aunt Jo Cady stood at the open front door.

"Come along, you two," she called over her shoulder as she went out onto the porch and down the steps and along the flagstone walk to stand at the gate. JoBeth and her mother followed.

The May morning was warm, bright with sunshine. Residents from eleven of the houses on the street were rushing out to the strip of grass on either side of the road. In the distance they could hear the drummers beating, the brisk sound of marching feet, the clatter of horses hooves. Then the line of gray-clad soldiers rounded the bend and came into sight. People began to shout 'hurrahs' and wave small Confederate flags. Where had they gotten them so soon? JoBeth wondered. North Carolina had only seceded a few days before. Although, of course, secession had been discussed for months, ever since Fort Sumpter and South Carolina had seceded, when President Lincoln called for troops from North Carolina to subdue the sister states labeled rebels, Governor Ellis' response had been immediate. "I can be no party to this violation of the laws of this country and to this war upon the liberties of a free people. You can get no troops from North Carolina." The state had enthusiastically rallied to the Confederate cause.

After that things happened with lightening speed. JoBeth's uncle Harvel Cady had immediately formed a brigade, and there had been no lack of men ready to join up.

As the soldiers marched by everyone began to clap. Their officers mounted on splendid horses, crisply uniformed with shiny braid and buttons, sash fringes streaming in the wind, sabers glinting . Harvell, astride his gleaming roan-colored mount in the lead, did not look at his relatives nor show any sign of recognition. It would have been unsoldierly to do so. But as he went by his mother, he seemed to sit a little straighter, jutting out his chin, with its bristle of mustache and well trimmed beard.

Among the rows of erect soldiers were many JoBeth knew; boys she had played with, gone to school with as children, later had danced with, flirted with, teased. Now they were almost unrecognizable with their military bearings, new, serious expressions, eyes straight ahead, not looking to right or left .

As she looked at the passing parade of familiar faces JoBeth felt an enormous sadness. Only one person was missing.

For her the most important one; Wesley Rutherford, at college in Philadelphia. And even if he were here, he would not have been in the group. Wes had already expressed his deep doubts about the division among the states, saying, "Both North and South fought to create the United States, we shouldn't break apart now."

Next month when he graduated Wes would come back to Hillsboro where he had made his home with his relatives the Spencers. JoBeth worried about what would happen then. Will and Blakley, twin cousins his own age, had already gone to Raleigh to enlist.

In spite of the warmth of the day, JoBeth shivered. A feeling of impending trouble, a kind of premonition. The bright day seemed to darken. Suddenly, even though surrounded by family, friends of a lifetime, she felt cut off from everyone else. All at once JoBeth realized that she was the only one in the crowd not happily cheering.

To read more, ask your local bookseller for *The Pledge* by Jane Peart.

How to Make Johanna's Quilt

Appliqué allows you to create your own design by stitching bits of fabric on a foundation material. The Carolina Lily quilt is easy to make if you follow the step-by-step instructions. Allow your creativity to blossom by selecting your favorite colors for your own lilies. No two lilies are the same on the Carolina Lily design, but our instructions will allow you to make the flowers look symmetrical to each other.

First, sew two diamonds. Stitch from the bottom of the diamond to the top seam. Second, sew two pairs of diamonds together making one Carolina Lily blossom. Be careful to sew from the bottom of the diamonds to the top—do not sew through it. Now, sew the long side of a triangle to the base of the blossom. You may need to trim the ends of the petals within 1/8 of the sewing line, while gradually tapering the points. Next, make the stems by folding green strips along each long edge. Put the center stem on top of the side stems. You may need to trim the side stems where they meet the center stem to avoid bulk. Hand-baste or pin the Lilies onto the foundation. Trim the stems, allowing 1/4" under the flower. Finally, using small slip stitches, appliqué the stems and the Carolina Lilies. If you prefer to work with felt, wool, or non-woven materials use the buttonhole embroidery stitch instead.

Now to assemble the quilt top, trim the sides of the appliquéd block so they are all equal in length. Make three vertical rows of four blocks, joined with long sashing strips. Press each seam toward the sashing strips. Each of these rows should have the same measurements too.

Now you are ready to layer and quilt. The backing fabric should be divided into two equal lengths.

Sew the two sides together. Outline-quilt around all the flowers and stems. Lastly, quilt the marked designs.

Finally, to complete the quilt sew the strips together in a continual diagonal seam. Stitch through all the layers around the quilt. When you reach the starting point overlap the ends.

Your Carolina Lily quilt will forever bloom the fruit of your needle art.

Acknowledgments

The author would like to acknowledge the following authors for their books, which proved to be invaluable in the research and writing of this book.

Dennis Duke and Deborah Harding, *America's Glorious Quilts*

Wilma Dykeman, *The Tall Woman*

John Parris, *Roaming the Mountains*

Suzy Chalfant Payne and Susan Aylsworth Murwin, *Creative American Quilts Inspired by the Bible*

Lillian W. Watson, editor, *Light from Many Lamps*

Books by Jane Peart

A Tangled Web

The Brides of Montclair Series

1 | *Valiant Bride*

2 | *Randomsed Bride*

3 | *Fortune's Bride*

4 | *Folly's Bride*

5 | *Yankee Bride/Rebel Bride*

6 | *Gallant Bride*

7 | *Shadow Bride*

8 | *Destiny's Bride*

9 | *Jubilee Bride*

10 | *Mirror Bride*

11 | *Hero's Bride*

12 | *Senator's Bride*

13 | *Daring Bride*

14 | *Courageous Bride*

Westward Dreams Series

1 | *Runaway Heart*

2 | *Promise of the Valley*

3 | *Where Tomorrow Waits*

4 | *A Distant Dawn*

5 | *Undaunted Spirit*

The American Quilt Series

1 | *The Pattern*

2 | *The Pledge*

3 | *The Promise*